THE
AMULET

AN ADVENTURE

BY

VICTORIA PAULSEN

ISBN-10 0615635504
ISBN-13 978-0-615-63550-7

Table of Contents

PROLOGUE

Life was prosperous and peaceful on the south coast of Britannia in 196 AD. The produce of the farms – grains, wool, horses – was sold throughout the Roman Empire. Most Britons cared nothing about the two power-hungry would-be Emperors competing for supreme rule of the known world. That would soon change, however, especially for Lydia (17) and her brother Darius (11).

You'll meet some people who really existed, like the two Emperors and the old schoolteacher, Numerianus. Other characters are perhaps fictional, perhaps not. From this distance in time, who knows? Enjoy the journey.

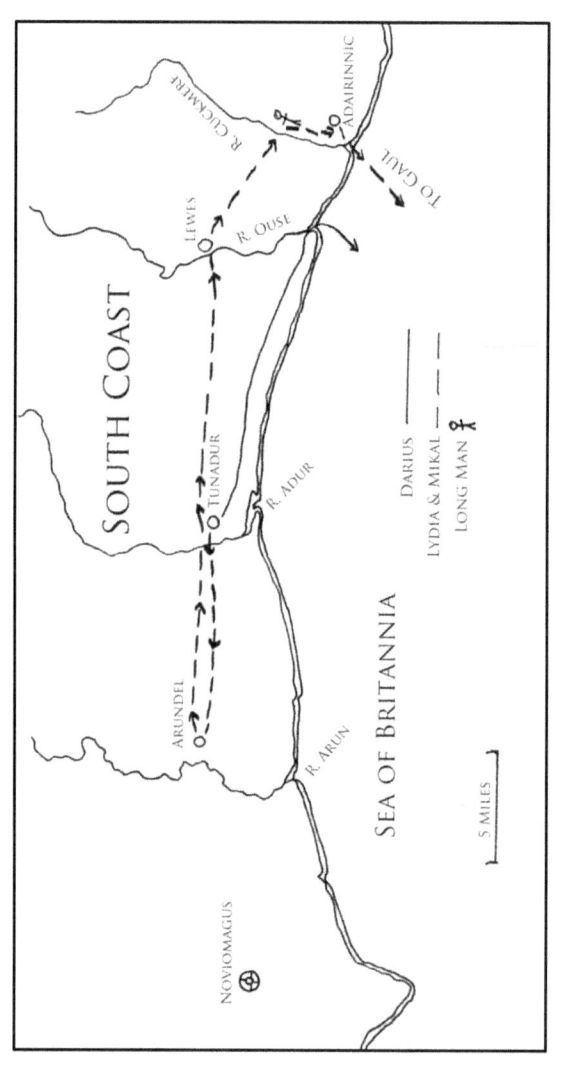

SOUTH COAST

SEA OF BRITANNIA

NOVIOMAGUS

ARUNDEL

TUNADUR

R. ADUR

R. ARUN

LEWES

R. OUSE

R. CUCKMERE

ADAIRINNIC

TO GAUL

DARIUS
LYDIA & MIKAL
LONG MAN

5 MILES

iv

The Amulet

1. A Bad Omen

"Everyone is ready to leave! Your mother sent me to find you." It was the young slave girl, Mikal. "You're a mess," she added bluntly.

Lydia had been concentrating so hard on finishing the little bronze statue of Minerva that she had lost track of time and hadn't even noticed the chaos in the courtyard. Whenever she worked in the forge, it was like that. In other things she could be scattery, but when it was something she liked doing, nothing got in the way.

Quickly wiping little the statue on her grimy tunic, Lydia mumbled, "I'll be right there. I'm ready."

"You don't look ready."

Lydia scowled at her. Mikal could be so annoying. "Is Coa still in the stable? If he is, ask Tar to bring him out."

Mikal shrugged and ambled slowly away, shaking her head.

"Don't do that!" Lydia yelled after her.

As she headed for the house, Culain, her wolfhound puppy who was tied up, began to whine pitifully. At just a year old, he was as tall as the sheep but thin as a post, with long shaggy gray fur that made him look like an old man. Stopping to give Culain a quick pat on his head, she ordered, "Hush, you'll be fine." Borac the blacksmith would take care of him while Lydia was gone.

She then ran across the courtyard and into the villa, hurrying down the hall to the baths. Enough water was left over from the morning to quickly rinse off her face and arms. She tore off the charcoal-stained tunic and replaced it with a clean white one. Draping it quickly, she tied a blue ribbon around her waist to hold the folds in place. It wasn't stylish, but she knew her mother would have packed something more elegant for her to put on later.

"Good enough," she said to her reflection in the hand mirror. The polished bronze surface showed an oval-faced 17-year old girl with large blue eyes, dark straight brows, chestnut-colored curly hair, and fair skin that blushed too easily. She ran her fingers through her curls, shaking loose what she hoped was the last of the soot from the forge. Tucking the little Minerva into a fold in her tunic, she returned to the courtyard only slightly out of breath.

There, Tar was waiting with Coa, her handsome grey gelding. Just fifteen hands high, Coa had been a war horse with the legion until two years ago when his left eye had been injured in a training exercise. He might have been killed for meat except that one of the officers, Titus Julianus, decided to keep him. Titus then brought the horse to Tunadur and gave him to her father as a gift.

Lydia, fifteen at the time, had instantly fallen in love with both Coa and Titus. The tall, sandy-haired Legionnaire was now, at thirty, second in command of the Roman legions in Britannia.

"Good Coa," she said, giving him a red apple and rubbing his nose. He took the apple eagerly and munched away while she massaged him with her knuckles from head to rump and down his legs. He eased into the pressure, loving it. It was her special way of checking him to make sure he had no sore spots. Today, there were none. Indeed, he seemed eager to be off on the long ride.

Taking hold of the reins, Lydia vaulted easily onto his back. He pranced and circled, impatient. She nudged him into line in front of the wagons and carriages just as an unearthly howl from Culain pierced the air. Startled, Coa reared up, catching Lydia off guard but she quickly recovered to calm him down.

"Easy, Coa," she reassured him, reaching for the reins that had been torn from her grip. "It's only Culain. He wants to come, too."

All would have been fine if the lonesome puppy hadn't let out another howl worse than the first. Coa's ears flattened against his head and he bolted for the low, closed gate. The flock of chickens scattered, squawking with feathers flying, as the horse raced through their midst. The always irate gander heaved himself into the air and flew to the top of the granary roof, honking loudly into the turmoil.

Lydia saw the gate looming ahead and adjusted her weight for Coa's jump. At the last possible moment, he changed his mind and planted his front hoofs firmly into the wet ground, catapulting Lydia through the air and over the gate.

"This does not bode well," she thought just before landing hard in the middle of the muddy roadway.

She didn't move for several seconds, catching her breath and wishing she could disappear. The gate creaked open. As a crowd surged forward, she heard Borac yell from the blacksmith shop, "Here comes Culain!"

A grey meteor shot through the gate and leaped happily into Lydia's lap, his tail wagging proudly. Culain licked her face and barked himself a welcome that Lydia, mortified, did not share.

His grey floppy-eared face was so happy and excited she couldn't bring herself to scold him. She knew they made a ridiculous picture sitting in the mud together and started to laugh.

Then her father was standing over her with his usual stern look that dried up her laughter.

"The rest of us will go ahead," Quintus said. "If you can still ride, you will get cleaned up and join us later."

"I can go by myself?" she asked hopefully.

"Mikal can stay with you."

"Where's Darius? I'd rather have him."

Quintus frowned and muttered, "We haven't seen your brother all morning. He probably took off for Lewes or is hiding somewhere. I wanted him to be at the ceremony tomorrow when I give the amulet he made to Titus."

Lydia was surprised. Was her young brother mad enough about the amulet to give up the chance to go to the festival? She knew he hadn't liked what she'd done to it, but it had been for his own good. So Father wouldn't be angry with him. "You really don't know where he is?"

At her father's look, she knew that question shouldn't have been asked. Quintus scowled, "He is not here. That's all you need to know. He will be punished when he gets back, but that is not your concern."

Lydia's grandmother, Rema, appeared from nowhere to say, "I will help Lydia get cleaned up since I am staying here. She can ride alone to Arundel. She's done it many times. Let Mikal go on with the rest."

Lydia felt a twinge of jealously even as she hoped her father would agree with Rema. It often seemed as if her family liked Mikal better than they did her.

"As you wish," agreed Quintus to Lydia's relief. "We will stop for awhile at the Jade Forest just before Arundel. You will meet us there. Do not get in any more trouble."

With that, he turned and strode back into the courtyard.

Coa was led to the stable. He went quietly like the noble horse he was and not the unbroken colt he had pretended to be.

Culain, however, raced around in circles, yipping and whining. Lydia was about to ask if he could come, too, when her grandmother, as if reading her thoughts, said a firm, "No."

Borac took hold of Culain's collar and started to drag him back to the blacksmith shop, but the dog stiffened his legs in protest. Lifting his head straight up, he howled again, a long eerie sound that sent shivers along Lydia's spine.

In the uproar, she didn't notice that the little Minerva statue had fallen out of her tunic into the mud. It would soon be pressed deeply into the earth by the passage of the wagons and horses heading to Arundel.

* * *

An hour later, Lydia was ready to try again. Rema stood at the courtyard gate, the only person to witness this second, more successful departure. She handed Lydia a bouquet of chrysanthemums for good fortune.

"Thanks, Grandmother," Lydia said, kissing Rema on the cheek.

"Now you can enjoy your ride, taking whatever route you choose."

"You know how much I like that, don't you?" Lydia smiled as she mounted Coa.

"I used to do the same thing on these very hills. In fact, if I wasn't two years older than the gods, I'd go with you."

Lydia knew Rema was at least half serious, and was glad she didn't have to have her as a traveling companion. Going alone was best.

There was one more thing she needed to say.

"When Darius gets back . . ." She wasn't quite sure how to finish that sentence.

Rema finished it for her. "I'll tell him you're sorry."

"I'm not, you know. I did the right thing," she said, wondering how much Rema knew.

"It won't hurt you if I say it."

Lydia was sure her grandmother would do whatever she liked. It was easy to see where Darius got his stubbornness.

Nudging Coa with her heels, she rode through the gate at a slow canter. Dutifully, she looked back to wave, but Rema had already disappeared into the villa.

The sun had burned off most of the early mist from the sea, some patches still hovering in copses and vales. On one downslope, the ground fog was so thick that Lydia couldn't see Coa's legs, though everything above was perfectly clear. It was like floating on clouds.

Rather than follow the wagon road the others had taken, she chose a different route across country and directed Coa to the lower ford over the Adur. Taking off her boots, she let her feet dangle in the cold rushing water. The strong horse moved steadily, finding solid footing among the rocks on the river bottom.

Once on the other side, he started an easy lope, but Lydia reined him in, preferring to take her time for awhile longer.

The golden light of fall seemed full of mystery and excitement after the hot honesty of summer. The air smelled fresh, as if the rain had cleansed it and was drying it on the rolling hills. Lydia felt that something wonderful was going to happen at Arundel.

How could she not begin to daydream about Titus? She was sure he had almost hinted at marriage when she last saw him three months ago. He had even kissed her, a quick kiss while they were walking near the hay barn. Then he had smiled, touched her on her left shoulder and gone back to the villa. Nothing more had happened, but a kiss is a kiss no matter how short, and the touch lay deep in her memory.

Just before joining the old wagon road, a rabbit darted out from under a gorse bush, startling Coa into a lively dance.

"Silly Coa," Lydia crooned, rubbing his neck. "Rabbits don't attack horses as brave as you who have fought with Roman legions."

Tossing his head as if he understood, Coa trotted proudly along the deeply-rutted lane.

Two hours later, rounding the hill where the Jade Forest began, Lydia caught up with the company. They had already begun getting back into the wagons for the short trip to the villa at Arundel.

A quick glance told her that Father wasn't there, though his horse, Fabian, was.

Her mother explained, "Titus met us. He said Quintus Antonius was urgently needed at Arundel and even brought Cormus for him to ride, knowing that Fabian might be tired." A slight smile lit Angwyn's face. "I daresay your father looked rather like an Emperor when he put his toga on."

Lydia ignored the toga comment because she knew her father hated to ride while wearing one. They were cumbersome, enormous sheets of fine wool that got in the way and often bothered the horses.

Having not been there when Titus came, however, made her cheerful feelings disappear and be instantly replaced by crankiness. She declared, "Father knows Fabian doesn't tire that easily. That's why he brought him."

"Cormus is almost the best horse to ever come from our stables at Tunadur. It was an honor rightfully his, and Titus showed great . . ."

"I know!" Lydia interrupted, wishing – wishing what? That the day would stop getting better only to get worse again. Titus had come and she hadn't been there because she got thrown off her horse, which hardly ever happened. She knew she should show more respect to her mother in public, but she couldn't help it. All of a sudden, it was a perfectly awful day!

Mother and daughter were silent for a few moments, then Angwyn asked, "Will you ride in the carriage for the rest of the trip?"

Lydia was grateful to be asked rather than ordered. She gave a nod and said, "Coa needs to rest. Can someone walk him?"

Angwyn motioned to Mikal who went to find one of the stable boys.

When Angwyn spoke again, it was in a low voice that didn't ask this time. "Let Mikal help you get dressed. I brought your over-tunic, the one that looks so nice on you. You must not arrive poorly attired."

Dismounting, Lydia gave Coa's reins to Chaton, the stable boy, who led him away. Nothing more was said as Mikal untied the ribbon around Lydia's waist and let the folded up part of her tunic fall gracefully to its full length at her ankles.

Suddenly Lydia remembered the Minerva statue. It should have fallen when the ribbon was untied. When it didn't, and she realized she'd lost it, it seemed like a bad omen. What more could go wrong?

Mikal draped the other tunic, a pale pink wool colored by dye made with roses and lavender from Tunadur's gardens, over the first one. She then fastened the shoulders with jeweled pins and encircled Lydia's waist in a double row of ribbons. Her boots were exchanged for soft white leather shoes. Lydia, trying to seem patient, even allowed the girl to untie her hair and comb it out. However, when Mikal began to rearrange it stylishly, Lydia protested in a tone that clearly showed how far from patient she actually was.

"Save that for later! Let's be on our way before everyone wonders where we are."

Mother looked at her and sighed. Lydia hoped an apology wasn't expected.

Neither of them spoke again until they were almost at the villa, then Angwyn said, "Titus was riding Zephyr when he came to meet us."

Lydia's heart leaped and she felt her cheeks flush, betraying her feelings. Zephyr was almost seventeen hands high and black as coal except for white fetlocks. She and Titus had picked him for a champion and he had proven them right. Last year in his first competition, he had overpowered all but the most experienced horses. This year he would beat them all. Lydia was sure Titus had ridden him for her benefit. He must have been disappointed not to find her with the company.

Mother continued, "When Titus asked your father to ride back with him, he seemed rather . . . I don't know. It's no matter."

Lydia smiled to herself. Mother, of course, couldn't guess that Titus was disappointed because he hadn't seen Lydia. Probably he wanted to talk to her father about her. She sat up straighter. It was a good day after all.

2. An Awkward Day

The main villa at Arundel, with its imposing neo-Roman style, dominated the view of the countryside. Even with all the wagons and people arriving from Tunadur, there was still room to spare in the vast courtyard.

When their carriage arrived, Lydia wondered where Diana and her mother, Fulvia, were. It was unusual for them not to be waiting outside when guests arrived.

"Maybe," Lydia mused to herself, "we're such old friends that they expect us to walk right in." She glanced at her mother. Angwyn motioned for Lydia to follow her as she walked toward the front entrance. Just before they got there, a large woman in red and orange flowing robes rushed out toward them.

"A thousand pardons! No, ten thousand! What a day this has been! You'll have to hear it all! Lydia, welcome. Diana will be ready to see you soon. We have such news! The men are in the library – Titus, Quintus and Brutus, of course, but also Lucius Barinius and two others from Londinium. They rode all the way today, can you imagine it? Changed horses three times but never stopped to rest. Something exciting is happening, can you feel it? You always were sensitive to these things. Ah! I can see it in your eyes, dear. You know, don't you?"

To Lydia, her mother's blue eyes were the same as always – inscrutable. That was a good accomplishment, given Fulvia's appearance. The normally dark hair had turned a preposterous shade of vermillion, the effect heightened by an extraordinary mountain of round curls set off by jeweled combs that held them on top of her head like a volcano. Fulvia's brightly colored overdress floated on the air as if spun from a rainbow. The border, woven with golden threads, was a marvel of intertwined geometric figures.

Lydia must have been staring, for Fulvia smiled broadly at her and twirled around, showing off the mysterious material.

"It's silk! From the eastern Empire. Titus was able to procure it for Diana and me from a merchant who stopped in Londinium in the summer. I've been eager to surprise you ever since. Only the finest people in Rome wear silk."

Angwyn smiled and said, "It's lovely, Fulvia."

Lydia's head spun. Titus brought silk for Fulvia and Diana but not for me? Not for Mother and me?

Fulvia trilled on, "And my hair? What do you think? One of our new slaves has been a hairdresser in Rome. She knows all the latest styles. I wanted my hair to be the same red as your Darius's hair. He's lucky it's natural, believe me. What I had to go through to get this, bleaching my old color out, putting the new one in. It didn't work the first few times. My dark hair refused to be washed out, and the grey! What a laugh that was! The grey turned almost green. But we finally got it right. By the way, where is Darius? I want to compare it with the dear boy's."

"He had to stay behind," Mother answered simply.

"What a shame. He would have enjoyed the festivities tomorrow. The gladiators are going to fight bears, had you heard that? Will Quintus be bringing him soon to be initiated into the temple of Neptune? He's almost twelve, isn't he? Or am I being too nosey?"

Mother smiled. "Quintus hasn't spoken of it yet."

"It will be soon, surely. I remember when your dear Ansonius was initiated. What a festival we had then! My, but he was big for his age, not at all like Darius. Oh dear, listen to me rattling on about Ansonius and making you sad again. I think of him being killed, his bones lying all alone somewhere in Gaul, and I turn all weepy."

Lydia wondered if Fulvia would start crying and risk having her thick eye paint flow down her powdered cheeks, but the colorful woman managed to keep herself in control. Mother seemed not to have heard. That was how she always acted when anything was mentioned about Lydia's older brother, Ansonius. He had been a wild one, but his adventurous high spirits drew people to him. He had the gift of making you feel more alive when you were around him. Curiously, Lydia had never mourned his death. To her, he couldn't die.

"Fulvia!" Angwyn said sweetly, "It's getting chilly and I think we should go inside."

"Well done, Mother," Lydia thought.

"Of course, how silly of me. Come along," Fulvia chortled. "Why stand out here in the cold when I've got so much to show you inside. We've been working for weeks redecorating. I hope you like it. Come!"

Lydia was relieved to see her best friend, Diana, approaching from the atrium at the end of the long corridor. The late afternoon sun angling in through the skylight touched the forest of plants growing inside and outlined Diana in a golden glow.

Never had Lydia seen her this way. Diana wore a long tunic of flowing silk, the softest blue, gathered under her breast and embroidered in white entwining flowers. Her blonde hair, usually hanging limp around her plain face, was beautifully arranged in soft curls atop her head with a few strands falling casually down her neck. Her thin body had filled out to lovely curves, and her face? It was beautiful. What had happened to transform her so quickly?

Lydia felt frumpish and awkward in her presence.

"I'll take you to your room," Diana said after a short and cool hug.

Lydia followed obediently, wondering why she was being given a separate room. On all other visits, she had stayed in Diana's room with her.

Diana continued talking as she led the way down the opposite corridor to a guest room near the smaller atrium.

"There are three guests from Londinium besides Titus," she said, "and that makes our numbers more than nine and uneven besides. We're expecting one other, a trader from Gaul, but he might not make it. Mother thinks it's unlucky not to have the dining hall arranged as usual, but I've finally convinced her that with twelve or thirteen people you have to do things differently."

Diana laughed then, and Lydia joined in half-heartedly, not sure how to react. Diana seemed older, more assured than she had been only two months ago. It was as if Lydia had stayed seventeen while Diana had decided to finally be her own real age of nineteen. The two years' difference had never seemed so long before. Diana had always been the follower. It was Lydia who encouraged Diana to try new things. Now everything was topsy turvy.

The wall panels of the guest room where Diana left Lydia were painted to look like a view to a strange southern sea. There were palm trees and brightly colored birds with long swooping tails. A geometric floor mosaic gave style but not warmth to the space. For the first time, Lydia didn't feel very comfortable in the home of her good friend.

Since a basin of water had been left in the room, she splashed her face and then impulsively dunked her head, shivering as the cold water dripped down her neck. She dabbed at it with a towel then stretched herself out on the couch. Staring at the ceiling painted like a stormy tropical sky, she tried to find an answer to what had happened to Diana. Had it been only two months since they were together at the Lughnasadh festival? Secrets about life and hopes and dreams – and Titus -- had been shared in complete trust, lying awake far into the night in Diana's bedroom.

"Your hair!" Mikal cried, standing in the doorway.

"You needed a challenge," Lydia said irritably, her musing interrupted. Remembering how elegant Diana had looked, she told the slave, "I'd like to look. . . well, nice, for dinner."

She was ready to scold if Mikal showed any hint of a smile since it was unusual for Lydia to care how she looked.

All Mikal said was, "I hope no-one else from Tunadur decides to get their hair wet because I'm the only one who can fix it properly."

Lydia was relieved. Mikal wasn't going to make fun of her. It didn't matter that Mikal was only a slave, and three years younger than her. She was a girl and her opinion mattered. Besides, she had a talent for knowing what looked good and what didn't.

While Mikal worked on her hair, Lydia decided to lighten her own mood by telling Mikal something that Fulvia had said.

"There is a hairdresser from Rome at Arundel now," Lydia said.

"No! Really?" Mikal gasped.

"Yes. She's done Fulvia's hair."

Mikal giggled before playing the diplomat and answering, "I think it best that I take care of your hair and your mother's."

The young girl's fingers massaged Lydia's scalp, relaxing her and making the meeting with Diana not seem so bad. Of course, Diana was just flustered from trying to set up the dining room in the right way. Everything would work out. It always did. After dinner she would find out from Diana all that had happened since August.

"Keep still," Mikal ordered.

As her hair got pulled and combed then piled on her head and secured with jeweled hairpins in a proper style, Lydia realized that she did not want to be alone in that strange room at night.

"I could stay with you," Mikal ventured.

"Would you mind?" Lydia asked, not noticing that Mikal had offered before being asked.

"I do not mind," answered Mikal, putting the final touches on Lydia's hair. "But I do not have a choice," she added. Her voice carried a slight accent, though she had been with Lydia's family for six years, since she was eight.

"Of course you have no choice," said Lydia, acknowledging the obvious. "But you can still have an opinion. You always do."

Mikal nodded and said, "I do have an opinion about a person, though I probably shouldn't say."

"A person?" Lydia asked, curious.

"Yes, Fulvia Marconius." Mikal smiled, quickly continuing. "I have never seen anyone as gaudy as she is. Her slaves say that the last few months here have been so hectic that everyone has been overworked to death. Titus has been practically living here for weeks on end – hold still! – and that means they've had to entertain officials from Londinium and Gaul and everywhere on Caesar Albinus's business."

Lydia felt more than the pain of pulled hair. If Titus had been in the region, he should have come to Tunadur. He always did. Why had he not come those times? What was his business at Arundel?

Brutus Marconius must be to blame. The ambitious master of Arundel had made himself high priest of the Mars temple and thus the highest ranking Briton on the southern shore. He even outranked her father, soon to be the Prefect of Noviomagus. Cold, fine-boned, pale and tall, he had power, but surely he could not also rule Titus, second only to Albinus himself in Britannia.

"Sorry, I should not have spoken," Mikal apologized.

Lydia shrugged. Annoyed as she was by the news, she had asked Mikal to speak. Slaves were often used as information gatherers, especially by women, who were not always aware of what their men were up to.

"You look fine indeed," Mikal complimented Lydia's hairstyle and the draping of the new tunic. "Tonight you will shine, believe me."

Lydia needed to believe, but without a mirror it was hard. There should have been one in the room, especially since Lydia knew that in Diana's room were several. It didn't really matter. Titus was the mirror that mattered. She smiled a bit, looking forward to seeing him at last.

There was a knock on the door which then opened slowly. Lydia's mother stepped inside and Mikal slipped out, leaving the two alone.

"I need to tell you something," Angwyn said, her usually placid face showing deep concern. They sat on the couch. "There is no easy way to give news like this which will cause you so much pain. Titus is taking Diana as his legal wife. She is with child even now."

"What?!" Lydia was overwhelmed. She could not think. She could not breathe. Nothing made sense. Her thoughts were a maelstrom of betrayal, both by Titus and by Diana. Were they a couple even in August when Lydia had confided so much to her?

Having delivered her news, Angwyn stood up and said, "I have to join the others for dinner now. Do you feel able to come?"

Lydia was still reeling from the news and wished to be anywhere else in the world, but she made herself nod her head. Titus and Diana must not be allowed to think she had any feelings to be hurt.

"Good," her mother said, hugging her gently. "I have always admired your courage and strength."

If only Angwyn had been more distant, the way she usually was, Lydia wouldn't have cried, but unfortunately kindness was harder to bear.

As tears engulfed her, she sobbed and sobbed, trying to erase from her mind what she had just heard. Angwyn rocked her back and forth, assuring her it was all right if they were late for dinner.

Lydia couldn't remember a time when Angwyn had treated her so tenderly, though maybe it had happened when she was a little girl. The closeness of her mother felt so comforting, she didn't want it to stop, but finally, calling upon the strength her mother said she had, Lydia willed herself to breathe deeply and compose herself.

When she could stand up, she promised herself and her mother, "I will not do that again."

"Cry, or fall in love?"

Without hesitating, Lydia answered, "Both."

"I hope not," Mother said, touching her cheek kindly.

After blowing her nose and flooding her face with cold water from the basin, Lydia asked, "How do I look?"

"A little flushed, that's all, but the lamps will be low in the room. You actually look quite lovely."

Before going out the door, Lydia confessed for the first and last time, "I thought he cared about me."

"I know, and I'm sure he does. I'm sure he does." She might have added that choosing Diana was the wiser political move, but didn't.

Entering the dining hall late was the hardest thing Lydia had ever done. She stood straight, head up, and tried not to think about how her knees were shaking.

Two square tables were placed together forming a rectangle, one side of which was open to allow the servants to pass food and pour wine. Couches were set up for the diners who would lie on them while they ate. Fulvia shared a couch with Brutus at one end, chattering with Titus and Diana. The three men from Londinium and Quintus had the other honored positions on the side. At the far end were places for Angwyn and Lydia.

Reclining gracefully she hoped, Lydia took a deep drink of watered wine from her silver goblet. Out of the corner of her eye she saw Titus place his hand on Diana's hip. It was her first glimpse of him in three months. Titus, with his tall, commanding bearing, his light brown hair and blue eyes set in a strongly boned face, was the most handsome man on earth. He, like the other men, was wearing a toga, which made him look more dignified than ever. Lydia wished she hadn't come. Why had she thought she could watch him and Diana together and not feel anything?

Searching for a way to get through the ordeal, Lydia decided that the solution was to pretend to be someone else. She could be like her brother, Ansonius, who had been so full of confidence he could make her laugh even when she was afraid.

She remembered how one night not long before he left for Gaul, the two of them had ridden home late from visiting Uncle Petrus in Lewes. The dark forests had been full of phantoms and chilling noises. Ansonius had sat her in front of him on his horse and held her tightly while he sang at the top of his lungs. He loved rowdy songs, the kind he learned from sailors whose ships anchored near Tunadur, and the kind that were not heard in the villa. Ansonius taught her to imagine the worst and face her fears. Usually that made them go away.

With her brother in her heart, she smiled directly at Titus, thinking inside, "Lucky for you Brutus is holding the meat-slicing knife. If it was in my hands, Diana would be a widow before the appetizers were finished." Hah! Ansonius would have liked that.

It was good sport, so she kept it up. Passing a bowl of fresh oysters to the men from Londinium, she thought, "You boors who grab the best pieces for yourselves, who do you think you are? Too soft around your middles to ever sit a horse well. I hope your kidneys and other parts are miserable from your long ride today."

Unexpectedly, she caught Titus watching her. It so flustered her that she let an oyster slip out of her hands onto the couch from where it oozed down to the floor, leaving a trail of juice in its wake. That was nothing compared with what came next. Titus laughed!

"Lydia seems to be having an awkward day," he teased. "I hear she got thrown by Coa, and now the errant oyster slides from her grip."

Everyone was looking at her. What sort of man would make fun of her in front of strangers!

"Oh, Lydia, how amusing," spoke Fulvia. "Do tell us all about it."

"Mother, please," Diana intervened, looking embarrassed.

Lydia knew she could not stay another minute.

"I must be excused, Brutus Marconius," Lydia said as she stood up. "It is a delicious meal, but I don't feel well."

How had she had the courage to say that? Her father would be furious. She did not dare look at him.

"Of course, my dear Lydia," Brutus crooned in a voice as slippery as the fallen oyster. "My slave will escort you so you don't lose your way. Please rejoin us when you feel better."

"Thank you." Lydia kept her eyes on the floor and left the room quickly without making further excuses.

Mikal, who had been helping in the kitchen, caught up with her in the hall. "You look awful."

How dare she say something like that? Lydia turned to scold her, but saw that one of Brutus's slaves had come out of the dining hall.

"We know where we are going," Mikal told him imperiously. She then took Lydia's arm in a vice-like grip and led her away.

Her hold on Lydia did not relax until they were entering the guest room. Mikal closed the door tightly.

"What happened?" she asked. "I saw Titus Julianus seated next to Diana. Is there trouble between you and Titus? I thought –"

"Quiet, Mikal!" Lydia said, collapsing on the couch. "I need to rest, that's all."

"Nonsense. You're as healthy as a young mare and you know it. Oh, I know what I said about looking awful, but that was just to back up your story in case that other slave was curious."

"You heard me? Did you also hear what Titus said?"

"I did."

"Well, don't tell me what you think."

Before Mikal could reply, there was a light knock on the door which opened to admit Angwyn. She took a quick look at Lydia, then smiled, relieved. "I had to be sure you were all right. Do you want food brought to you?"

Pleased by the unusual attention from her mother, Lydia nevertheless answered, "No thank you. I'm not hungry. Seeing Titus and Diana together made me lose my appetite."

"I don't blame you," said Angwyn softly, then added in a determined voice, "We must get you back to Tunadur tomorrow."

That was unexpected. "How can I? Father is to be sworn in as Prefect."

"I will be at the ceremonies and so will many others. He won't notice your absence."

In spite of what had happened, Lydia wanted to see Titus conduct the ceremony while wearing the amulet she had made.

"Mother, do I have to go back?"

"You would torture yourself? If you stay, you will have to keep Diana company. Titus, after all, will be with your father and the other officials. Do you want her to tell you all about how Titus makes love to her?"

"Of course not!"

"Well?"

Lydia sighed. "All right, I'll go back."

"Good, because there's another reason. I'm worried about Darius. I have a feeling he's in trouble. I need you to make sure he's all right."

Lydia shrugged, indicating a less than enthusiastic assent. Her brother was known to take off on his own every once in awhile. Never more than a day. Why worry?

Mother took Lydia's hands and looked right at her, saying quietly, "I think I would die if I were to lose either of you. Please."

A rebellious little brother and two traitorous friends had made this an awkward day, just as Titus had said.

Lydia didn't hide her annoyance. "I'm sure Darius was only sulking. He's probably home asleep by now."

"You may be right, but I feel uneasy about him. I will convince Quintus that if he wants to see you alive again, he'd better let you return to Tunadur. He knows that Rema is the best person to tend to sickness."

"What's supposed to be wrong with me?"

"You will have a fever. I know how to induce one that will fool everyone." Turning to Mikal, she added, "It would ease my mind to have you go with Lydia. You could drive the carriage for her."

"Carriage?" Lydia was dismayed.

"Yes, carriage. No arguing. Coa can be led by a rope tied to the back so you'll have him at home. Don't ride him anywhere near here where you'll be seen."

Lydia could see she had no choice. "All right, Mother." She noted how Angwyn had implied that after she left Arundel and was out of sight, she could ride.

"I will return after dinner with the fever potion."

"Will I be really sick?"

"No, just uncomfortable. I hope you can pretend."

"I can, believe me."

"I can help," Mikal offered eagerly. "I'll mess up your hair and make your face pale with powder, black under your eyes. Can you cry? That would be perfect!"

"I'll be laughing too hard to cry," Lydia declared, wishing it was true.

"You're in good hands," said Angwyn. "Dinner will last another two or three hours so don't get anxious waiting for me. Thank you, Mikal."

"Oh, Madame Angwyn, I thank you! This is going to be fun!"

"I hope so," Angwyn said, leaving the girls alone.

3. Reeling from the News

The potion tasted worse and was much stronger than Angwyn had promised. In fact, Lydia felt terrible for a few hours afterwards. The painted walls of the room seemed to sway in and out as, sweaty and delirious she tried to turn herself into a tiny hollow ball and roll along one of the black stripes in the mosaic floor toward the sands of the strange southern sea that pitched and tossed all around her.

During that horrible time, Diana came. When the fever cleared from Lydia's mind, Mikal told her how full of concern Diana had been.

"She was pretending," Lydia sullenly declared.

"I don't think so. She seemed genuine."

"I doubt it. And me? Did I seem really sick?"

Mikal grinned. "You were ghastly sick."

"Good." Lydia was glad. She hoped Diana would tell Titus and then they would both feel sorry for what they had done to her.

"Do you really think so?" Mikal asked.

"What? Did I speak?"

Mikal hesitated before mumbling, "Not exactly."

"How did you know, then?"

"Know what?" Mikal asked, not looking at Lydia.

"You said 'Do you really think so?' and it was just after I was thinking something all to myself. So tell me. I order you."

Mikal looked at the floor and finally admitted, "Sometimes it's as if I know what you're thinking."

Lydia stared at her, hoping she had not heard what she had heard. If it was even a little bit true, then there was no telling how much this girl knew about her.

"Why didn't you tell me before?"

"I couldn't. You might have had me sent away. Maybe you will now. I can't make it go away, you know. You couldn't stop your thinking even if you knew I might hear it, could you?"

"I could try!" Lydia declared. "Do you know how embarrassing this is, to think that you know so much about me? You're a mind reader. That's evil! Do you read everyone's mind?"

Mikal shook her head, still looking at the floor. "No. I can't do it all the time to anyone. I never want to do it at all. When your thoughts are really strong, then I sense them. Darius's, too. But certainly not your father's or mother's."

"How about Titus?"

Mikal's expressive face closed like a strongbox. No answer was given.

"Why won't you say?" Lydia asked.

"I have only seen him a few times at Tunadur. His thoughts are strong, but strange to me. If I were to tell you, you would judge him through me and that is wrong." Mikal gave a little laugh. "This so-called talent doesn't seem to do anyone any good. It's not a useful talent like yours."

"What do you mean?"

"You have practical talents like making things and riding horses. How powerful it must feel to transform a lump of metal into a beautiful pin or amulet, or even a pot for the kitchen. When you ride Coa over the fields, you look so free. I watch from the house and envy you."

Lydia had an idea. "Mikal, you shall ride tomorrow on the way back to Tunadur."

"I can't –"

"Of course you can if I say so. As soon as we're past the Jade Forest, no-one from Arundel will be around, so I'll drive the carriage and you take Coa. Riding is easy. You'll love it."

"But Coa threw you over the gate!"

"That was an accident. He's really very gentle."

"He's a giant! I'm afraid of him."

Mikal argued a bit more, but saw it was hopeless.

"If you say so, I guess I have to try."

"Good."

The hour was late. Because they weren't used to having rooms heated by a furnace system, or hypocaust, at home, the guest room was too warm for comfort. Mikal opened the door a crack for fresh air. It was then that they heard the men's voices.

Immediately, Lydia extinguished the wick on the oil lamp. A dim, fluttery light came from the atrium.

"We save the best for midnight," Diana's father's smooth voice was easy to recognize.

"I hope we can be in bed before then." It was Titus. Lydia would know his voice anywhere.

"The bridegroom speaking?" She did not recognize that voice, and decided it was one of the men from Londinium.

"Don't be a fool. Do not think I forget my office because I take a wife. There are ceremonies to conduct tomorrow and I want them to go well. Quintus, are you prepared?"

"You know I am." Her father sounded weary.

"Of course."

Another voice, rich and resonant with a lilting undercurrent, asked, "Is there more wine?" Lydia was certain she'd never heard him before.

"Give Marius some of the elderberry wine. It's our finest. You missed it at dinner by coming so late."

"Thank you, Brutus. I gather that's not all I missed, either."

Lydia was shocked. Had Titus told him how he had ridiculed her when she dropped the oyster? Or about how she had to leave the dinner because she got sick – or pretended to get sick?

"Let's get down to business," Titus ordered, ignoring the man's comment.

Lydia scarcely realized how intently she was eavesdropping until her foot fell asleep after being squashed too long in the same position on the hard floor tiles. She stretched and moved closer to the door, standing behind Mikal.

From the shadows of the room, Lydia could see into the atrium. Though a garden of small trees and tall flowers obscured most of her view, she caught glimpses of the men as they stood and sat about twenty feet away.

Titus seemed to be in charge. He asked the questions; the others answered.

"The first two legions are leaving soon for Gaul to meet up with Albinus who is in Lyon. Albinus wants more British soldiers, especially cavalry. How many men can you have for him in, say, six week's time, Quintus?"

"Probably no more than 200."

"Not enough," interjected one of the others.

Quintus spoke again, saying, "The southern coast has been the unflagging supporter of Rome in Britannia. If the visitor from Londinium has objections, perhaps it is because he does not understand our position."

Titus spoke. "Upon what reasoning do you base those figures?"

"Upon our population, of course." Father's voice, though raspy was confident. "Men are in short supply in the south."

"Give me a figure for horses."

"At Tunadur there are 73 fully trained six-year olds. Fifty-nine seven-year olds. The four- and five-year olds aren't ready yet. There are 150 of them. How many at Arundel, Brutus?"

Father had played his hand well. Lydia knew that Diana's father couldn't match Tunadur in horses or livestock.

"We have had no luck with our horses these last few years," Brutus's oily voice answered. "Of six-year olds, only twenty could be ready if we have enough time to train them. Of older ones, maybe another twenty. That would leave only a few for the farm work."

"The other villages have even less," Quintus declared. "Can you see, Titus, the folly of Britons taking on the entire Roman Empire?"

"Watch what you say, Quintus," Titus answered. "It is hardly the entire Empire. Septimius has the east and most of Germania, that's all. Albinus's claim is as strong as his, and Britons are the equal in battle of any Roman legions."

"Perhaps," said Lydia's father. "But in defeat we become the whipping boy of the Empire. We lose our lands, our lives, to strangers. I don't know that I want to risk that simply because two men can't figure out how to run the Empire together."

"The risks of war are always great."

"I am aware of that," Quintus answered coolly.

"Albinus has great respect for Britons as soldiers," Titus said, shifting the subject slightly. "What do you think, Brutus?"

Diana's father quickly answered, "I will follow Caesar Albinus, of course. He is our leader."

"And you, Quintus?"

A long silence this time. Lydia strained her ears to hear her father's answer.

"Quintus?" One of the strangers repeated the question. The air became stifling as Lydia waited.

"Albinus may have my horses and 200 south coast men," her father spoke, but some of his intensity seemed to be missing.

"Well spoken," Titus said. "Marius, you've been quiet so far."

"Yes, and I'm going to remain so, friend, and so remain friend. My business is to trade, that's all. Give me merchandise to sell in Gaul or Rome or Asia and you have my loyalty."

"You know of Septimius from your uncle in Rome.

"Yes," Marius sounded less amiable.

"How do you compare him to Albinus?"

"Titus, that isn't fair. You know Septimius better than I do. I only know of him second hand."

Lydia shifted her weight again and noticed that Mikal did, too. Neither dared speak of the extraordinary discussion going on so close to them.

"I'll go first," Titus declared. "Septimius is fierce and his soldiers love him. Under him, an army will fight to the last man."

"Albinus is too nice," Marius added. "People don't take him seriously. He could never lead an army."

"Don't be too sure of that," Titus interjected. "You haven't watched him in the north."

"No rebuttals yet," Marius objected. "I say Albinus is nice. Septimius is ambitious, fierce, determined, and cold. Lose to him and you lose everything."

"He allowed Albinus to be called Caesar of Britain. Is that the act of a wise man?"

"Yes," Marius answered. "To keep Albinus from taking over Rome in his absence, Septimius decided to pacify him with a grand title."

"Which Septimius has now revoked," Quintus added. "Remember Sophocles' advice, '*Enemies' gifts are no gifts and do no good.*' Does this have to be decided tonight?"

Titus replied, "Not tonight, but soon. I personally will take responsibility for getting the horses and troops to Gaul."

"It is imminent, then?"

"Yes. The last courier said that Septimius is in Rome. I believe he may already be heading up to Germania through Pannonia and then over to Gaul to meet Albinus. Time is crucial."

"I propose a toast," Marius declared. "To history, and the fact that Emperors never learn from it.

Lydia saw a goblet raised, presumably Marius's. His was the only one.

"Sorry, Marius," Titus said softly. "Even if we agreed, we couldn't drink to that. How about, 'To my unborn child, may he or she be able to grow up on the peaceful southern shore'.

Hearty "aye's" followed, and the sound of more wine being poured.

Lydia wished she hadn't heard Titus's toast. She wanted to scream horrible things at him and Diana, but of course she couldn't. Instead, she crept back to her bed and pulled the blanket over her head. She heard Mikal close the door softly. It was a long time before she slept.

4. The Wrong Place

Tied to the gunwale of a dilapidated trading ship, the young runaway was not able to appreciate his last view of the chalk cliffs of Britannia from the ocean.

If only he hadn't fallen down that cliff. It was just that he hadn't eaten all day and the smell of cooked fish made him ravenous and careless. Leaning over the edge of the cliff, the sand gave way and down he tumbled, landing at the big man's feet. Hector. The skinny one was Acteon, mean as a snake.

At first the ruffians thought he was the courier they were waiting for, the same one who was now propped up by the mast babbling on and on about the women of Gaul. The boy had never met anyone so irritating. With more than a dozen arrow wounds, the man should have died, but no. The gods must have protected him for their own weird reasons.

Acteon planned to sell the boy as a slave. He said that the boy's bright red hair made him worth a lot of money. Acteon gave him a name, too. Flea, spoken like a curse because of all the fleas on him from the sand. The man thought it was such a clever name. The boy thought it was a stupid name, but he decided to go along with it. "Flea" sounded more slave-like than his real name.

When he tried to escape, Hector caught him and tied him up on the ramshackle boat next to bales of wool and iron. All afternoon he'd been there, stiff and cold and miserable, waiting for the courier to arrive.

Being a courier was obviously fraught with peril. If the man had died from his wounds, or been captured by his attackers, the boy wouldn't have had to listen to his feverish ranting..

Once they put out to sea, Acteon escaped below deck to get away from the courier's prattle.

"Why not untie me?" the boy asked Hector. "I can't go anywhere, can I?"

Once free, he was able to look around. It was fascinating to watch Hector wield the huge oak tiller.

"How can you tell where you are going in the dark?" the boy asked,

Hector pointed behind him to a long rope trailing in the water. "If I keep the rope straight, I'll not go wrong. We head straight for the mouth of the Seine. If it wasn't for that rope, we might end up in Spain or falling off the edge of the world."

"Really?"

"Sure. Right off the edge, just like how you fell down that cliff. No telling what happens after that."

The boy didn't argue, figuring that Hector probably never had a tutor to tell him the world was round like a ball.

"Can I watch the rope for you?" he asked.

"Sure. Tell me if I go astray and I'll just look ahead, following that star cluster."

It would have been a nice night on the water if the ranting of the courier could have been stopped.

"What good am I?" the courier droned. "A miserable sliced-up imitation of a man. Gloriana will never forgive me. Gloriana my soul, my duckling. Waiting in Lutetia forever for her poor Optimus Maximus. My sweet dumpling with big soft oranges waiting to be plucked by her strong Imperial soldier . . ."

Hector roared, "Gloriana of Lutetia? Speak! Is that what you said, you miserable excuse for a man?"

Optimus hesitated then nodded his head. Hector exploded.

"Take this!" he ordered the boy, plunking the tiller into his arms. "Don't let it get away from you!"

The big man stomped to the front of the boat, leaving the boy with a bucking, twisting hunk of wood that refused to obey him. Wrapping both arms around it, he braced his legs against the gunwale and held on. It was harder than wrestling sheep at home during shearing season.

Hector was yelling at Optimus. "Gloriana is my sister, you blustering swine! Guess what? We are taking you to Lutetia. When we get there you are going to ask Gloriana if she wants you, and if she does, though I can't think why she would, you will marry her. Give her babies. You don't deserve her, but if she wants you she'll have you or I will personally twist your neck into a double-jointed hangman's noose that will never come untied! Understand?"

The boy stared in wonder. He hadn't thought the big man had so many words in him. It was astonishing to see the courier cringing, his bluster gone.

"Oh, yes indeed," the little man agreed. "Marriage to Gloriana. Should I survive. But there is a problem."

"What, you worm?" Hector looked murderous.

"My message for Septimius Severus. It cannot be delayed by marriage ceremonies. But I have a remedy for that."

Hector glared at him without saying a word.

"In my condition, I can't carry out my duty to the Emperor, but I can commandeer someone to do it for me."

"What are you getting at?"

"You! Slave!" Optimus yelled at the boy.

"Me?" He hadn't been listening because he was fighting so hard with the tiller.

"Are you really a slave to these blockheads?"

"They say so." The tiller almost knocked him in the head.

"What is your name?"

"Flea, so they say." He was wary of giving his real name to anyone. "Hector! Help! I can't hold this any longer!"

Hector moved quickly to take the tiller back from the Flea, righting the course again.

Optimus declared, "Flea, you are now my slave. I am going to purchase you and allow you to take my message to the Emperor!"

The boy was dumbfounded. That was the stupidest idea he'd ever heard.

Acteon, who had come on deck when Hector first yelled, shouted, "Hold on! Just hold on! Hector and me, we have plans for the Flea. See that red hair? He'll make our fortune. People pay good money for boys like this."

The courier looked at him with scorn. "Your Flea will never be the plaything of a money-grubbing banker."

"And who are you to say that?"

"By the power of the Emperor Septimius Severus, I can take whatever I need to complete my mission. If you're not quiet, I won't even pay you for the boy because I don't have to."

Acteon looked as if he wanted to argue, but the thought of losing money kept him silent.

"Here's what will happen," explained Optimus. "You two will protect the Flea and make sure he reaches Lyon. I hope you know where that is?"

Acteon nodded. The largest city in Gaul was far south, on the Rhone and Saone rivers.

"There, my contact will take over and make sure the message gets to Septimius. If the boy succeeds, you will be rich. If he fails, you die. We all die because Albinus will be Emperor and anyone not on his side will be slaughtered. Understood?"

The boy was stunned by how quickly his fortune had changed. He hardly heard when Hector asked the courier, "What will you do while we go to Lyon?"

Optimus smirked and said, "Lutetia is a fine place to recover from my wounds, and Gloriana will be a loving nursemaid."

Hector's heavy brows knit together and his eyes shot fire as he growled, "Only if you marry her, you dog."

The boy crawled over to a spot between bales and wrapped a woolen blanket around himself. Looking up at the stars, he found the shapes of his enemies, the gods, watching him. Were they laughing? Had they planned this joke? Now, instead of becoming a metalworker's apprentice, as he had planned, he was a slave and a courier. He almost wished he was back home.

5. Such a Homely Man

Lydia had scarcely fallen asleep when she was awakened by Mikal.

"It's time, I think," Mikal said. "First light already. I've got everything ready except you. How do you feel?"

"Like a piece of twisted iron. I'm so stiff I can't move."

"Good! That will make you look sick in case anyone's out in the courtyard. Come on, up with you!"

Lydia was no match for Mikal's determination, so she got up and dressed herself in her old tunic and boots. Mikal patted some white powder onto her face and rubbed dark charcoal under her eyes.

"Perfect!" the slave complimented herself. "You look terribly sick."

"Thanks," Lydia grimaced, draping her long shawl over her head and around her arms.

Opening the door slowly, they crept into the corridor. It was deserted. Obviously the men, and the women too, had stayed up so late they were sleeping in before starting for Noviomagus.

Lydia pulled the shawl around her face to hide her makeup and followed Mikal to the kitchen where slaves and servants, who rarely got to sleep in, were busily cooking. They ignored the girls who passed through to the courtyard and stable area.

"We need to find someone to help us," Mikal said. "You sit on the bench and look sick while I go look." .

"Ah, Miss Mikal, you're a minute or two early." It was young Chaton, Tar's assistant at Tunadur. "We've got everything almost ready. Madame Angwyn told me last night you'd be leaving early. Is Miss Lydia not feeling well?"

Lydia tried to look sick as Mikal answered curtly, "That's right. Her mother thought she would be better off at home."

"You going, too?" Chaton asked, looking closely at Mikal.

"Of course. You can see that Miss Lydia is too sick to go alone."

"Yes," but he kept looking at Mikal.

"Now hurry with the carriage," Mikal ordered, obviously enjoying the chance to be in charge. "And Coa, too. Tie him to the carriage," she added after a poke from Lydia.

"Sure. Have a seat and I'll be right back."

Mikal sat down next to Lydia. When Chaton was out of sight, Lydia said, "He must like you. He never took his eyes off you."

"Insolent young man. I hate him."

"Why are you smiling then?"

"The smile lies," Mikal said, blushing.

Unexpectedly, Lydia noticed a man approaching from the main entrance of the villa and immediately covered her face again with her shawl.

Dressed in a simple long-sleeved white tunic cinched at the waist, leg-wrappings and boots, he strode purposefully toward the stables but stopped when he saw Lydia and Mikal.

"Good morning, ladies," he said courteously.

Lydia recognized the voice from last night. He was the one they called Marius. From habit, Lydia looked up and returned the greeting. The man immediately exploded in laughter.

Lydia was furious. "Sir, why does my greeting call forth such a reaction? You must be truly barbaric to behave with such bad manners."

Marius merely pointed to her face and choked out the words, "Forgive me, please, but your face . . .?"

"What's wrong with my face? No, I wouldn't want to hear it from such an ill bred, rude boor as you!"

The man nodded his head and bowed at the same time. It was hard to fit the melodious voice of last night with this medium-height, ears-sticking-out, dark-haired, dark eyed man with a short beard. How dare he laugh at her face!

"I am truly sorry," he apologized. His deep-set eyes seemed to glow with humor as he went on, "It was unforgivable, but please, ask your friend here if your face isn't uncommonly striped with black and white. If it is the new style on the southern shore, I beg your pardon. My reaction has been most uncharitable."

Lydia turned quickly to Mikal and realized from the look on her face that the man was right.

Mikal whispered, "The charcoal and powder seem to have streaked together," and then couldn't hold back her own giggles. Lydia hated being the center of so much early-morning amusement.

"Wipe it off immediately!" she ordered Mikal, who used a corner of her own tunic to do so without further comment except for a few repressed titters.

"It seems we are all going a-journeying this early morning. Are you heading to the festival?"

"No, sir," Lydia answered impatiently, wishing he would realize he was not welcome.

He went on, "You must be the young woman who left the dinner before I came yesterday. Quintus Antonius's daughter from Tunadur?"

"Yes," Lydia replied with thinly disguised hostility. What had the others told him about her?

"I trust then, that you are returning to your home? Tunadur?"

"Yes"

"I, too, shall miss the festival. Business calls me more strongly. I would have liked to see your father invested. He is a good man. But I was told you have a young brother. Is he here?"

Lydia didn't bother to hide her dislike for Marius as she said bluntly, "I have two brothers. The best one died in Gaul five years ago; one is alive but he's a spoiled brat and wouldn't lower himself to come. My grandmother always stays home, so Father has only my mother to watch the ceremony today. Now, since I am quite ill, I would appreciate not being disturbed further."

Marius murmured something, turned away, and walked to the stables. Lydia was relieved to be rid of him.

"There's Coa," Mikal whispered as Chaton led the horse out toward them. "He's enormous! I could never ride him, Lydia. Please don't make me."

Lydia, with no patience left, answered, "Don't be silly. You will ride him today and you will enjoy it. I know you will, so do not complain or I will have someone beat you."

Mikal sighed and in a small voice, answered, "Yes, Ma'am."

To Lydia it felt good to have let off steam. Besides, Mikal was being childish and deserved to be threatened.

To Chaton she asked, "Where is the carriage?"

"Coming, miss. There was a mix-up. A new stable boy put our livery on one of the Arundel mules. He's making the switch, so the carriage should be ready shortly. Here, Mikal, hold these reins and I'll go see how he's doing. Come on, Coa won't bite."

With trembling hands, Mikal took the reins and held tightly.

Lydia wished Chaton would hurry. For one thing, and it was ridiculous, she didn't want that man, Marius, to see her riding in a carriage. It was too humiliating.

Part of her wish came true because just then Marius rode out on a fine horse, sitting tall in the saddle, looking straight ahead and not acknowledging Lydia at all. He rode well for such a homely man.

Chaton now came out leading the mule and carriage. He ably tied Coa's lead to an iron ring attached to the back board and helped the two young ladies to their seats.

"Who is driving?" he asked.

Mikal didn't hesitate. "I am. Miss Lydia is much too sick to drive."

Chaton seemed to take extra seconds handing the reins to Mikal. Lydia wrapped the shawl around herself and pretended not to notice.

Soon they were through the gates, joggling along the roadway leading to the Jade Forest. From the top of a small rise, glancing back to Anglesey as she always did, Lydia was again struck by the elegance of the villa set among its surrounding oaks and birches, with vines climbing up the arches and covering the walls in places. In the springtime when the vines and the flower beds blossomed, Arundel was rich with fragrance and color. It was so well-suited to its surroundings that it might have been put there by divine providence, except for the recent events that spoiled it for Lydia.

After they entered the forest, Lydia began to breathe quickly.

"What's wrong?" Mikal asked, her voice full of concern.

"I hate too many trees, that's all. They block the light and keep out the fresh air so I can't breathe. Don't you agree?"

"No. I like forests."

"I don't. I should, since there are so many everywhere, but I don't. In a forest you never know what's watching you. Brutus Marconius gets his game in these woods, did you know that? Not just deer, either, but wild boar and foxes. There have even been wolves here."

"That may be, but I don't mind. The tall branches form a kind of roof overhead and make me feel protected."

It was obvious that Mikal's normal exuberance was gone. It was like talking to a blob of bread dough, and Lydia was sorry now that she'd threatened her with a beating.. How could she let Mikal know that without directly apologizing? Not finding any way, she reverted to her normal bluntness.

"Look, when we're out of these woods, you are not allowed to be gloomy anymore. Understand? I'll teach you to ride Coa and you'll like that. Now cheer up!"

Mikal sighed then gave a small grin. "I appreciate your kindness."

Lydia knew sarcasm when she heard it. She certainly didn't deserve it since she'd tried to help Mikal feel better. She absolutely would not apologize. You don't do that to slaves.

"I'm sorry I got mad at you back at the stables." Where had that come from? She hadn't meant to say it! "It's just that riding horses is fun. It makes you feel free and strong."

"I will try, truly," Mikal answered, looking at Lydia for the first time in a long time. "Thanks."

"What a relief," said Lydia, who couldn't stand it when people sulked. "Now I can be the gloomy one."

"Oh? Why?"

"Short memory you have. Titus."

"Ah. Love doesn't always work out the way you want it to, does it?"

"You're young to know that, but I think it never does. I'll end up an old maid somewhere, taking care of Darius's children."

"I doubt that. Losing Titus isn't the end of everything."

Lydia bristled at the lack of sympathy. "It feels that way! It's the end of trusting people, that's for sure."

"Only some people." Mikal got a mischievous look in her eye and said, "I know a love poem. Would you like to hear it?"

"Not really, but go ahead if you want to."

"It's from an old book I read in one of my owner's houses..
'My beloved is fair and ruddy,
'A paragon among ten thousand.
'His hair is gold, finest gold,
'His locks are palm fronds,
'His eyes are like doves beside brooks of water . . .'"

In spite of herself, Lydia burst out laughing. "Palm fronds? Like the ones on the wall of the guest room? I can't imagine anyone having hair like that! But I like the doves beside brooks of water. That's romantic. How did you learn it?"

Mikal didn't answer.

"Tell me?"

"I'd rather not talk about it," Mikal answered testily.

"Oh, well, if it bothers you. Because of your family? Because of where you read it?" Lydia found herself curious about Mikal for the first time since she'd known her.

"Miss Lydia, I don't want to talk about it."

"Certainly." Lydia was quiet for a moment, then couldn't resist asking, "Are they slaves, too? Do you miss them?"

"Stop it!" Mikal was mad. Her face was turning red and her dark eyes glared right through Lydia.

Lydia somehow managed not to react. It was the first time she'd ever tried to have a real conversation with a slave, and was puzzled over why it hadn't gone better. She had just discovered that slaves didn't have to share their feelings if they didn't want to. With this new idea prompting her, she decided it would probably be best to hold her curiosity in check for awhile. There would be another day.

She tried to remember how Mikal came to the family. Six years ago, Lydia would have been eleven and Mikal eight. Somehow she didn't think that Mikal had been bought at the slave market in Noviomagus. Maybe it had been the market in Londinium.

It almost felt like one day Mikal wasn't there, and then she was. Lydia remembered coming to the kitchen for breakfast and seeing Rema with a scraggly haired, dark eyed little girl. Maybe she had wandered in during the night. From where? Alone? She watched Mikal, trying to recall that little girl. The dark hair and eyes were still there, but not the little girl look. Neither of them was a little girl anymore.

By then the woods were thinning out, giving way to the rolling countryside of the Downs with clear views to the southeast where it looked as if there might be rain on the sea. A strong breeze sent wavy cloud shadows flying over the hills. Rain might catch them before Tunadur, but for awhile, at least, it would be fine weather for teaching Mikal to ride Coa.

"Do I really have to?"

"Yes. He is as gentle as a new-born lamb. He won't hurt you. You just have to get acquainted with him."

"I've been butted by hundreds of new-born lambs," Mikal argued.

"Nonsense. Stop the carriage and I'll get him ready for you."

After untying Coa, Lydia gave Mikal a boost up. It was hard to remember what it felt like when she'd first learned to ride, because it had been so long ago.

She took the reins, leading the horse and told Mikal to hold onto Coa's mane and to press into his flanks with her knees.

Even at a walk, Mikal looked like a little bug bouncing all over Coa's bare back.

"Grip with your knees," Lydia instructed.

"I am!" Mikal yelled as four inches of daylight appeared rhythmically between her bottom and Coa's back. "Ooowww! It hurts! Can't we stop? It's torture!"

Was Coa disturbed by the yelling or the bouncing rider? Was that why he stopped and lowered his head to the green grassy field so that Mikal slid unexpectedly but gently down his neck to the ground?

Sitting where she landed, Mikal declared with finality, "I have no talent for this, Miss Lydia."

But Lydia, for whom riding was as easy as breathing, reassured her, "All you need is a blanket to sit on. When we get to Tunadur, you can try it with a blanket."

"Not Coa, please. He's too smart for me, and by now he knows it."

"All horses are smart," Lydia told her. "You've got to make them think you know more than they do, that's all."

"But I don't."

Lydia took Mikal's hand and pulled her up to stand. "Horses are different in other ways, too. At Tunadur I'll get you one of the smaller mares and you won't have any trouble, believe me."

Mikal sighed in resignation. "I don't like riding," she said just to make sure Lydia knew.

"Maybe you don't like it now, but you will." She remembered that she'd said those very words to Diana about four years ago. Her former friend had been a more willing pupil than her slave.

For the rest of the trip home, Mikal seemed content to drive the carriage while Lydia, on Coa, raced ahead, then back, circling all over the familiar fields. The faster she galloped, the easier it was to outrace thoughts of Titus. She imagined that each time Coa's hooves struck the ground, they crushed another memory of him or another sweet word of Diana's. Someday she would get even, but until then, she wouldn't waste another moment of her life thinking about them.

6. No Sympathy or Compromise

Lowering clouds turned the downlands to soft tones of grey and brown, but the rain held off until Lydia and Mikal were within a half mile of the River Adur. After a brief sprinkle, it began to pour. Pools of water collected rapidly in old wheel tracks and overflowed, making miniature streams and waterfalls.

Coa, rested by a long period of walking, was energized by the rain and loped like a young stallion the whole distance to the river, splashing mud everywhere and leaving Mikal and the carriage far behind.

On the opposite bank, too far away to see details through the mists, one hill stood taller than the others. That would be the villa at Tunadur. Lydia was glad to be home. After yesterday's fiasco, she had no intention of ever leaving again.

Turning Coa's head, she was about to start upstream to the ford when from the underbrush along the far side of the Adur, she saw a movement, heard a loud bark and then saw a splash! A moment later, a small head surfaced. The dog made almost no progress against the river. Because of the rain, at this spot it was deeper and faster than where she crossed yesterday.

"Culain!" Lydia shouted, horrified. "Go back! Go back!"

If he heard, he did not heed.

The dog looked tiny against the waves as he bobbed up and down, disappearing behind the swells. Kicking her heels into Coa's flanks, Lydia plunged recklessly down the steep bank and into the swirling water. Coa never broke stride charging through the shallows.

Lydia's arms and legs clung desperately as Coa plowed through the torrent. Her voice grew hoarse from shouting over the sound of the rain and river. Her shawl, heavy with water, weighed Lydia down. She unwrapped it and gave it to the Adur. The river wasn't appeased. It wanted her.

When they were just past midway, Lydia was horrified to feel something pulling her down. In desperation, she kicked out at it, god or monster, and was instantly flipped off Coa's back like a leaf. Her left hand still held his mane but her right hand flailed helplessly against the water. She twisted her wrist to get a better grip on the mane, but instead it was yanked out of her hand! Triumphant, the Adur carried her toward open sea.

"Come on!" she commanded herself. "Forget demons! Stroke!" Choking on dirty water, she fought with all her strength, but the current was stronger. The water swirled around her, dragging her under.

Suddenly something bumped into her and latched onto her tunic with its teeth. Culain! There was a forward surge and Lydia knew the young dog was pulling her. She was much too heavy for him. He would kill himself. They would drown together. She tried to help by grabbing his neck, but only caused both of them to go under. Kicking hard, she surfaced. Culain hadn't loosened his grip on her. How was he breathing?

When she came up, she glimpsed Coa already on land, shaking the water off himself in a halo of spray. Culain was swimming valiantly but Lydia knew she was dragging him lower in the water. Somehow she managed to kick again, using her arms to keep her head above water. As long as Culain was fighting for her, she would fight, too. She blotted every thought but survival out of her mind and continued to kick and stroke, though she seemed to make no progress.

At last, one of her boots touched something. The sludge drifted away instantly, but the next step felt more solid. The next, she could stand, though the raging water kept pulling at her, making it impossible to keep her balance. Wrapping her arms around Culain, she let him help her to the shore. Water from the river, rain and tears all blended together as Lydia realized that her valiant young wolfhound had saved her life.

On the opposite bank, which now seemed very far away, Lydia saw Mikal jumping up and down, waving her arms in a victorious dance. The river had not won this time! Lydia waved for Mikal to go upstream to the safer ford, and watched as she turned the cart in that direction.

Culain, leaping and bounding along the shore as if he hadn't done anything remarkable, occasionally stopped long enough to shake more water off himself.

Lydia knew she had to get to Tunadur quickly. She was completely soaked and exhausted, shaking already from the cold. She called Coa, but he ignored her as he bent his head to nibble the damp grass. She called Culain, but he, too, took no notice.

Giving up, she trudged on unfeeling feet to Coa and took his reins in her cold hands.

"Come on, let's get home," she coaxed him. He lifted his head and she started up the muddy bank. The last person she expected to find at the top was her grandmother.

Rema looked amused rather than concerned as she held out a huge woolen blanket for Lydia to wrap around herself.

Lydia was too tired to ask the questions that filled her head. Rema probably wouldn't have answered them, anyway. How had she known? How could she have seen them with all the wind and clouds and rain? How could she have known they were coming?

She would have liked to ride Coa, but it didn't seem fair to the horse or to Rema, and she didn't want to wait for Mikal and the carriage, so she trudged beside her grandmother the half-mile to the villa.

Rema broke the silence. "Don't put Coa to pasture. He must go to the stable. Tar can take care of him, make sure he is dried off and has some good oats."

Lydia shrugged and led the horse to the stable. Rema rarely allowed such a treat but Coa deserved it.

How quiet her home was with almost everyone gone to the festival. The flock of geese huddled together under an overhanging eave, ignoring the horse this time. Just as well. Coa might swim stormy rivers, but his fear of the sour-tempered gander could well prove stronger than his courage.

Tar nodded a greeting to her, patted Culain and took Coa's reins.

How good the stable smelled; how kind and comfortable old Tar looked.

Eyeing the puddle she was dripping on the ground, Tar remarked, "The Adur must be high. I expect you'll be warming up in the kitchen where there's hot food and drink waiting."

"Culain deserves a treat, too, so I'll take him along. How did he get out? I thought Borac had him."

"Aye, but Borac was called away to help the smith in the village this morning. Is it trouble for him?"

Lydia laughed. "Not at all! Lucky, in fact. Now tell me if you can, how is it that we seem to have been expected?"

"You ask me?" Tar said with a twinkle in his eye. "Ask your grandmother. She's the one who knows such things."

"All right then. How did Rema know?"

Tar shrugged his heavy shoulders and shook his head. "Ask her yourself," he repeated.

Lydia suddenly realized she was famished. Rema would be in the kitchen. Hurrying across the courtyard, patches of color showed that the clouds were beginning to lift. Leaving her muddy boots at the doorway, Lydia entered the kitchen, Culain close behind.

Immediately, Rema handed her a bundle of dry clothes and ordered her to change.

"Right here in the kitchen?"

"It's warmest here."

"Then make sure no-one comes in," Lydia grumbled and started to undress.

"That, too," Rema ordered, pointing to Lydia's undergarments.

Lydia slipped them off quickly and reached for the dry ones, feeling much better when she was dressed again. Rema bundled up the wet clothes and took them away to the laundry area of the bath wing. She seemed to have a lot more energy than she showed when the family was all home.

"What would you like?" Lydia asked Culain. "Stew?" Culain's tail wagged. "All right. It's a small enough reward for saving my life. Of course, if you hadn't gone into the river, I wouldn't have gone in either, and none of this would have happened. But it did happen and it turned out fine for both of us."

Taking a wooden bowl from the shelf, Lydia dished up a generous helping of stew and put it on the floor. "It's hot!" she warned, but Culain had already found that out for himself.

Lydia tore off a hunk of savory bread from the loaf, dipped it into the rich dark mutton gravy and began to eat. A few drops of gravy dripped onto the table. They reminded Lydia of something but she couldn't remember what.

How unmannerly I am, she mused, and then deliberately spilled more sauce and sopped it up with more bread. Suddenly, between mouthfuls, she started laughing and couldn't stop. It was the oysters! Spilling the oysters at Diana's. What was it Titus had said? "The errant oyster slides from her grip"? What a conceited fool he is!

Culain gave a little yip and perked up his ears, looking toward the door. Noises from the courtyard signaled that Mikal had arrived safely. Lydia dished up another bowl and set it next to her own on the table. In a moment Rema appeared with a new stack of dry clothes.

It was time to ask. "How did you know I was coming back? I didn't even know."

Her grandmother merely said, "Your mother and I knew."

Mikal entered before Lydia could ask another question. Wet through, the slave girl had to go through the same undressing ritual. When she had her dry clothes on, she took her bowl and was going to move to a stool in the corner, but Lydia stopped her.

"Sit here," she ordered, then added an uncharacteristic word, "Please."

Rema also took a seat at the table and finally explained, "Your father mentioned several times meeting Titus unexpectedly at Arundel, hinting that it was more than Province business that took him there. We all knew that Titus would be there yesterday and Diana of course, so when your mother asked me to mix up the fever potion for you, I knew I'd see you today. How did you like the drink?"

"Terrible, but effective. Go on."

"Guessing when you would arrive wasn't hard because you would have to leave at the earliest possible time."

"And Mikal?"

"Your parents wouldn't send their sick daughter home alone, would they?"

Lydia smiled. "I thought you were maybe a sorceress or something."

Rema was amused. "Well, I did not know you would go swimming in the river. I went to watch for your coming and had the blanket just in case you needed it. So I guess I'm as good a sorceress as almost anyone else. It only takes thinking and reasoning. Now Mikal, she may have the real gift."

"Mikal? What gift?"

"From the Old Ones," Rema answered. "It's said that their descendants still retain some of the power."

"But Mikal isn't from the Old Ones," Lydia objected.

"Not our Old Ones, but others perhaps."

Lydia turned to Mikal. "Are you?"

A shake of her head because her mouth was full of bread and stew was Mikal's answer.

"See, Grandmother? She's not." Then Lydia remembered the way Mikal had been able to read her mind back at Arundel. She'd even said she could read Darius's mind. Maybe that's what the "gift" was.

"Mother said she was worried about Darius," she said to both Rema and Mikal. "Has he come back?"

Rema answered, "No. That's why you're here. I trust your mother's feelings in this. She suspected yesterday that Darius hadn't merely gone away for a day, and she's worried. Like it or not, finding your brother is your job."

"You're sure he's not hiding in the barns or in the pottery shop?

"I'm sure."

Lydia knew what she'd be doing for the rest of the day.

"Good bread and soup, Grandmother," she said, meaning every word but wishing she could enjoy it longer.

"To stoke your furnaces," Rema replied.

"Furnaces? I have only one."

"Mikal has the other."

Up came Mikal's head. "Me? I'm going with Lydia?"

"Of course. You will be of great help finding Darius, as you well know."

A heavy sigh accompanied Mikal's return to eating.

"It will be a fine afternoon," Rema stated, taking a seat at the table. "By the way, how did you like Fulvia's dining hall?"

Lydia almost choked on her food. "It's very elegant, with gold plates and candelabras. I spilled an oyster and it slid all the way to the floor, very slowly. Everyone was watching and Titus, especially, had a good laugh. Thank you, but I prefer to sit in sensible chairs rather than lie on couches."

"Roman ways are not always best," Rema agreed, then pointed to some skin bags stacked in the corner. "Your provisions. Bread, dry fruit and meat, some milk for today. Uncle Petrus will fix you up tomorrow for whatever you need to do."

"We're going all the way to Lewes, then?"

"Yes."

"Is Darius there?"

"I don't know. I hope so."

A long silence followed. Lydia sopped up the rest of her soup with the last piece of bread and then, in what she hoped was a nonchalant way, turned to Mikal.

"Did you know about this?"

Mikal looked embarrassed, fumbling for words. "I didn't, not really, but I knew master Darius was in trouble. That's all."

Rema looked directly at her and said, "If you allow yourself to reach out to him with your mind, you will be able to find him."

Mikal shook her head doubtfully. "How are we getting there? Walking, I hope."

This time Lydia could read Mikal's thoughts. "We're riding the horses. Anything but horses is too slow. I will take Coa. Tar can saddle Kem for you. She's small and gentle."

Mikal's face fell. Lydia had no patience for people who didn't get along with horses. No sympathy or compromise was to be forthcoming.

"How long will it take?" Mikal asked.

"Four or five hours," Lydia answered. "If we leave right away, we'll probably get there in time for part of their festival. Uncle Petrus will let us go, won't he, Rema?"

"Don't count on it. There's been trouble up there with some of the Cantii who don't like Romans. Festivals, especially ones like the Bacchus festival, seem to bring out the worst in people like that."

"After 200 years you'd think they'd be reconciled to the Romans like we are. It's stupid."

"Maybe so."

"What if Darius won't come back with me?" Lydia knew how hard it would be to persuade him after their big argument about the amulet.

"Try to convince him that it's better coming with you now than with his father later. Don't let him forget that Quintus has absolute power over him. Over you, too, and your mother. Quintus is a good man, but power can lead even good people to do bad things."

Mikal pushed back from the table, her bowl empty, and declared, "I'm ready. Show me this gentle horse and I'll do my best to steer her in the right direction."

The Amulet

Lydia was pleased with Mikal's new-found determination. "Don't worry," she said. "Kem will follow Coa all the way. Thanks for the food, grandmother." Gathering up the skin saddlebags, she added, "Guess we'll see you tomorrow. Oh – what if Darius is not with Uncle Petrus?"

"Find him wherever he is and bring him back."

The look on Rema's face left no doubt that she had given Lydia an unbreakable command, a command that would send the girl far from Britannia.

7. "I Don't Really Need a Horse"

Two hours into the ride, Mikal pleaded to be allowed to walk. "If I sit on this horse any longer, every muscle I have, every bone in my body, is going to be permanently bent out of shape. Please, Lydia, have pity. I wasn't born to this the way you were. I can keep up by walking, really I can."

It took at least ten minutes of moaning and supplication before Lydia began to think that Mikal might not be pretending.

"You must not be doing everything I told you," she scolded.

"That does it!" the slave shouted. "Nothing I say has any effect on you. It never will. I give up. I don't care what you say, I am getting off this bony beast and I am going to walk the rest of the way to Lewes. Whip me if you want. Nothing could hurt more than riding this razor-backed nag another six miles."

Moaning all the time, Mikal slowly pulled her right leg over Kem's back and dropped all the way to the ground, landing in a heap. Stretching out, she lay flat on the rough ground.

"Praise god," she cried. "There is still life in my poor body. Something inside here" – she held her sides – "is killing me."

"That's your kidneys," Lydia told her, looking at her in disgust. "They don't like being bounced around. You'll get used to it."

"Not me. Not ever again."

"Rema said you had to come with me."

"I know. I will obey. But I will walk. I will walk to the end of the earth. There is no other way for me."

Lydia sighed. Six miles wouldn't make a lot of difference today, especially since Coa should continue to walk also, but what about tomorrow? Mikal didn't make any sense to her. Culain, just a puppy, was racing everywhere in spite of having been nearly drowned earlier. Why was Mikal so weak?

Maybe tomorrow she would be better. Darius could ride double with Lydia while Mikal rode Kem. No matter how much she complained,

Mikal could not walk all the way back to Tunadur. She would have to ride.

"You win for now," she told Mikal. "Keep a good pace."

Mikal soon found a walking stick and looked as stiff as if she was going on three wooden legs, but she never complained.

The countryside was rough and more wooded than around home, especially along the streambeds. Steeper hills, lower vales, marked their entrance into mining country. Lewes was a crossroads for iron going by road or river to Londinium or the south coast. Most of the buildings on the farms they passed were round, in the old style, with stone walls and tall pointed thatched roofs. Stone marked the boundaries of the fields.

Near the entrance to Lewes, a few temples with colonnades surrounding a tile-roofed sanctuary showed the Roman presence, but there was none of the elegance of Noviomagus in either the buildings or the people.

Lydia didn't care about that. What she liked about Lewes was visiting Uncle Petrus's bronze casting workshop. It was a fascinating place with white hot fires and the huge bellows heating the cauldrons until hard metal was transformed into rivers of molten bronze. Petrus made plaques, hinges, and sometimes a small statue for a god offering, all by pouring the liquid into molds which then solidified. After they cooled, which took a day, sometimes more, the hard work of scraping and polishing began. With enough work, the bronze could develop a brilliant shine that looked almost like burnished gold. Petrus was one of the best artisans in Britannia. His love of form and grace showed in every piece he made.

It was Petrus who first introduced Lydia and then Darius to working with metal. For a girl to work in a foundry was unusual because many people were superstitious about it. They thought the god Vulcan, being masculine, would resent it. What eternal laws would be broken if, for instance, a woman turned out to be better than a man at it? None of that bothered Petrus.

Working on small pieces was what Lydia loved. At first, she and Petrus kept her work a secret from her parents, not knowing how they would react. Now, of course, they knew because Borac had let her work in the blacksmith shop with him. The iron hinges and smaller implements that she helped him with did not seem cursed by any gods, but it was probably best to let people assume that Borac or Darius had done the work. Lydia's greatest pleasure was in creating jewelry and fine decorations for ordinary household things, like putting a dove on the handle of a soup ladle. No other villa had such creative kitchenware.

One secret remained between her and Petrus, though. Many of the statuettes she made, like the little Minerva, were sold at the market. Knowing that people gave money for things she made, pleased Lydia so much she would have loved to tell her parents, but knew they would think she had disgraced them.

Darius, on the other hand, didn't allow his work to be sold. Fortunately for him, he let the work he did with Borac be used on the farm. If he hadn't, father would have put him to work in the fields instead.

Lydia didn't know the reasons for her brother's actions. She just knew he was strange. That's probably why he made such a huge mistake with Titus's amulet. He had done what he wanted, and not what Father wanted. There was a big difference. One day he'd thank her for changing it without asking him..

A fifteen-foot thick, twelve-foot high wall surrounded Lewes, with four passageways which should have held gates but didn't. It was as if the town itself had decided that the protection of the forests and hills was all that was needed.

It was dusk when Lydia and Mikal entered Lewes and the festival was still in full swing. Jugglers, acrobats, games, food, and much strong drink had brought the outlying populace to the streets of the small town.

Lydia dismounted because it was usually forbidden to ride horses in Roman towns. To avoid the crowds, she took a left turn up a narrow lane that led the long way to Petrus's home. Mikal limped behind, leading Kem by her bridle.

"How much farther is it?" she asked.

"Not far. See that corner where the road starts uphill? Uncle Petrus lives just beyond that at the top."

A pack of excited little urchins spilled out of a nearby shop. Seeing the two girls with horses and a huge dog, they stopped to stare, then to beg and pester. When that brought nothing but cold stares, the children started to follow, throwing sticks and shouting things that little children shouldn't know about.

Barbarians, Lydia thought, cursing them silently. Coa's ears were laid back flat on his head and twitched nervously. Lydia implored Epona, the Celtic horse goddess, to make him and her dog behave. Up to now, Culain had never growled at or bitten anyone, but after all, he was a wolfhound and sooner or later his heritage would show through.

Lydia's prayers went unanswered. A hard-thrown pebble nicked Coa's flank. He reared up and pranced, undoubtedly looking like a gigantic monster to the rascals who, scared to death, fled down the pathway and disappeared around a curve. Only the echo of their screeches was left.

"Good horse," Lydia told Coa, rubbing his neck. Mikal looked terrified, but Kem, with nerves of steel, had stood like a statue during the ruckus.

Culain stayed close to Lydia as if glued there. His tail hung low between his legs as he whimpered and peered around for enemies.

By the time they arrived at Petrus's house, Lydia was ready for something good to happen. She gave Coa's reins to Mikal who now held both horses, and went to knock on the heavy wooden gate.

No-one could doubt that this was the metalworker's home. Bronze shields decorating the door gleamed from a recent polishing. Lydia lifted the large iron knocker shaped like the beard of a gnome, and let it fall onto the gnome's chin, making a loud clang. No-one answered. She tried again. The house and courtyard seemed empty. Of course! They were probably at the festival with the rest of the town. She felt let down, unwelcome.

"What do we do?" Mikal asked.

"I don't know."

The street was deserted now, but from the center of town came sounds of revelry. Coa tossed his head and stamped his feet, impatient with indecision. Culain whimpered and crouched low to the ground. Lydia nudged him with her foot to get him to stand up and be brave. Instead, he whined and looked up at her with soulful eyes.

Mikal, softer of heart than Lydia, knelt down beside Culain and wrapped her arms around him, which meant that both horses were momentarily free to leave. And leave they did.

"Look what you've done! Idiot!" Lydia screamed as Kem followed Coa back toward town.

"No, it's your fault," Mikal defied Lydia. "This dog saved your life today and you treat him as if he was nothing. You deserve to lose the horses!"

"Merciful gods, I didn't kick Culain, I nudged him. You really should watch your tongue, you know. Now get up and help me catch those horses before something bad happens."

Mikal snuggled her face into Culain's fur then stood up, pulling him up, too. The dog looked at Lydia who, unsmiling, patted his head and said, "Good dog."

Now they all rushed off in the direction the horses had gone. From out of a dark doorway, a slovenly, stinking fellow lurched into their path.

"Eh, lovie," his slurred voice mumbled, "Where'r ya headed?" His thick rough hand caught Lydia around the waist and pulled her against him. Without hesitating, Lydia brought up her knee between his legs and the man collapsed, writhing in pain and cursing wildly.

Mikal gasped. "That was rough."

"My brother taught it to me."

"Not Darius, I take it."

"Of course not. Ansonius. He taught me that there isn't always time to be nice and polite."

"I'll remember that," said Mikal.

The horses seemed to have vanished, a good trick for one huge and one large animal.

"Which way?" she asked Mikal. It felt like being in a forest with tall trees on every side, except that these were tall buildings hemming them in, making it impossible to see more than twenty feet in any direction. Mikal turned around slowly then declared, "That way," pointing to the street leading down to the forum in the center of town.

"How can you be sure?"

Mikal pointed. "Droppings in the road. Near the shoemaker's."

"Let's go!"

At the corner, a commotion caused them to turn right and head down a winding little road lined with small workshops. Squeals and laughter could be heard, but each bend in the road brought them no closer to the horses.

Suddenly Lydia went cold. The words she heard were, "What a sacrifice for the gods, eh, Madoc? A whopping big fee the priest will give us for this one."

"What about t'other?"

"I'm keeping her for meself. Sweet thing. Sell her for a pretty penny when I've had me fun w'her."

Lydia glanced at Mikal and saw that she, too, was aware of what lay ahead. How she wished she had a weapon, any weapon, now. Even if she didn't know how to use it, she could threaten.

Unexpectedly, Culain growled, pulled his lips back over his teeth and leaped forward. Lydia and Mikal raced after him, arriving just in time to see him explode into a crowd of drunken revelers, men and women. Fierce and frightening, tall as a wolf, he stood there, menacing the crowd who backed off. Only the men holding Coa and Kem were left. Culain snarled at them, taking a short ominous step forward.

"Now, now, doggie, hold off," said one. "Bertie, I don't really need a horse, do you?"

"Not any more I don't."

Both men dropped their reins and hurried off after the crowd.

Culain was on Coa's left side, the one with the bad eye. The horse sidestepped and then backed into a wall trying to escape the unseen growling monster beside him. Kem, at last upset by the chaos, whinnied in fright, adding to the tumult. Coa was now trotting up the road toward Lydia and Mikal, so Kem followed. Culain, coming behind, made sure the crowd stayed put.

As Coa raced past, Lydia grabbed for his trailing reins and held tight even though her arms were almost torn off.

"Easy! Coa! Easy!" she urged, trying to calm him as he dragged her over the cobblestones.

Wild-eyed and trembling, Coa finally slowed down and let her lead him.

The more even-tempered Kem, who never stayed frightened for long, allowed Mikal to take her reins and followed nicely. Lydia was astonished at the change in Culain, who walked at her side, tail and head held high. Without any training, he'd done exactly the right thing. She rested her free hand on his head and praised him for real, "Good boy. Smart boy."

Soon they were back at Petrus's door, wondering if the family and Darius had returned.

"Miss mind reader, can you tell if anyone's home?"

"No. I wish you wouldn't tease me about it. I can tell you that Darius hasn't been here, though."

"What?! How long have you known?"

"A long time, I guess. I know I'm stupid, like you said, but you wouldn't have listened and I couldn't be completely sure, not until we were through the gates of the town. That's when I really knew. Now you can send me back to Tunadur if you want to. I'll walk all the way."

"Quiet!" Lydia ordered imperiously. The girl really was annoying sometimes. A horrible thought was forming and she needed to concentrate on it. If Darius wasn't here, where was he? Mother, Rema, and Mikal all said he was in some sort of danger, but if he wasn't in Lewes, where could he be? Her breathing came fast as she worried about what this might imply..

"Mikal, where am I supposed to look? How can I find him?" Unwelcome tears of panic began to gather in her eyes but she wasn't about to give way entirely to her fear. Turning to the gate, she pounded desperately on it.

8. "No-One Should Venture Alone"

From down the road, a boisterous crowd of men and women surged toward them. Frantic, Lydia continued to bang on the gate until her knuckles hurt. It was obvious no-one was home, but she couldn't think of anything else to do, so she kept pounding while Mikal kept a tight hold on the horses.

From the midst of the approaching horde came a call, "Well look who's there! It's our Lydia!"

Uncle Petrus, older than his sister, Lydia's mother, by nearly six years, had none of her reserve. Not much taller than Lydia, he made up for his height with a wide body and bighearted personality. A jovial smile lighted his face as he strode toward them followed by his wife, Georgia, a shorter, female version of Petrus.

Lydia was relieved to see that they seemed fairly sober. She wiped her eyes quickly on her sleeve, glad of the dim light.

"What brings you here this day?" Uncle Petrus asked, not waiting for an answer. "Come to join our festival? Not in Noviomagus? But I don't see Darius? Where is the boy? Is he with your father? Come in! Come in!"

He threw open the gate and led them all into his courtyard.

"Here, you girls come inside," Georgia said, opening the door to the house. "Petrus can take care of your animals. What about the dog?"

Culain nudged Lydia's hand and sent a mournful look to Georgia.

"I guess he wants to come in," Georgia laughed, her rosy face a picture of goodwill. In her presence, Lydia always felt at ease. She began to relax. "Fine-looking young hound, isn't he? Have you eaten?"

"Some," Lydia said, forgetting that it had been many hours earlier.

The kitchen was small compared to Tunadur, with a low beamed ceiling and tiled floor. Georgia lighted a few candles and had the girls sit at the table. On the hearth were at least ten heavy iron pots and many large spoons of both metal and wood. All had been made by Petrus.

Georgia stirred a large pot that hung in the fireplace, releasing enticing aromas of stew. Ordinarily that would have whetted Lydia's appetite but not now. She was too anxious about Darius if, as Mikal said, he hadn't been here.

"Now who is this?" Georgia asked Lydia, indicating Mikal.

"Sorry, my mind is elsewhere," Lydia apologized. "This is Mikal, one of our slaves. Grandmother sent her with me."

"You are welcome here, Mikal," Georgia said, smiling.

Lydia remembered that Georgia and Petrus did not choose to have slaves. Georgia continued, "No-one should venture alone these days."

"Oh?"

"There has been trouble around here that would curl your hair if it wasn't already so curly." Georgia laughed heartily at the old joke, making Lydia smile.

Petrus then blasted into the room, making it seem to shrink to half its size. Whisking off his knit cap, his graying red hair flowed out. Once it had been almost as bright as Darius's but Darius did not have Petrus's stocky build nor his disposition. Petrus and Georgia were easy to love.

Her uncle pulled up a richly carved stool to the table and took a good look at Lydia before asking her what was wrong.

"Darius." She then explained as much as she could, leaving out the details about changing the amulet. When she was done, the older couple shook their heads.

"It's a shame," Georgia stated.

"Certainly," Petrus agreed. "The boy is different from all of us. And already a far better artisan in many ways even than I am. Gone, you say? Maybe two days?"

"Yes."

Petrus took his time before speaking again. Georgia, in the meantime, put a large bowl of meat and vegetables on the table and spoons for everyone. At her house, everyone ate from the serving pots.

"He should have come here," Petrus said and Georgia readily agreed with him. He grabbed a meaty bone of pork and started to eat, looking thoughtful. Finally he gave his conclusion.

"This is how I see it. Darius chose not to come here, probably figuring that someone would be sent to take him home, like you have been. There's no reason he would have gone west for that's where everyone from Tunadur was heading. To the east, however, the land and people are less well known. Less settled. The woods edge right up to the open downland.

High cliffs by the sea. He must have gone east by the shore, yes, but he might now wish he hadn't."

"Why would he go east? What's there for him?" Lydia asked.

"Canterbury. If he ever got there alive. A haven for artists like him. Easy to find work."

"But he's only eleven!" Picturing her scrawny little brother alone in the middle of a strange city made Lydia feel awful. She was ready to forgive him anything if only he would be all right. She looked to Mikal.

"Yes," Mikal said slowly and deliberately as if choosing her words carefully. "I think he went east. But I – I don't know this Canterbury. It may be so, but I don't feel as if Darius is there or even going there."

Petrus laughed loudly and Georgia asked, "What is she? Rema sent a witch along with you? What a stroke of luck!"

Lydia was dismayed. "No, no, Mikal is not a witch, she just gets feelings about people."

"What do you think a witch does?" Petrus asked. "But alright, if it pleases you, she's no witch. Still, getting feelings is a good skill to have when you're looking for someone."

Lydia nodded then changed the subject. "Could you draw me a map of the area from here down to the coast? Lewes is as far in this direction as I've ever been."

"Get us a piece of charcoal, love," Petrus asked Georgia. She found a good-sized one and handed it to him.

Talking as he drew on the table, Petrus said, "Here we are, right on the Ouse which goes down to the sea, here. And this is Tunadur. About eight miles beyond the Ouse, that's the Cuckmere. Where it cuts through the hills it's rough and the cliffs are tall. Only brigands live there, and wolves. Cliffs along the ocean front, here, where this big head of land juts out. You travel that way and get to Adairinnic. A decent settlement there, near the sea and a wild sort of coast. Not the best harbor, but it's all you've got along there so people use it anyway."

"If Darius went on the coast, would he pass by there?"

"Likely. He'd be wet, too, crossing two rivers."

"How long would it take him?"

"He'd need more than two days. At least, say, three. But people there aren't as friendly as on your coast. You'd best start as soon as you can in the morning if you expect to be in Adairinnic while it's still day. It's a good 10 or 11 rough miles I'd guess."

"We've got horses. They can go faster than a walker can."

"That's usually true, yes, but as I say, it's rough country. The horses should walk, not trot or gallop for most of the way," Petrus said reflectively. Pointing to a spot about halfway to Adairinnic where the pathway curved, he said, "You'll pass by the great Long Man. Have you heard of him?"

"Who is that?" Lydia asked.

Petrus laughed and Lydia sensed a story coming. "Even before the Old Ones came, the Long Man was there, carved on a hillside with the white chalk underneath showing through. You never want to see him at night; he'll scare the life out of you in the moonlight. But by day, he's right friendly like. You can't miss him. This path goes past him and the barrow he guards. But take care. Cults of one kind and another worship there and do things you wouldn't want to be bothering with. Some people think he's a kind of Mercury or Apollo, or even Bacchus. Ride on by, but take your chance to look. You'll tell your grandchildren about him someday."

"Sounds bizarre," Lydia said, looking at Mikal whose eyes had grown big and round. "We'll take a look at him. Is the path hard to find? Is it overgrown or anything?"

"Easy to find. I'll set you on your way. You won't even have to cross the Ouse except by bridge, and the Cuckmere's a gentle lass up this far. Given the weather stays nice, you'll have a fine day of it and find your brother at the end of it."

"Thanks. I hope we will."

"You're not worrying, are you? You know that my mother, Rema, would never have sent you on a venture like this if she wasn't sure you could do it. Since you have the little girl here to keep you company instead of one of the strong men, it shows she didn't expect trouble. Don't fret. She is almost never wrong."

"Well, she sent me up here instead of over the coast. Wasn't that wrong?"

"Was it? Haven't Georgia and I enjoyed seeing you and talking with you after all the time between? I don't call that wrong, and you can be sure my mother doesn't, either. But just in case that's not all, I'll give ye something to ease your way. Bring me the box, love."

The Amulet

Georgia took a small carved box from a locked cupboard and set it before Petrus. He wiped his hands on his leather tunic, then opened the box and brought out an exquisitely formed chain, the links intricately joined in a grapevine pattern.

"Oh, Uncle Petrus!" Lydia gasped. "It's in the old style, isn't it? I wish you could have seen the amulet Darius made. It had this same feeling of vines and branches and roots going deep into the underworld."

"It's yours."

"Oh, no," she protested, overwhelmed by the offer. It must have taken him weeks to make. Besides, mentioning Darius had restored her guilty conscience.

"But it is yours," Petrus insisted. "I made it in my spare time for you, so you must take it."

"I don't feel worthy of it, truly. Maybe you could keep it until I deserve it."

Petrus laughed heartily. "Humility from you? See, love, our Lydia is growing up after all! But she'll have to take it with her, won't she?"

Georgia nodded and said, "He loved making it for you, knowing how much you would like it. It may bring you luck."

"That's right!" Petrus agreed. "Hock it if you get in need of money. It will bring a good price."

"Sell? Uncle, I would never do that," Lydia exclaimed hotly.

"Good. Show your spirit. Now let's have some nice mead before we put these two to bed for a long rest. Looks like they be wearying."

It was true. The early departure from Arundel, the wetting in the Adur, and riding and walking to Lewes, plus chasing after the horses – it had been a long day.

The mead, made from honey, was warm and sweet. It soothed Lydia into a deep sleep in the bed Georgia had made on the floor for her and Mikal. At home, as at Arundel, Lydia would have been in her bed and Mikal on the floor, but such social norms didn't matter at Petrus's house. She slept soundly.

9. No Time to Waste

"You stay here with the Mouth," Acteon ordered the Flea as soon as they docked at the harbor of Juliobone. "Make sure he doesn't die on us or you'll die soon after, you can take my word."

They had had to stay outside the harbor for half the night waiting for the tide to change, which had not helped anyone's humor.

The boy had no doubt Acteon would do as he threatened. He glanced at the messenger who looked a lot worse than he had when they set sail from Britannia. Some of his wounds were turning red around the edges, getting the better of him, and the one on his thigh was disgustingly ugly, oozing green pus.

Acteon and Hector left for the public houses where they would hire men to row them up the Seine against the current. Using the sail as a supplementary aid, they could expect a fast trip to Lutetia.

From the deck of the boat, the boy looked out at the city, whose tall buildings and monuments seemed to dwarf everything and everyone in the harbor. An extraordinary assortment of men and women, animals and children, strolled along the quay hawking food, trinkets – or themselves. He had never dreamed he would ever be in such a place, where great ships from as far away as Alexandria might be tied up right next to him. Here, even an elephant could appear. How he would love to see one of those giant beasts with huge long tusks and legs as thick as houses. It was said that a single elephant could carry ten fully-armed men on its back.

While he was thinking about elephants, a sailor approached with a monkey riding on his shoulder. At first the boy thought the monkey was a small dog, then a malformed child, and finally a piece of magic. The man drew closer, as the boy had hoped he would.

"Ho, boy!" called the sailor. He was a youngish sort, dark with only a scant beard, wearing a vividly embroidered linen vest. "From the wild lands of the Picts with hair like that, I gather. Slave you must be to the captain of this leaky barge?"

The Flea was wary about talking to him, though he was curious about the monkey. Acteon had warned him to keep away from the people of the quays, but it couldn't hurt to be civil.

"Yes, I'm his slave," the boy answered, still not quite sure if he was the slave for Optimus or Acteon or Hector. He also wasn't sure if he should call himself a Pict or not. As a fugitive from Tunadur, it might be sensible to join, unofficially, the untamed Pictish tribes of Caledonia, but he didn't know much about Picts or their ways, and doubted they spoke Latin. If this fellow knew more about them than he did, it would not be smart to try to fool him. In the end he said nothing, but watched the monkey.

"My little manikin here – you like him?"

The boy nodded.

"Many there be where my ship is sailing in four days time. Africa. Ever heard of it, Red? Then Greece. And up the passages to where Tartars live. Ever think you'd like to see that?"

The boy had heard of these places from tutors and saga singers, but they were like places in a fable to him.

Now the man was so close that he sat down on the dock, his feet dangling over the edge almost touching the gunwale. His monkey was attached to the man's belt by a long light chain, exploring as far as the chain would reach.

"His name is Sinka. You want to hold him? Sure. Come right up here."

The man held out his hand to the Flea, ready to hoist him up to the dock. The boy saw that the hand was trembling. He then looked directly at the man's face for the first time. The dark eyes gleamed like a dragon's would, guarding its hoard of gold.

"Hold!" Optimus shouted from the bow where he had supposedly been sleeping. "Out of here you scurvy water rat or you'll not see the shores of Greece again! The penalty for stealing a man's slave will be yours in a thrice if you so much as look at my boy again. Off with you!"

The man spat out an oath, scooped up his monkey and sauntered off the dock into the crowd.

The Flea stared at Optimus, wondering how he could have so much energy after the feverish night he'd spent tossing in delirium. Indeed, the messenger must have gathered up all his strength for his speech to the monkey man, for now he lay in a faint upon the pile of wool that was his bed. His head was wet with sweat, but when the boy touched his skin, it was cold.

Trouble, thought the boy.

More of the many wounds were running with pus. The boy got mad. How could such a conceited person as Optimus let this happen to him? Stupid, that's what he must be, to get himself this messed up. Even more stupid to be making love to the sister of Hector! If he died, which seemed likely, Septimius Severus would never get his precious message because Optimus refused to part with it. The boy couldn't very well deliver a message he didn't have, and that meant he'd be stuck with the surly Acteon. Given a choice between Acteon or Optimus, he'd pick Optimus. Actually, he'd pick Hector. It didn't look as if he'd have a choice, though.

The boy dipped some rags into the bucket of water close by and applied them to Optimus's face and shoulders since that's what he'd seen Hector do. When that didn't seem to help, he tried to wash off some of the pus from the wounds. It seemed as if he was just moving slime from one place to another, so he gave up, realizing there were a lot of things he could have learned at home about taking care of injured animals if he'd only paid attention.

Then he started thinking about the slaves at home. He'd never thought about how they might feel, but now that he was a slave himself, it was different. Mainly he wanted to be free again. He knew that some slaves became freedmen by doing a brave deed or saving money to buy their freedom. He doubted Acteon would go for either of those ideas. Besides, he didn't feel brave and he had neither money nor any chance of getting some.

Not fifty feet from the boat loud screams erupted as a mob of rushing bodies hurled along the quay. The sound of a whip ripped through the air, then a loud crack as it crashed down upon something – or someone. Again and again! Moans and cries from the midst of the crowd became angry shouts of "More!" and "Make his blood run thick!" The mob parted for a moment and Darius caught a glimpse of a shiny heap of red flesh lying on the stone pavement.

A man in the toga of an official kicked the mound and said to the one with the whip, "Take him to the dormitory. If he comes around, he's a galley slave. Weld the iron collar around his neck so everyone will know he ran away."

A chilling terror shook the Flea from head to foot. A runaway slave!

Kneeling close to Optimus's ear, the boy whispered, "Hey, my friend! I'm not a slave, not really. I'm a Briton. A Roman Briton. My name is Darius and my father's the Prefect of Noviomagus."

The messenger opened one heavy-lidded eye and said, "Too bad. Don't let anyone know."

"Oh wonderful," the boy whispered in exasperation. "Now if you die someone else will steal me and take me off to Ethiopia or some other ungodly place and I'll never get home." Optimus made no response. He was unconscious.

An hour passed, then two, with nothing to do but observe the noise and confusion of the city, and watch Optimus look sick.

Eventually along the waterfront came Acteon and Hector, weaving from side to side at the head of a parade of six hapless-looking men. The oarsmen, Darius guessed. From the look of them, it would be a slow trip to Lutetia.

Optimus grabbed Darius's sleeve. "Get me to Lutetia. Don't fail me. Big money . . ." Then he was gone again.

The boat careened as the new crew leaped aboard. They reeked of all kinds of human body odors.

"Slave!" Acteon yelled. "We leave at once. Show these fine gentlemen to their places and put oars in their hands. Lutetia, flower of the Seine we are coming!" He then sank slowly to the deck and passed out.

Darius doubted that the rabble would do anything he told them to, even if he knew what that was. He looked to Hector for help. The big man seemed to be in slightly better control though his eyes had to struggle to focus on Darius. Muttering under his breath, Hector shoved the oarsmen into their stations, three on each side, one sitting at each of the oar holes. He had to move some of the bales of wool to the center of the boat to make room for them. He then pointed below to where the oars were kept and said loudly to Darius, "Get those out."

Darius went down the hatch to the hold, bumping his head on the crossbeam because there was only about four feet of head room. The oars were stacked one on top of another, as tall as trees and almost as heavy. He had to kneel down to try and lift up one end, and could only budge it a few inches before letting it fall painfully on his foot. He was relieved when Hector leaned through the hatch, put his arms down, grabbed three oars at once and lifted them up to the deck. Darius ducked just in time to miss getting whacked. Hoisting himself back onto the deck, he saw how easily Hector had placed the oars in the slots on the rail and was going back for the remaining three. That was a kind of talent Darius knew he would never have.

As drunk as the new crewmen were, they knew what they were doing. Yet what a miserable way to make a few coins. Darius wondered if they were freedmen, ex-galley slaves, or only poor people.

"On-shore wind," Hector explained. "Good to catch it in the mornings. Speed us upstream." Singlehandedly he hoisted the large sail. Darius felt useless.

"You stay with the Mouth, Flea. Keep him alive if you can, because if he dies Gloriana will kill me. My sister has a fierce temper when something goes against her. Aye, lad, as disgraceful as this man is, she'll want him alive. Then she can kill him herself or keep 'im. Up to her."

Darius tried to picture a female version of Hector. She would be huge, with dark hair piled on top of her head, not hanging loose and scraggly like her brother's, and no beard. Or maybe a light shadow of a beard like some women had. It didn't make sense that a woman like that could lure a gigolo like Optimus Maximus. If, indeed, Gloriana had any of Hector in her, she would squash poor scrawny Optimus, or perhaps the slave who let her lover die.

"What's so funny, Flea?" Hector, at the tiller, asked.

"Nothing. Really nothing," Darius choked out.

Optimus stirred and opened his cloudy eyes, searching for Darius. "Come close," he whispered in a grating voice. "The message. Remember it. You have a memory? No matter. You have to now. Remember this even if you've never remembered anything in your short life. Yes?"

Darius nodded. His memory was good enough, thanks to his tutors making him memorize long speeches by dead Romans and Greeks. Optimus then continued, though each word sapped more of his diminishing strength.

"You go to Lyon. In the countryside near Lyon there is a man, Numerianus, who calls himself a Roman Senator. Find him. Beware of all the roads and the post houses. Albinus rules the part of Gaul south of Lutetia. Enemies in the city. Kill you. No post houses. Only Numerianus. Yes?"

Darius gulped then nodded. He didn't know where Lyon was. Italy?

"Numerianus will trust you. You trust him. My old teacher."

Optimus stopped, closed his eyes. His breath was quick and shallow. Scared, Darius shook him, whispering urgently, "What's the message? Come on! What's the message?"

"Yes . . . moment. Listen."

"I am listening! Tell me!"

"Keep me alive. You must."

"I'm trying to," Darius answered in desperation. If the fellow went delirious again, he might never give him the silly message and then, horrors, Darius would be stuck with Acteon in Gaul or wherever he went.

A heavy cough wracked Optimus's weakened body.

"Septimius Severus. Emperor. Tell Numerianus that Albinus's British legions are coming. They will sail in three weeks and join Albinus by mid November. Numerianus will know where Septimius is. He is not in Rome. Albinus means to have the Praetorian Guard in Rome declare himself Emperor. What day is this?" Optimus grabbed Darius's wrist and held it with surprising strength.

"I don't know. Yesterday was Bacchus festival?"

"I hope it's no later. You hurry to Lyon. Tell Numerianus. Don't fail."

He fainted or died, Darius wasn't sure which, but he felt a lot better having gotten the message out of him. He repeated it over and over so as not to forget. Three weeks, legion sailing from Britannia. Mid November in Lyon. Albinus Emperor. Get to Septimius Severus. No time to waste.

The boat went slowly, laboriously around a bend in the river and the distant sea disappeared, shut off by the last view of the port city. Already the sun was halfway to noon, but it did little to warm the autumn air.

One of the rowers began to hum a tune, a low, soft sound. Another joined in and then another until the song of the rowers fell rhythmically on the waters.

10. "What If We Walk Off a Cliff?"

Following Petrus's instructions, Lydia and Mikal rode southeast on the rough, rugged path toward Adairinnic. A northeast wind made it cold even though the sun was shining. The hills were steeper and sharper than on the gentler Downs. Oaks with trunks as thick as small houses grew in frequent groves interspersed with ash and beech, making tunnels with bare branches intertwined overhead.

Lydia did not like it. It was too easy to think about wolves lurking in the shadows. Mikal, on the other hand, hummed little tunes and seemed to be unbothered by either the ride or the surrounding trees. If she ached from the previous day, she didn't mention it.

About the future, Lydia was uncertain and wanted to remain so. Not knowing what was coming, she could be optimistic. Whenever her thoughts meandered toward ideas like "What if Darius is hurt and can't --," she quickly shoved them to some other corner of her mind and paid special attention to Coa's ears or the way the wind blew the fallen leaves.

"I must not be much of an adventurer," she thought. "I'd just as soon be home, riding Coa over familiar fields, than here." She had no doubt she would be back at Tunadur soon; if not tomorrow, then in a few days, no more.

In the distance was the familiar white line of chalk cliffs along the seashore. Birds skittering in the brush or soaring overhead were the same as at home. In fact, if she looked west and squinted her eyes, peering hard in that direction, she could imagine seeing Tunadur. It was only imagination. Sea mists, forests and rolling hills obscured the real view.

She and Mikal made good time, so when the sun was just past overhead, they stopped by the grassy banks of the Cuckmere to eat the lunch Georgia had packed for them. The bread was crusty on the outside, soft inside. Dipped in the light wine, it went well with Georgia's homemade cheese. Some sweet apples rounded out the meal. The horses grazed hungrily in the tall grass; Culain lay close by, chewing on meaty bones included in the lunch just for him. Mikal stretched out on her back, looking at the sky through the twisting branches of an ancient oak. In a sweet, slight voice, she began to sing,

"The Lord is my shepherd; nothing shall I want.
"In pastures of grass, he makes me lie down
"and leads me by the waters of peace."

Lydia commented, "That's beautiful. Did you write it?"

"No, no. People who owned me before you did taught me. They knew lots of beautiful songs.

"That's strange," Lydia said. "Were they minstrels, then?"

Mikal laughed. "No. But they sang well. The Father especially. He was a very smart man.

"And you like to be mysterious. Who were they? You were about 8 or 9 when you came to Tunadur, weren't you?"

"Yes, eight. Six years ago. When I was very young, I lived in Gaul in a fine big city. I remember our house. It was large with a wide porch that looked out over the whole land for miles and miles. You've never seen anything like it."

"The house of your master?"

"No. Of my parents."

"Slaves can't own houses like that," Lydia scoffed.

"My parents weren't slaves! You aren't listening. There was some trouble, an awful night, and I was taken away. I don't know where my mother and father are now, or my baby sister."

"I don't understand how your family could have been wealthy one day and slaves the next. Your father must have been a murderer or a traitor to have had that happen."

"Be quiet!" Mikal said hotly. "You know nothing of it, living safely in Britannia. You probably don't know where any of your slaves come from. It doesn't matter to you. We are nothing. Well guess what? Britons can be slaves too. You do one thing wrong or one person doesn't like you, and you will find yourself without any rights or family. It happens. Do not accuse my father of being a traitor. He is loyal and hard-working."

"Enough!" Lydia ordered. It was not right for a slave to be so forward. She had allowed Mikal too much freedom on this ride and it would have to stop. She reminded herself that she must treat Mikal as a slave, not a friend. And so it would be from now on.

Mikal was silent.

The gentle sound of the Cuckmere, plus the generous lunch they'd eaten, brought on an inescapable desire to rest. There would be plenty of time to reach Adairinnic. They could relax here for an hour. Relaxing, it was impossible not to sleep.

While they slept, clouds appeared, first high wisps then puffs, then enough to block the sun and cool the air even more. Lydia awoke at the change in temperature and shook Mikal.

"Get up! Time to be going. Looks like rain soon."

They worked together to round up the horses, neither of them speaking. Culain was eager to cross the Cuckmere which was shallow and slow at that point. He leaped in and splashed to the opposite bank. Coa with Lydia, Kem with Mikal, followed.

The next leg of the journey had steep uphills and downs where they had to go slowly to save the horses. No sense wearing them out when there was still a long trip home once they found Darius. The sun disappeared behind dark wind-driven clouds as they rode up a short hill and made a curve to the left. Lydia suddenly pulled Coa to a stop, astonished at what she saw.

"What in the world --?! " She stared at the apparition before her.

Mikal came alongside and whispered, "The Long Man, it must be."

The enormous outlined figure of a man was striding across the entire hillside opposite them. Ghostly white, he was carved into the white chalk that underlay the thin soil of the region. According to Uncle Petrus, no-one knew what gods made it or which people worshipped it. To Lydia, it was alien, far remote from anything familiar or reasonable. As ancient as it must be, she couldn't help feeling a kind of unpleasant power emanating from it.

At that instant, a crack of thunder tore through the air followed by brittle lighting and a stabbing torrent of icy rain. Both girls screamed at once!

The horses, terrified, scrambled in opposite directions. Mikal instantly fell off, while Lydia managed to hang on until Coa headed for the heavy, low-hanging branch of a tree. She knew he would try to knock her off. It was a trick he played sometimes when he was panicked. She made a simple choice and slid off just before the branch hit. Coa kept going.

The ground came up hard. It always did. Shaken, but no bones broken, she slogged back through mud to Mikal, who was also unhurt.

"Let's find some shelter till the storm passes. Follow me," Lydia ordered. A tree trunk that had fallen and become wedged on the lower branches of its neighbor seemed to promise some hope of dryness.

Just as Lydia ducked under the log, a bolt of lightning turned the world white and split a huge oak only yards away. Lydia screamed, her arms and head and feet buzzing from the electricity. Mikal skidded in beside her, shivering from the cold and from fear. Culain followed, quivering, and snuggled close to them.

"This is awful!" Lydia gasped, hardly daring to breathe.

"Yes!" Mikal agreed, staring petrified at the storm that swirled around them.

"I think the Long Man wants a sacrifice, but the horses ran off with our food," Lydia shouted as lightning exploded all around them. She had an idea. "The priests sing at the temples when they make a sacrifice. Maybe a song will be enough. Sing, Mikal, sing! Now!"

Mikal shook her head.

Fed up with Mikal's disobedience, Lydia slapped her face, screaming, "Sing! Now! He's going to kill us. It's the Long Man! He has magic and all we have are your songs! I order you!"

Mikal shook her head.

"Gods aren't something you toy with," Lydia yelled, realizing she was hysterical but unable to stop herself.

"You sing, Lydia. I can't," Mikal said quietly.

"You know I'm a terrible singer! It would only make it worse!" She picked up a large stick and shook it in Mikal's face, on the edge of madness, wanting to hurt her.

Mikal looked away, as if unwilling to see what was in Lydia's eyes.

Terrified, Lydia expected each bolt of lightning to be the one that killed her. Realizing Mikal was not going to give in, great huge sobs shook her whole body. She'd never been in a storm like this in her whole life. She knew she was a coward. She hated herself for that. She hated Mikal for everything. She hated Darius for running away.

The storm kept its strength for almost an hour, lightning, thunder, rain and all. In the end, Lydia was surprised to find that she was still alive. The stick was still in her hands, her fingers stiff and her knuckles white from gripping it so tightly. The Long Man, oblivious to her, still strode the opposite hillside.

Now that the storm was over, she had to face a big question. What was she going to do about Mikal? Horrible things usually happened to disobedient slaves, and Mikal had definitely been disobedient, arguing and even refusing to sing. How hard would it have been, especially when Mikal knew so many songs? The best thing would be to send her back to Tunadur for punishment. How? Lydia could not go with her. She had a job to do: Find Darius. If she sent her back by herself, Mikal might run away, and then the penalty would be horrible. As angry as she was at her, she did not want Mikal to suffer that kind of treatment.

Rema and Mother had both said Mikal would be able to help. If she kept the slave until they reached Adairinnic, she could figure out what to do depending on what they heard about Darius. It seemed the best solution, at least for now.

With a big sigh, she crept out from under the tree, stood up and ordered her slave to do the same. "We have to find the horses."

Culain shook himself all over, delighted to see action again. After having been a shivering mass of fear during the storm, he now pretended to be their brave leader, prancing down the little rise. Turning southwest on the muddy pathway, they started toward Adairinnic. Lydia guessed it was only about an hour away.

Even though the clouds had started to lift, they let through very little light, making it seem later than Lydia thought it should be. The oaks began to grow more closely together. Thick roots pushed up through the ground, putting unexpected stumbling blocks in their path. In fact, it was a far less pleasant route than when they had started from Lewes.

Lydia walked quickly, often slipping in the mud but anxious to get away from the woods and out to open country again.

"This is foolish," Mikal complained from behind her. Lydia would have ordered her to be quiet but she was too busy trying to keep from tripping and falling.

Mikal continued, "It's getting so dark I can hardly see you, let alone where we're going. I just tripped for the fiftieth time. What if we walk off a cliff or something?"

"Stop complaining! Culain will warn us of anything bad."

"I can't see him, either."

"He's right in front of me. I can hear him even if I can't see him. Stop worrying so much!"

That, of course, was the moment Lydia's foot caught on a root and she went tumbling full forward, thrusting out her hands to cushion the fall. Mikal, who had caught up, almost fell on top of her but managed to sidestep at the last moment, landing by chance on wet grass-covered ground.

"Are you all right?" Mikal yelled.

"Of course," Lydia answered, angry at herself for being clumsy. When she tried to stand, however, a sharp, sick pain shot through her left arm, making her cry out. A cold sweat broke out on her forehead. She lowered her head between her knees to stop the dizziness and wished she was home.

Kneeling beside her in the mud, Mikal asked, "Where does it hurt?"

"I'll be fine," Lydia whispered, trying to wish the pain away. All she needed was a few minutes of sitting and she'd be ready to go.

"It's your arm. Let me see it." Lydia had been cradling the left one in the right and didn't want to let go, so she just shook her head.

Mikal sighed, and didn't move.

Lydia reluctantly admitted, "I'm not sure I can go any farther right now. Can you make a fire?"

"No. I didn't know we would be needing one so I didn't bring the flint and steel. Besides, all the wood is probably too wet."

They sat awhile longer, then Mikal said, "We have got to move. My feet are getting numb and my bottom may become part of the mud if we don't get up. Can you stand?"

Lydia thought about it and said, "Help me."

Mikal did, being careful not to jar Lydia's left arm. It was hard to do because the path was so slippery from the rain. Their cloaks, though caked with mud, had kept them from being soaked. It was true what Mikal said about feet. Lydia's were almost senseless in her boots.

"Guess we better walk," she said halfheartedly.

"Do you know how far we've come?"

"No idea. But the villa couldn't be more than a couple of miles farther, don't you think?"

"Lydia, you are my mistress, but you are in no condition to walk two or three miles in the black dark. Neither am I. The villa will still be there in the morning and that's when we'll go. You stay here. I will find us shelter, or make some."

The clouds had broken up a bit, letting through dim moonlight by which Mikal was able to make a sort of shelter. It wasn't much. A group of close-growing oaks with intertwined branches provided a kind of roof. She scraped the thick top layer off of some wet piles of leaves, exposing the underlayer that had been packed together so long it formed an almost comfortable mattress.

Once Lydia lay down on it, she drew her cloak over her because, even damp, the wool could keep her warm. Mikal then lay down and covered them both with a thick blanket of dry leaves right up to their chins. Culain, wet and messy but warm, snuggled close and soon fell into a snoring slumber.

From the deep sound of Mikal's breathing, Lydia knew that her sleeping slave wasn't bothered by any of the things that troubled Lydia. Her nose started to itch, then her neck where fine dirt drifted down inside her tunic. Then her ears felt as if little bugs were crawling inside them. Every breath she took seemed thick with dirt. Any movement of her arm hurt fiercely, so she lay on her back, her arms crossed on her chest. Every once in awhile, when she couldn't stand it any longer, she'd shift her legs to a different position, trying not to wake Mikal. She was warm enough, but far from comfortable.

Remembering Culain's courage at the Adur and in Lewes, she prayed silently that his protective instinct would wake him if danger came near. After that, she dozed fitfully.

When morning came, Mikal determined that Lydia's arm might not have broken completely. The bone was probably cracked just above the wrist because it wasn't far out of place.

"But it sure hurts if I don't hold it."

"Oh, it's as bad as a full break," Mikal explained, "but it won't be as hard to set right. I'll find a straight stick for a splint and wrap it tightly so you can let go of it. Then we'll try to find Adairinnic."

"I hope they have a bath there, and my horses," Lydia mumbled.

"Yes, you are mud from head to toe, and your clothes are awful!"

"Well, look at yourself," Lydia observed. "You look worse than I do, with leaves sticking out all over your head."

Mikal laughed. "You have them, too! We are both disgraceful."

Lydia wasn't ready to see the humor in their situation. Her stomach was empty. "I hope Adairinnic has lots of food."

"Me, too. I'm starving."

Mikal found the splint, tore the bottom few inches off her tunic, wrapped up Lydia's arm, and they started walking.

"Watch for hoof prints," Lydia said.

Mikal took a quick glance ahead and said, "Look, Coa's big prints and Kem's little ones. Going fast, by the look of it. They sure stirred up the mud."

"The gods be praised. We'll find them soon, I know it."

The road was not a neat, well paved Roman road by any stretch of imagination, but there was periodic evidence that flat stones had once been spread over certain areas in a half-hearted attempt at smoothing it out.

As they slogged forward in the mud, Lydia ventured, "Do you have a song for this?"

She was relieved when Mikal didn't take offence, but instead answered, "Maybe. I'm working on one. My owners used to hire a certain minstrel to sing at parties sometimes. That man knew poems that lasted an hour or more, about anything under the sun."

"Like the minstrels that come to Tunadur?"

Mikal giggled. "Better. I'm sorry, but he really was better."

"How better?"

"His singing, for one thing. It was beautiful. The ones at Tunadur or even at Noviomagus have boring voices with no emotion in them, and they only play one instrument, and that they play badly."

Lydia of course took offence at this. "I like them!"

"Yes." Then Mikal added, as if she couldn't help herself, "That's because you haven't heard the ones in Gaul. There's a big difference."

"I doubt it," argued Lydia. How it irritated her when her slave acted this superior way just because she came from Gaul. "You were just a little girl and everything probably sounded good to you."

Mikal didn't say anything.

The mists of morning hovered in little patches. The air was brisk but the skies were clear again. Each time they came to a glen or vale, Lydia looked for Coa. She called him a few times, even whistled, to no avail. She wasn't worried though. How far could he have gone? His tracks led right on down the half-hidden road.

The smell of the sea was stronger now and the roadway looked better travelled. Paving stones became more frequent, which helped them make slightly faster progress.

11. A Welcome Place for Strangers

Far in the distance Lydia spied a traveler. He was riding toward them on a large horse, leading a smaller one. She decided that, coming from that direction, he must know Adairinnic and planned to ask directions of him.

Mikal touched her arm, the good one, and said, "I think those are your horses."

Lydia squinted her eyes, looking more sharply, and saw Coa! The man was riding her horse! He must be one of the thieves Uncle Petrus had warned them about, and now he had both her horses.

Furious, she knew she was going to fight him for them. It didn't occur to her that two ragged and filthy young women on foot, one with a broken arm, might not be an equal match for a vicious highwayman.

"Find another big stick," she ordered Mikal. "Quickly!"

The horseman had closed the distance to within a hundred feet or so before Mikal found a stick good enough to use for a weapon.

At that distance, Lydia was astonished to recognize the big-eared, homely Marius whose business had taken him from Arundel two days ago, the same morning that they had left. Oh heavens! She hoped he would not recognize her.

"Those horses do not belong to you!" she challenged. Her bluff voice did not match her demeanor as she looked at the ground trying to hide her face.

"Is that right?" he answered in that deeply melodious voice she remembered. "I wondered who would be out here on these horses, and now I see – or think I see – that it is the young mistress Lydia Quintilla and her friend. You seem to be disguised as mud people, or perhaps it is the illness that troubled you before?"

"Sir! That is a rude way to talk to my mistress!" Mikal dropped her weapon and faced him, chin out, arms akimbo.

"I apologize," he said.

Lydia ventured a glance at his face and sure enough it was smiling, teasing her. She couldn't think of a thing to say and wished this wasn't happening.

Finally Mikal asked, "Have you come from Adairinnic?"

"I have."

"Is it far?"

"Not by horseback. Will you ride?"

Mikal looked at Lydia who shrugged and whispered, "It would be better than walking."

"Miss Lydia, then, will ride the horse you are on if you will kindly dismount. I will ride the other."

Marius laughed. Lydia didn't think anything was funny.

He dismounted and handed Coa's reins to her which she took with her good hand, but immediately knew she needed that hand to hold her splinted arm.

"I can't," she whispered to Mikal, handing her the reins.

Coa turned his head to nuzzle her and look at her with his good eye. Lydia then looked at Mikal, wondering what to do.

After too long a silence, Mikal spoke to Marius, "Sir, Miss Lydia has hurt her arm as perhaps you can see."

"Yes, I see it has a splint on it."

"I'm fine!" stated Lydia, burning with embarrassment under the mud on her face. She had finally figured out that she could immobilize her left arm by tucking her hand into the ribbon that held the tunic around her waist. "I just need a hand up."

"Yes," agreed Marius. "It would be difficult if you could not use both arms. Unless, of course, you knew how."

"I don't think she does," Mikal ventured after quite a long silence. "Besides, it might injure her arm even more." Marius seemed not to have heard, so Mikal took a deep breath and spoke loudly, "Sir, will you please help my lady to mount so we can continue our way to Adairinnic?"

"Of course," he replied amiably. "But you see, I question what she will do once she gets up on this big horse. How does she plan to handle him?"

"Well, why don't you help her up and then we'll find out!" Mikal sounded exasperated. Lydia wished to be invisible. She hated this infuriating man!

"A good idea!" Marius exclaimed too heartily to be sincere. Without another word, he took the reins from Mikal, grasped Lydia around the waist and hoisted her up on Coa's back as if she were no heavier than a feather. Aside from the initial surprise, Lydia felt strange being up there again and not being able to use both arms.

The next second, though, Marius had boosted himself up behind her and settled the reins in his own hands, ready to be in control

"What are you doing!" she protested.

"When your father hears about this," he explained, "I had better be a hero or he'll cancel my trade contracts now that he's the Prefect. Can't afford that, Miss Lydia, not even for you. So come along; we're off to Adairinnic. Heavens, you're filthy." Looking back at Mikal who had gotten up on Kem, he asked, "Are you all right there?"

"Fine," Mikal answered, coughing perhaps to cover up what might have been a laugh.

Humiliated beyond belief, Lydia could think of nothing insulting enough, so she kept quiet.

Marius, ignoring her, directed his questions to Mikal. He was awfully curious as to why they were there. Lydia wanted to ask him the same questions. Why, indeed, was he here? It wouldn't surprise her to find out that he was one of the thieves Uncle Petrus had warned them about. Was he only pretending to rescue them? Would something worse happen to them at Adairinnic? Could she trust him?

Mikal, bless her, answered his questions briefly, telling him only that Darius was missing and was thought to have travelled near Adairinnic.

"No-one there mentioned it," Marius said seriously. "But why should they? A young boy like that is no concern of theirs, nor mine either. Except that now he has become my concern."

"We don't need your concern," Lydia snipped. She was extremely uncomfortable riding in front of him. Under any circumstances, two on a horse was bad, but this was worse. His arms were practically around her rib cage, his chest and her back touching, as well as legs. It was like when she was a little girl riding with Ansonius, except that now she was a big girl and Marius was certainly not her brother.

With great relief, she saw the village come into view. The look of the place was not inviting. The buildings were round with thatched roofs, their walls a mixture of wood, plaster and stone. It had a gloomy atmosphere.

Instead of being open to the view of the distant sea, trees grew thick around it, making it look as if it was hiding something.

Four large ill-tempered dogs in varying shades of brown and black raced out to meet them, challenging Culain and running in circles around the horses. Lydia tensed, expecting Coa to shy and afraid of falling if he did. She could feel Marius's knees working to keep the horse calm, doing all the right things.

"Luppa!" he called. "Get these curs away from us before I kick their tails off!"

Around the far corner of the house ambled a low, stubby-bearded man in clothes of grey that hung on him as if thrown there months ago. He spoke to the dogs and they immediately ran to him, wagging their tails like new puppies. When he smiled at Marius, most of his front teeth were missing. His eyes were worse. One looked straight ahead while the other wandered over the sky; then they switched and Lydia couldn't tell which one he was really looking through.

The man gave a rough rhythmic wheezing sound that could have been laughter.

"Back so soon are ye?" he asked Marius. "Dug these ladies up out of the mud, did ye?"

Marius chuckled and dismounted. "These are polite young ladies, Luppa. We have to treat them with respect."

Once more he grasped Lydia's waist and pulled her off and then dumped her unceremoniously onto her feet.

Luppa grinned at her. "Awright, I'll be so incredibly perlite they'll think they was in Albinus's bedroom hisself. Now I'll be puttin' the horses inta the pen w' t'others. The dog can stay, too. Me pets won't do him no harm. Do ye think will they be stayin' long? A power crowded we be w' all the visitors."

"Do as suits you best," Marius said. "But I think the puppy will want to come with his mistress."

If my father could see me now, what would he think? wondered Lydia. Her instinct told her to be aware of all around her. Adairinnic was, after all, a place for outlaws and thieves.

Marius started across the yard so Lydia and Mikal followed, there being no choice. She couldn't figure him out. Making fun of how she looked after the kind of night she had spent wrapped in wet leaves! And then he paid no attention to her broken arm, and didn't give her any sympathy. He needed to be put in his place, and she would do it once she got cleaned up. He'd be surprised, having only seen her with her face full of powder and charcoal at Arundel, and today with mud everywhere. He thought she was a joke! She'd make him notice her, not that she wanted him to, not exactly, but her pride was wounded. He didn't even know what a good rider she was! Getting back at him would be balm for her soul.

Marius obviously knew his way around. Entering one of the back doors into a hot, smoky room, he called out, "Hola! Bearta! Anyone here?"

A plump, middle-aged woman with a large bosom that threatened to escape her low-cut formless dress, came bustling into the room. Her unkempt brown hair hung to her shoulders. An apron stained from years in the kitchen was tied around her waist. Lydia took her for the cook or housekeeper, rather than the mistress of the house.

"Shame on you, Marius, hola'ing so loud and the meeting going on in t'next room."

Her voice was warm and her smile friendly. Lydia felt better.

"Bearta, meet friends, Lydia and her companion Mikal, from the south coast. Ladies, Bearta's house is a welcome place for strangers. You won't be sorry you passed here."

"So these be your lost ones? And these be theirs?" she asked, pointing to the saddlebags that lay on a side table, to Lydia's relief.

"Yes. Easily found, too. The big one here has hurt her arm. Would you take a look?"

"Big one?" Lydia protested. Marius gave her a teasing grin which she made her realize how filthy she still was.

Bearta intervened. "Off you go, Marius. Surely I'll look at her arm and clean them both up, too, but Fonuc has been waiting for you to begin the talk. Go!"

As Marius passed into the next room, Lydia caught a glimpse of a medium-sized pillared hall, paneled in wood and darker than it ought to have been. A quick scan of the wall showed many ornaments hanging there looking suspiciously more like weapons than decorations.

Bearta examined her arm. "Ye're holding it tenderly. Be it broken?"

"I don't know. Mikal says it's cracked. All I know is I can't use it at all."

Without another word, Bearta unwrapped Mikal's bandaging and felt along the forearm. "Aye, most likely almost cracked through. Lucky ye are. T'will heal straight, and a pretty lass like you wants to have strong straight arms to hold your man."

Lydia wondered if Bearta was making fun of her for how grubby she was, but the woman smiled kindly and went on, "Ye do need cleaning up, so we'll just wrap this a bit and do the final touch after ye're done washing. Come!"

The girls followed her to a small storage room off the kitchen in the center of which sat a huge cauldron which Lydia guessed was the bath.

"Take hot water from the stove if ye like and mix it with some cold from the cistern. There's plenty. If you're hungry, take whatever you like from the kitchen. There's plenty but ye have to look for it. Busy I'll be takin' care o' the rest o' the place before time to fix dinner for the men. Bless me, clean clothes ye'll be needing, won't ye? Be right back."

Lydia looked at Mikal, who seemed just as perplexed. There was nothing hanging over the door to block the view from anyone entering the kitchen. For the second time in three days they were going to be undressing in almost public view. She didn't plan to get used to it.

"Here ye are, clean dresses and somewhat to dry yourselves with. After, there's a spare room I can put you in, small but it has a rare window looking out. It do get dark in this place, the way the woods hover over it and block the light – but then they blocks out a lot more, and that's good."

What did she mean by that? Lydia wondered.

Left alone, the girls examined the dresses. Not in the Roman style, they hung shapeless and long, with sleeves set in. More coarsely woven than wool from Tunadur, one was a ruddy rose while the other, almost white, seemed to have once been blue.

"I'll take the white one, I guess," Lydia offered since it was the softest.

"You'd look better in the rose, I think," Mikal suggested.

"What do I care which looks best? But all right. After we bathe."

They first scraped as much mud off themselves as they could, then poured water into small pottery bowls and washed the worst of the dirt onto the floor. Still not in the tub, they rinsed and washed again, paying attention this time to their hair. Mikal had to do most of the work because of Lydia's arm. After several washes and rinses, they were finally clean enough to soak in the hot cauldron.

Lydia, of course, went first, with Mikal standing guard at the door wrapped in a large cloth. As she felt the heat relaxing her abused muscles, the horrors of the past night slowly melted away and she began once more to feel as if she could handle whatever was in store for her, even with a cracked arm.

"That's a relief," said Mikal from the doorway.

"Stop that!" said Lydia.

When she was finished, Mikal helped her maneuver the rose dress on. The dress style was not likely to make Marius notice that Lydia was sometimes thought to be an uncommonly nice-looking girl. Not that she cared what he thought.

After that, she watched the door while Mikal soaked.

Where had Culain gone off to? He had been with them as they crossed the yard, but didn't follow them into the kitchen. Surely he would have made a racket if the other dogs had attacked him again. Anxious, she was about to order Mikal to hurry up when she realized that the girl must be as exhausted as she had been. In an unusual move for her, she kept quiet and tried to comb out her own hair with the comb Bearta had left for them. With only one hand, it was almost impossible. Her scalp pulled till it hurt so much that she had no choice but to wait for Mikal to do it for her.

Bearta returned to the kitchen and hurried about laying out onions, carrots, spices and other foods on the cutting boards. She moved so fast she seemed not to notice Lydia standing guard in the doorway. After putting out bowls and knives, tankards, and finally shouting to someone in the yard, "Uncover the boar! And keep those hounds away! I want the whole thing in the kitchen and no foolishness!", she turned to Lydia with a sigh of relief.

"Whew! Such a hassle! My you look nice, don't you, except for your hair. I put grease on mine to keep it smooth. Would you like some?" She indicated a wooden bowl on the shelf which presumably held cooking grease.

Looking at Bearta's wild hair, Lydia's answered, "No thanks."

"So be it. Wait till you see the boar. The best boars in the world live around here. Feel lucky you didn't meet up with one last night. Fierce as dragons they are. Most of our dogs get killed one day or another by them. But tasty! Oh my, yes. Tender and juicy out of the pit, with his eyes a-bulging out. That's what we'll all be dining on this noon, so, my girls, I need help from you and lucky I am you came. With my cook gone to tend a sick grandbaby and everyone else off to who knows where, who do you think has to do all the work while the men sit in there jawin' about wars and tribes and emperors and all that nonsense. Me. Who else? But I loves it, I do. Children gone to sea for better or worse, bless their souls. My daughter, though, just close down the road three miles. Won't leave her house, with first baby on the way soon. Ye'll find out, ye will. Fine lasses like you, ye'll be getting a man soon. Oh! Maybe you have one! That Marius, he's a good man, he is."

Lydia found herself blushing again! That awful habit had to stop! Bearta wasn't done yet, though. She rambled on and on until Lydia thought her ears would burst from so much listening.

"We won't be staying long," she managed to interject as Bearta took hold of her left arm and pulled, causing an exquisite sharp pain as the bones slipped back in place.

"Aaaa!" Lydia screeched, feeling tears coming to her eyes.

"There. Now it won't hurt anymore. See?"

Lydia nodded, realizing that the pain was gone. Still she had to sit down and catch her breath as Bearta expertly re-splinted and wrapped her arm with heavy wet material that hardened and shrank as it dried.

"We're on a search, Marius may have told you." Lydia wasn't sure how much or what to say about Darius, so she stopped there.

Bearta smiled amiably. "Searches can wait. But famished and weary you must be so you will at least stay to eat. And help me get it all ready. After lunch we'll see to your room. There be fourteen, I think, mouths to feed this noon. How does the arm feel now?"

Lydia tested it and was pleased at how much better it felt with the hard cast all around it. It was so heavy, though, she definitely needed a sling to hold it up. The cloth Bearta provided looked as if it had once been part of an old dress. The important thing was, it worked.

Mikal, refreshed and clean, offered, "If you tell me what needs to be done, I'm sure I'll be able to do it."

"Bless you, child. Good fortune the goddesses gave me today if you can slice and peel onions and pop in carrots and spices. It's a feast we'll be having if we ever get started. Lydia, you sit by the window here while Mikal and I get to work."

Lydia realized her hair would have to wait, so she sat in the window and ran the fingers of her right hand through the curls. It was a lot easier than using the comb, and after not too long her hair seemed almost free of snarls.

Everything about the kitchen was different from the one at Tunador. It was crowded with cutlery and baskets and wooden pots and bowls and metal cooking pots. Even the charcoal fires on the several hearths were different. Thick shelves on all the walls held more dishes than Lydia had ever seen in one place. Bearta and her husband must have a lot of parties, Lydia thought.

The smells were different, too. Heavier spices, old grease, unwashed dark walls.

Certainly Bearta wasn't anything like either her mother or Rema or their cook. Her constant chatter, for one thing. Lydia was used to people who spoke only when something was worth saying.

"Nice to be having a friend go with you when you're on a search," Bearta was saying, and Lydia perked up her ears, sensing a warning here.

"Yes," she answered, giving Mikal a severe look that meant don't say anything about being a slave. She certainly didn't want to have Mikal stolen away to become a kitchen wench here at Adairinnic.

Suddenly the courtyard exploded with growls, yips and yelps. The yelps she recognized as Culain's and ran out to rescue him.

The lop-eyed Luppa was in the midst of the fray, wielding a short whip right and left until the other dogs had all slunk away. Lying on his back, legs curled up, Culain was the epitome of vanquished puppy.

Luppa called to her, "Ye'd better take 'im in, Miss, or he'll be supper to these hungry mutts. The smell of the boar is driving 'em mad." He then bent down and gave Culain a rub behind the ears that set his tail flapping. "Don't worry about him. He'll be all right and one day he'll be a fine brave one. The wolfhounds come from strong stock, that I know. He's no match for my ones now, but in a bit, he'll be bigger and stronger than them. Go ahead, take 'im. Old Bearta, she don't mind."

"Come here, Culain," Lydia commanded and he came running. When they were back inside and Lydia at her seat near the window, Culain lay on her feet watching everything but staying out of the way.

12. Magical Folk of the Woods

"So, Mikal tells me your brother ran away? Was it for the coming war? What call did he have to be going?"

Why couldn't Mikal have kept her mouth shut! All right, Bearta's questioning was probably hard to resist after awhile, but still, now Lydia had to explain and she wasn't ready.

She weighed her words carefully. She decided to avoid talk about wars, so said only that Darius was eleven and not a fighter. He was an artisan looking for work, was how she put it, amused at how simple it all sounded when said that way.

"We think he came this way. I wonder –" she almost didn't dare ask the question. "I wonder if a small red-haired boy has been here? It would have been yesterday or maybe the day before."

"Nay. None like that. None at all. Sorry I am to tell ye."

"Well, that means we better leave soon," Lydia said, wishing the answer had been different. Her panicky feeling returned full force with the realization that she had no idea where Darius had gone.

"You can't leave till ye've fed yourselves up proper and rested a bit. Then we'll put ye on the good road west, for that's where ye'll be heading since the boy hasn't been by here. He's likely gone home or perished along the way."

Lydia glanced at Mikal and could tell the girl didn't agree with Bearta. Did she believe that Darius had not been there, or that he had not gone back home? Or, hopefully, that he had not perished?

"Here's the boar!" called out Bearta with pride and excitement.

Borne on a slab of oak by four foul-looking youths came a crackling-skinned forest monster, head lolling to the side and wicked tusks that could never again gut its prey.

"That's the biggest thing I ever saw!" Mikal exclaimed.

"Where you been, then, that they raise puny little runts?" one of the boys joked, guffawing. Lydia saw that half his ear was missing under ragged hair.

"None of your business, Kwalin," Bearta scolded. "Now out with all of you. Ye'll get yours later."

Out the lads went, pushing and cuffing like young pups.

The smell of the boar was rich and savory, making Lydia remember how hungry she was.

"Mikal, you and I will serve," Bearta ordered. "Lydia will be of no help so she'll sit out at the table in the big room. Come along. There will be seats for us, too, but first we have to get the men fed."

She grabbed two bowls of onions and potatoes and motioned for Mikal to bring carrots and a brown thick sauce. Lydia pushed open the heavy plank door out to the hall, pleased that she had thought of something she could do.

The men around the table all turned at once.

"Good Bearta! Just in time before my insides would be turning inside out looking for food," jested a swarthy rough-bearded man. The others joined the laughter which Bearta cut short.

"I need two of ye weak souls to fetch the piglet we scared out of the woods yesterday. Hot and tasty he be, the puny little thing."

The two at the end got up quickly and went to do her bidding. The others were as repulsive a lot, except for Marius, as Lydia had ever seen. If any of them dared talk to her, she vowed she'd not answer. The only possible place for the women was at the end of the table. She took the middle of three empty seats, grateful to be far from the next man.

Marius glanced quickly at her, then away. Did he notice how nicely she had cleaned up? He should have smiled. It would have been polite, but obviously he was not polite. She knew that already. If Titus – but then she remembered how mean Titus had been to her and decided not to think about any men ever again! All worthless, just like the ones around the table.

Marius spoke then to the man next to him. "Looks like your good Bearta fixed up the lady's arm very well."

Ah, so he had noticed something.

The other man turned to look. "Well, so this is the one. Surely Bearta has practice enough in fixing broken bones and wounds. A little scrape like that would be nothing to her."

"Aye, and fixed her with clean clothes, too, that make her a right becoming young lady," Marius said with a quick smile that lit his eyes.

Now all the other eyes were on Lydia so of course she blushed, though she hated to, and hadn't the faintest idea how to act or what to say in such company.

"Some piggy!" shouted a man across the table. Lydia scowled then realized he was speaking about the huge boar that was being brought into the room.

Bearta and Mikal sat down at the places next to her and with Mikal's help she managed to get her share of meat and vegetables. The delicious flavor surprised her.

"This is excellent!" she said and was pleased to see Bearta's sweaty face wrinkle up in a grin. The woman reminded her of the old stories of the magical folk of the woods, good people who helped travelers. What she was doing in this band of thieves was a question Lydia would have loved to ask.

As the men's appetites became sated, the talk began again. Talk of pirates. Talk of war. Talk of Albinus. The company did not seem to mind that she and Mikal were still present. That was certainly different from her father's or Brutus's houses.

It seemed that Marius's role was to convince these men not to use their boats in service of Albinus when troops were sent to Gaul. But all the others spoke strongly in favor of helping the Caesar of Britannia. Lydia remembered how Titus had argued for the resources of the south coast, and how her father and, yes, Marius too, had not agreed. She wasn't sure which side was right, or if there was a right side.

Bearta's husband summed up the feeling of most of the men. "We have no love for the Romans. You know that. Albinus knows that. But all of us here would put our boats to his service. Roman or not, he would make us rich. He's our Emperor."

Lydia held her breath, feeling like a spy. None of them could know her father so they wouldn't care that his loyalties seemed to be more for Septimius than Albinus. How weird to find herself in the middle of a political dispute affecting the whole Roman Empire when all she wanted was to find her little brother and take him home.

"Got clean away," a tall lanky fellow was saying. "My men shot him with a fortune of arrows. The fool should have died straightway."

Others laughed. One said, "Some fool that one! I'd not mind being such a fool and live forever."

"I doubt he's still alive, Tom."

"Your men's arrows might only have wounded him. Maybe he had armor on. The question is, did he live long enough to give them his message?"

"Aye, that's the question, isn't it?"

"The two villains in the boat – where do ye think they be headed?"

"Two? Then I know not. But if ye say three, and one small with a flame of hair" – Lydia's head jerked up at this, but she quickly lowered it again and listened intently –"then I tell ye they've headed straight out. Set sail for Gaul or I don't know me own name. The boat, though, was a poor ugly thing that didn't look as if it could make it halfway without sinking. I'll bet me socks there be three and a half new-drowned men in the sea this day."

Her bowl of food seemed to float before her eyes. She prayed that nothing she did would betray her feelings. It was imperative that she find a way out of Adairinnic, and quickly! She could make no sense of what they'd said, but that it was Darius the man had seen, she had no doubt.

"Do we follow them?" Heurac asked the company.

"Hold!" the tall thin one ordered, looking down the long table to where Lydia and Mikal sat, both trying to look as if they had no idea what was happening. "I want those two," pointing to the girls, "out. They shouldn't be hearin' what we say."

"Aye." All assented.

Marius spoke up, "I suppose then that I should not be here either, friends."

"Aye, that's so, friend. No hard feelings."

"None."

Had she wings, Lydia would have flown out the door, she was so happy to be dismissed. Mikal followed, and then Marius, who did not speak with them.

Bearta had also come out. "To your room, then," she ordered loudly. "Come, I'll show you. Come, come."

That was not what Lydia wanted, but Bearta was not to be argued with, not with ears perhaps still listening from the dining hall. The girls followed her hastily to a small square room just off the main hall. Closing the heavy door behind her, Bearta pointed to the window and whispered, "Out that you will go. Marius knew this might happen, so he will meet you with your dog and horses. In a few hours, Adairinnic will not be safe for any of you. He knows that. Once the men start on the mead and singing a saga about war heroes they'll be off after your red-haired brother and the others. Nay, wait a few minutes and then go! Fare ye well. Do be taking care of the arm, Lydia. Six weeks and it will be strong again, but not before then."

Lydia was overwhelmed. She could only guess at the risks Bearta was taking to help them.

"If only I had something to give you," she said, feeling inadequate.

"Nay, go on your way. Quickly." Bearta hustled out the door.

Heart beating wildly, Lydia went to the window, wondering how she could boost herself up high enough to reach the sill and then jump. Mikal had the answer. She pushed a stool underneath and helped Lydia up. Standing there, Lydia was able to sit on the sill then pivot around, ending with her feet hanging outside. The eight-foot drop was scary, but she took a deep breath and fell just as Mikal warned, "Wait! It's too high."

Halfway down, she wanted to change her mind. She hit the ground hard, rolling to her right, which cushioned her fall while only jarring her arm.

Mikal came next and landed lightly near her. Around the corner of the villa came Marius riding Coa, leading Kem, followed by Culain. This time Lydia had no complaints as he hoisted her into the saddle behind him, but she hesitated before putting her right hand on his waist. Well, a person has to hold on somewhere, so she did. Mikal on Kem trotted close behind as Marius directed Coa to an obscure path hidden from the house by a thick covering of bracken.

"We have to move quickly," Marius ordered. "The path is easy until we get to the cliffs. Hold on!"

Lydia wondered where they were going. Back to Tunadur? If so, who would the family send after Darius? There really wasn't time to dwell on these thoughts as Marius kicked Coa into a trot that turned into a lope and then a gallop. Only a strong horse like Coa could have carried two adults at such a pace. The big horse took commands without hesitation, as if Marius had been his master since day one.

Once clear of the house, Marius slowed him to a trot. She glanced around and saw that Kem and Mikal were almost keeping up, and thought that Mikal must be scared to death.

Culain raced ahead. When the trees and underbrush thinned out and the sea came into view, they halted to let Coa rest and Mikal catch up.

Tall white chalk cliffs edged the south coast of Britannia like ripples of lace from the west to the east. She knew that across the sea, barely visible, was another line of white. Gaul.

Far below them a river, probably the Cuckmere, cut through the chalk. In a small harbor, were eight boats. Two large merchant vessels were tied on either side of the dock and six smaller ones that were probably fishing boats were pulled up onto the sand.

"The two big ones are mine," Marius said. "They were both going to Juliobone, in Gaul, but now one of them will take you back to Tunadur and then cross the channel."

Without hesitation, Lydia made her choice. Rema had told her to find Darius, and that's what she would do. "I'm for Gaul!"

"What? Nay, nay, you must return to your family."

It wasn't the time or place to argue, so she kept quiet but didn't change her mind.

The trail, scarcely wide enough for a horse, descended to the river in long switchbacks. Mikal would have preferred to walk, but Marius convinced her that it was actually safer for her to ride.

Each step was treacherous. Many times the horses created small landslides when one of their feet would slip, tearing out small bushes and dislodging chalky shale.

When at last they reached the bottom, Marius reined in Coa until Mikal on Kem joined them. The poor girl was shaking, her face streaked with dust and tears.

"I thought I was going to die," she moaned. "I thought Kem was going to fall and we'd crash down on top of you and then we'd all die a horrible death. Never again!"

"You made it, though," Lydia reminded her.

"Pah! It was horrid!"

Marius broke in, "What matters, Mikal, is that you showed real courage by doing something that frightened you so terribly."

"Thanks," Mikal mumbled.

Lydia was miffed. She felt she deserved a special compliment for something – maybe for riding well or for having a sturdy horse like Coa.

"We still need to hurry," Marius said. "The horses will enjoy a short canter across the sand, and then we'll shove off." A small signal from Marius, and Coa was trotting as if he hadn't just exerted every muscle coming down the mountain. To Mikal's dismay, Kem followed his lead.

When they reached the docked boats, Mikal got off Kem as fast as she could, while Marius dismounted and helped Lydia down.

It was time, now, to argue. "I am not going to Tunadur!" she declared. "I must go to Gaul. It's my grandmother's will that I do so."

Culain barked and wagged his tail, agreeing with her.

"It may not be your father's will, and that's what's important to me," Marius countered. "Keep your voice down. The fishermen here are not so innocent as they might appear to you. My crews are ready to sail immediately. I am taking you to Tunadur whether you and your grandmother want it or not. Come!"

"I'll not leave the horses. How will they get home? And I'll not go to Tunadur."

"I stay with Lydia," Mikal added in a small voice.

Marius sounded impatient. "Your horses are too tired now to ride all the way to Tunadur and you can't stay in Adairinnic, not after that meeting you overheard. My ships are built for live cargo, including horses. Come along. It won't be long before we'll be followed." He took Coa's reins and started to lead him to the dock.

"Which boat goes to Tunadur?" Lydia asked sweetly.

"That one," and Marius pointed to the right.

Lydia took off as fast as she could toward the left boat. Bearta's long dress and the sand made running almost impossible. Marius leaped onto Coa, gave a kick, and within a few strides caught up with her.

"No you don't!" He reached down, grabbing Lydia's waist yet again, and hoisted her up in front of him. Frantic, she tried to break loose, but Marius's grip was too strong. In seconds, they were aboard the ship.

"Be ready to take up the ramp as soon as the other horse and the dog get aboard," Marius shouted to his crew of about ten men. "We're underway the minute they are here."

Dismounting and pulling Lydia off also, he kept a strong grip on the girl who screamed, "I won't go! Mikal, do something! I have to go to Gaul! I have to!"

Mikal was helpless. She had led Kem onto the ship and given the reins to one of the crew who took the mare to a stall at the back of the boat.

Shouting commands to both crews on the ships, Marius was not gentle as Lydia struggled and wailed. Below deck, six rowers on each side pulled at oars and the boats slowly moved away from the shore.

Coa was taken to a stall next to Kem and several other horses. Culain growled at Marius but hid behind Lydia, tail drooping, ears flat. The rocking of the boat made him unsteady and perhaps less courageous than if his mistress had been kidnapped on land.

"A rope!" Marius ordered one of his sailors. "Bring me a rope. And cast off!"

"You cannot tie me up!" Lydia warned.

"You are a nuisance to me. You get tied up. Stand still!"

Lydia whirled on him. The heavy wrapping on her left arm was like a cement block. It hit him square on the chin, sending him staggering back a few steps and loosening his grip on her. Free, she raced to the railing but found that she was not brave enough to leap into the deepening waters below. She was trapped.

Marius ignored her, wiping blood from his face.

"Hoist the sail!"

There was no limit to Lydia's despair as she sank to the deck knowing that she had failed. There was no limit to the anger she felt at Marius, her eternal enemy. If Darius died, it would be Marius's fault and none other's. Some day, some way, she would get revenge.

As they moved slowly into the channel, Mikal stood by the rail in her long British dress watching the shoreline grow smaller, less distinct. Lydia wondered if Mikal felt any of the misery she did. Sometimes slaves stayed so long that a family got used to them. The question was, had Mikal gotten used to the family enough to care about Darius? For herself, it was unbearable not to follow him.

Off to her left was Gaul. To the right, Tunadur, Mother, Rema. How could she face them?

Culain came and sat beside her, laying his big grey head in her lap. "I failed" kept running through Lydia's head. She felt an overwhelming emptiness. "A head of flame," the man at Bearta's had described him, and now Lydia missed that flame hair so much she would have forgiven him all his faults to see him again.

The white coast sank lower and lower on the horizon, but Lydia had no interest in watching. The gods could do what they wanted now. They had played with her enough.

Mikal finally left the railing and joined Lydia. She sat beside her stroking Culain's head. Finally she murmured, "I think it's going to be all right."

"How can you say that? " Lydia countered angrily.

Ignoring that remark, Mikal continued softly, "There's no land behind us now. I saw Marius send a signal by flags to the other boat, and then we seemed to turn to follow it."

Lydia didn't understand.

Mikal added, "I'm sure we are going to Gaul."

Map of Gaul

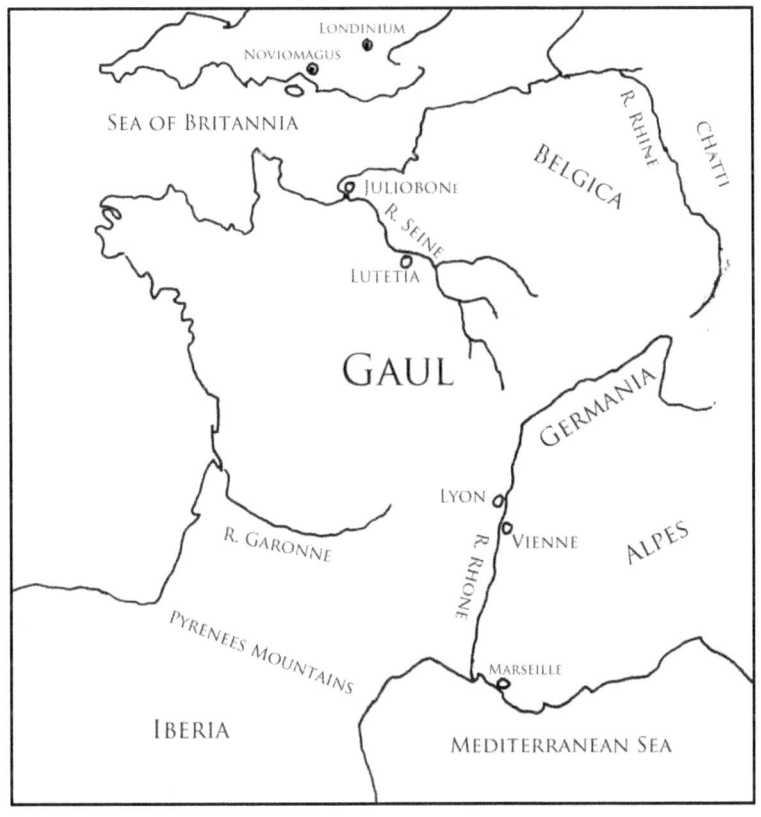

13. "We Have to Go to Lyon"

After five long tedious days on the Seine, with Optimus still barely alive, the struggling boat arrived at the city of Lutetia. Darius was awestruck by the monumental size of the buildings that seemed to soar to the sky. On an island in the river, he could see a beautiful temple that was at least twice as large as the one in Noviomagus. There seemed to be palaces everywhere, and arches and colonnades. It was overwhelming for a small boy from rural Britannia.

They pulled up to a quay and Hector, after tying the boat to a post, yelled, "Back in a minute!" In high spirits, he leaped onto the dock and raced off down a curving lane, leaving everything else in the charge of Acteon.

The six oarsmen demanded their pay which, surprisingly, Acteon was able to give them. Darius wondered where he got the money. Certainly not from Optimus, who had been unconscious most of the entire trip up the river. Last night, in fact, he had been so ghastly that the crew complained about having a dying man on board. Bad luck, they grumbled, not realizing that Optimus was the entire reason for their employment.

In minutes, it seemed, Hector returned, running as fast as if he'd been a thinner man.

"Ready! We're ready for 'im!" he gasped, going straight for Optimus. He knelt down, put his arms under the courier's shoulders and knees and lifted him easily. Stepping onto the quay again, he was off at a fast trot. Just before he disappeared into the lane, he turned around and yelled back to Darius, "Well? Come on, Flea! Speed yourself up!"

Thrilled to be getting off the boat and away from Acteon, Darius climbed onto the dock and immediately stumbled as the world seemed to sway around him.

"Go slow at first!" Hector called. "Ye're too used to the boat rocking."

It took awhile, but Darius finally caught up with Hector and followed him through the narrow, straight streets. It wasn't long before they reached the fuller's shop where Hector kicked open the door.

A lovely, sighing, "Ohhhh!" was the only thing Darius heard before a mist of blonde curls engulfed the yet-to-expire Optimus. The hand that touched the man's face was tiny and smooth, more graceful than anything Darius had ever seen. He was instantly, completely, captivated.

"Away, sweet," Hector growled as he carried Optimus down the two steps into the main part of the shop. "You want him dead or you want him alive? Let's have mum take a look at 'im."

"Yes, oh yes. She's here, in the room . . ." Her voice was as delicate as the down of a dandelion in summertime.

Gloriana, for who else could she be, led them down a tight corridor and into a sweet-smelling white-walled room where Hector deposited Optimus onto a clean, soft sleeping couch.

The mother, a robust woman looking more like Hector than his sister did, took charge. Off came Optimus's tunic to expose the festering sores which covered his body. Darius's stomach turned over. A furtive glance at Gloriana showed him that she was enchanted with the sight, so he took a deep breath and tried to be brave.

As the girl leaned over Optimus, Darius caught a glimpse of what "oranges" might refer to. He blushed crimson.

"Hot water," the mother ordered, and Gloriana hurried to the door. Darius stepped forward to block her way.

"I'll go," he stammered, "if you would just point the way."

She smiled. What glory in her smile! He would have leaped the Dardanelles for her.

"How nice you are," she said. "I'll show you, then you can do it the next time." She lightly touched his shoulder as she passed.

Into the fuller's workroom they went where great vats of steaming and cool water were filled with soiled garments or newly woven wool. Five workmen labored at washing and dying them. Taking a ladle, Gloriana poured water into a large pottery bowl and handed it to Darius.

He could feel nothing, for no blood had left his heart since seeing her for the first time. By some miracle, his hands held onto the bowl.

"Mother will need herbs from the kitchen. Come with me," Gloriana said, leading the way.

In the kitchen, from a high shelf she took down a large box with small compartments filled with various herbs. Darius felt his heart constrict even more as she stretched to lift it down. Never had he noticed how wistful a waist could be, or the graceful way a calf muscle curved. In a daze, he followed her back to the little room where, finding a stool, he sat in a corner and watched his goddess, silently vowing eternal devotion.

She took no notice of him. Her every motion, every breath was for the man lying on the bed. Optimus was wounded from mere arrows and spears that hadn't touched his heart, Darius reflected. If mortal wounds were in that room, the lovely nursemaid would do well to look at the young boy with hair like flames who languished in the corner.

"Well, mum, what do ye think of him?" Hector asked.

"He'll do," she declared. "He's come this far alive; he'll live more."

"Bless you, mother!" Gloriana sighed. "Oh, my dear sweet Optimus!"

"Hmmpf," grunted Hector. "A scoundrel he is and you know it. But you'll have him, be sure of that. Yes, you'll have him."

Tears, sweet trails of diamond dust, ran down Gloriana's cheek, turning Darius to water. Unfortunately, his reverie was interrupted by the great fist of Hector on his shoulder lifting him up and pushing him out the door to a far corner of the workshop where lengths of woolen cloth lay drying on racks.

Hector whispered, "Where've we got to go now? What's this message he was going to give ye to deliver? Acteon will likely kill us both if ye haven't got it."

Taking a deep breath to clear his mind, Darius answered, "We have to go to Lyon. Do you know it? Is it in Italy?"

Hector scoffed, "No, Flea, it's the main city in Gaul. Everyone knows that. "

Darius was embarrassed. If his tutors had ever told him of the place, he'd forgotten it. Why remember something you'll never use?

"What else?" Hector asked.

"There's a man I have to give the message to. That's all. And we have to go fast, as fast as we can if it's to do any good."

"Then we'll probably need horses so we can change them at the post houses."

"Uh, no post houses. He said not to stop anywhere like that."

"But the horses can't go all the way by themselves. They get tired and have to rest."

"Could we take the boat?"

Hector laughed, "A good idea except that this river doesn't go to Lyon."

"What can we do?"

"I know! It's slower, but we can trade the boat for a cart and two good mules. We'll make pretty good time and mules don't need to rest as much as horses do. Can ye drive?"

"Of course, but carts are so small . . ."

"Aye, and I'm so big. I know it, lad. Acteon and you make up only one together, so we'll be fine. A bit tight but fine. Come along. We can't delay. Couriers mean it when they say fast."

"Can I say goodbye?" Darius hoped Hector would think he meant say goodbye to Optimus when it was Gloriana he needed to see one last time.

"No. Now means now." Hector opened the back door and out they went.

When they reached the quay, Acteon was impatiently drumming his fingers on the railing.

"Well?" he asked, scowling as usual.

"We got to sell the boat and get us to Lyon," Hector answered quickly.

"Lyon?"

"Shhhh!" Hector ordered. "It's got to be a secret so shut your hyena mouth for a bit, won't you?"

Instead of going into a rage as Darius expected, Acteon said coldly, "So we're all official couriers now? We have no choice?"

Hector seemed confused by the question. "Didn't you – I mean, wasn't that why we sold the Flea to Optimus and brought him here and –"

"Idiot! I meant how are we going to sell the boat and the cargo? Do we lose it all? Don't couriers have ways to travel? Where's the money? He says he's rich. How are we supposed to go anywhere without money?"

Darius knew that Optimus had given no money yet, and Hector confirmed it.

"We get it when it's over," he assured Acteon then pleaded, "Look, this is the only way just now. The man's almost dead – no no, Mum says he's going to recover. He'll be good for the money, I swear. If he wants my sister, he'll pay up. Now hurry up because we got to get us a cart and two good mules."

"Why a cart?" Acteon asked, climbing out of the boat onto the quay. "We could probably go faster on foot."

At that Hector gave a huge guffaw and replied, "You haven't been on nothin' but ocean roads, have you? When you see this road to Lyon you'll see it's straight and smooth as a rock, so smooth you can practically fly over it. We'll be there in four days at the most. Forty to fifty miles a day if the mules are up to it. Can you beat that walking?"

"Sounds like a tall tale to me."

"Don't matter, you'll see. Time's getting away from us. Come on!"

Darius couldn't imagine anyone travelling 50 miles a day in a cart and couldn't wait to see the Roman road that made it possible. Since meeting Gloriana, he felt as if Gaul was the perfect place to be. If he'd gone to Canterbury and become an apprentice in some hot dirty shop, he never would have met her. Life was good. It was, that is, if Hector could keep Acteon in line. Besides his knife, the little man carried a whip, and Darius had no desire to feel its bite.

The party of three headed quickly back into the busy streets of the city, Hector leading the way.

"Where are we going?" Acteon asked impatiently.

"To the baths. My father will be there and so will his friends."

"This place has baths, too?" Darius asked. In Britannia, only large cities had public baths. Suddenly up ahead, there they were, more imposing than any buildings Darius had ever seen. The arched exterior rose high into the air, making everything around it look small by comparison.

Without a pause, Hector barged through the wide doorway, followed by Darius and Acteon. In the foyer, Darius stared at the enormous arches holding up a vault that must have been fifty feet high. A geometric mosaic covered the floor. The walls were painted with scenes from stories of the gods. Monumental statues of heroes and emperors stared down at him. He almost fell backwards, craning his neck to see everything while trying to keep up with Hector and Acteon.

A slave tried to stop their progress, directing them toward the changing rooms, but Hector ignored him. He knew where he was going and his size was enough to deter anyone from stopping him.

"*Felicitas*, Papa!" he shouted as they entered a huge room colonnaded on all four sides. A large steaming pool was filled with naked men soaking, eating, and carrying on business.

At the end of the pool, a man sitting on the edge looked up,

"Hector! Son!" the voice boomed up to the domed cciling and back again, echoing over the waters like thunder.

The father was husky, with light hair, light eyes, and a grey beard. Smiling broadly, he wrapped his arms around his son, who was a few inches taller and a lot broader than he was.

"You and your friends, get your clothes off and join us. Relax! Enjoy! Great Jupiter, look at the boy's hair! Is he one of those wild ones from the frontier?"

"Nay, nay. But I'm sorry to say we're in a mighty hurry. We brought Gloriana a fine present back at the house; you're in for a surprise yerself. But now we need to find us a cart and two mules, good 'uns that'll take us where we need to go at a quick pace for a long way, though I cannot rightly say where."

Hector paused.

"Well, son, what are you paying?"

"A good solid boat and its cargo. It's not big, but it's strong enough to go o'er the great seas."

Darius pictured the boat in his mind and hoped Hector wasn't exaggerating any more than was expected.

"Done!" said his father. "Lucius, come speak to my boy. He wants to do you a favor."

In the end the bargain was concluded. If Hector returned the mules and cart in good condition after a reasonable time, he could have the boat back at no charge, such was the esteem in which his father, the freedman and fuller, was held in Lutetia. Others would sell the cargo and pay the creditors.

With a great grin lighting his face, Hector led his group to the marketplace where they bought squash, carrots, apples, dried meat, bread and a cask of wine for their journey. They then proceeded to the stables where they found the mules and cart ready. Soon they were heading out of town on the paved highway leading to Lyon.

Darius noted that Acteon was now the follower while Hector had become the leader. He felt much safer with the change.

Hector drove first, standing, while Darius sat on the seat and Acteon drank in back. They had chosen a light cart with just two wheels so the mules could travel as fast as possible. They seemed to be good animals, one a darker brown and the other black. The stableman, Lucius, was proud of them, calling them the most obedient and strongest mules in Lutetia. He had given them names, but each person who rented them changed the names so it didn't matter.

Darius prayed that there would be no big bumps, for he didn't like the idea of Hector falling back onto him. But then he grinned, imagining that if something like that were to happen, and all his bones got broken, Hector would have to take him back to Lutetia where Gloriana would nurse him back to health. The mere thought of such a heaven put him into a different world. Fantasizing, he passed farms and villages, streams and fields, and woods without seeing them. Gloriana was always before him, yet far above him, with her tiny waist and golden hair.

Even when he was driving, Darius was lost in that other world. He designed in his mind a medal with Gloriana as Ceres, goddess of the earth, surrounded by flowers and grasses waving in an invisible breeze.

"I said stop!" Acteon yelled, whacking him in the center of his back for emphasis. Darius stumbled but didn't fall off. Embarrassed, he hoped he hadn't given any hint of the secret life he'd been leading. He pulled on the reins, bringing the mules to a halt.

He was surprised to find that night had fallen. A large half moon was rising behind a stand of trees, turning the ploughed-under fields to white. They were near a small woods where a brook of clear, cold water bubbled past.

"We'll sleep tonight over near the water," Acteon ordered in a voice that slurred in the cold air.

"Here?" Hector sounded incredulous. "We'll freeze to death. At least you and the Flea will, with your skimpy little bodies. Look beyond, over there. A farmhouse. There'll be a pot o' good stew on the fire, you can count on it. And welcome company after the meager talk we've had today what with your drinking up all the wine and wi'out adding water to it, neither."

"I agree," Darius spoke up, and since he still had the reins, he clucked to the mules and pulled the left reins to guide them down off the Roman road and onto a well-worn farm road that would soon pass by the house.

"And I say NO!" Acteon grabbed at the reins, which made the cart list dangerously to the left. Darius lurched forward and would have kept on going had Hector not caught him and at the same time hit Acteon so hard that he lay in a stupor across the seat.

"All right, lad?" Hector asked.

"Fine!." He was too busy trying to regain control of the mules and cart to check if he really was all right.

A mumbling came from Acteon that sounded like, "What if these farmers are thieves? What if they sneak up and kill us in the night, then what?"

Darius ignored him, but Hector said, "These are gentle folk. Ye've been in rummy ports too long. I'll wager all that's left of that jug of wine that these folk will treat us well. What reason would they have for killing us, do you think?"

"The Flea, of course," Acteon growled. "Maybe this country doesn't welcome secret couriers."

"And who is going to tell them? They don't know Albinus or Severus a'tall. I'm sure of it. Growin' crops and makin' a living is what they knows."

The farmhouse was of stone in the round style with a thatched roof and a couple of small round windows. Inside, as Hector had promised, was a stew bubbling in an iron pot. The dispositions of the old farmer and his wife were, however, not friendly. Being near the main road meant they had too many visitors.

Despite the cold, the wife made them eat outside from a large pot, but she did supply them with a small jug of plum wine and some woolly blankets. "Ye're lucky to get that. The soldiers come through here like locusts and rob us of everything in the name of his high and mighty Emperor-ness Clodius Albinus. If ye take them blankets away, ye'll pay for it and don't think ye won't," she warned before going back inside.

The mutton stew was thick with meat and vegetables and more than made up for the lack of hospitality. With his belly full and a warm blanket wrapped around his shoulders, Darius leaned against the cart and looked up at the sky. The half moon washed out some of the stars. He could relax without the gods staring at him. He wondered which of them crossing the heavens had chosen this fate for him. It must have been the gods themselves because a human surely could never have planned it. Curling up under his blanket, he hoped the weather would stay mild. It wouldn't do for an Imperial courier to be frozen to death before completing his mission, would it?

Wait, what had the wife said about soldiers stealing in the name of Albinus? Were the British legions already here? No, that wasn't possible. These must be other soldiers, for it was said that Albinus had the loyalty of much of Gaul. Did that mean that since he, Darius, was carrying a message for Septimius, that he was the enemy here? He felt very very small and vulnerable under the wide moonlit sky.

While he was musing, his thoughts turned to Ansonius. He had barely known his brother, being only six when Ansonius had left. He remembered that Ansonius had been travelling the road to Rome when he was attacked by bandits, or so they said. Maybe it had been on this very road, by this very farmhouse. If, as they said, Ansonius was dead, then maybe he was in the underworld helping the gods carry out this ridiculous scheme. "Help me, brother," he whispered very quietly.

Suddenly the sound of running hooves could be heard coming closer until, through the trees, Darius made out the shape by moonlight of a fine horse and rider galloping northward.

"What's that, do you think?" he whispered to Hector who was next to him.

"Don't fret yourself, Flea. Just a lovesick husband returning home to his wife after a frolic wi' his girlfriend."

That brought a cackle from Acteon which was so loud the farmer threw open his shutters and leaned out yelling for silence.

There must have been silence because Darius was suddenly asleep and just as suddenly he was being kicked awake by a hung-over Acteon.

"Breakfast, Flea," he said, handing Darius a bowl of lukewarm oats. Rather than argue, Darius ate, though eating oats made him feel as if he was a horse. He missed the bread warm from the oven that he always had at home with fruit and cheese.

The cart and mules had already been harnessed, ready for another hard-going day. Darius had slept through it all.

Acteon drove. Darius noted a few farm wagons rolling between fields, pulled by oxen or draft mules. The local people avoided the highway, which was for long trips like the one Darius was on.

The second and third nights, having made fast time all day, they travelled farther off the road to farms that saw fewer visitors. Here the hospitality was warmer, the food just as hearty, and the company friendlier as long as Acteon kept his mouth shut. But the nights were too short to take away Darius's exhaustion. By the fourth night he was so worn out by the fast pace, the long days, and the lack of sleep that when morning came, he couldn't rouse himself. Even though it was the final, crucial day, no part of him could move. Through the thick fog of sleep he heard Hector calling. He felt Acteon' kicks. But his sleep wouldn't lift.

Finally Hector carried him to the cart and laid him in the back, making Acteon drive again. It wasn't for another two hours that Darius was finally able to open his eyes and realize that morning had come. The cold wind against his face eventually brought him fully awake.

This part of Gaul was so different from Tunadur. There was no smell of fish, no sea birds, no breeze off the ocean. Fields of wheat ready for harvest shone like gold in the sunlight from the road to the river.

"Richest farms in the Empire," declared Hector.

Haystacks dotted some of the fields. Orchards of apple and peach trees covered acres of ground. Inside farmhouses, apple cider and fruit wine flowed hot and spicy every evening, not for our travelers but for the family and their hard-working farm laborers.

They were almost to Lyon, the foremost city in all of Gaul. Here, Darius must find Optimus's old teacher, the Roman Senator. How that would happen was not at all clear.

14. "Change Course"

As Marius's ship slid down a trough of water, the bow was buried then leaped up, sending a wave of cold water surging over the deck. It splashed by the mast where Lydia and Culain sat huddled on top of boxes like two dejected heaps of raw wool. Each time the water struck, Lydia was brought back to her predicament which was so uncertain that, rather than face it, she tried to daydream. It didn't help. Daydreaming about Titus was no longer fun. She didn't need more misery.

She envied Mikal, who stood by the railing hour after hour most of the night, facing the spray, head up, hair wet and flying in the wind like an Argonaut sailing to find the golden fleece.

Now she watched the girl eating breakfast. It looked like bread and water, the usual Roman breakfast, but Lydia could not face food. She knew that if she tried to eat, it would come right back up.

Mikal must be excited about going back to her homeland, but Lydia was going away from hers and everything she knew. She wished she felt braver. She wished Darius was not such a headstrong, sensitive, stubborn, childish – she couldn't think of any more words to call him and besides, whatever he was like, whoever he was, he was still her brother.

She wondered if her family would ever know where she had gone? If she never made it back, if she died, as seemed a real possibility the way the ship lunged through the ever higher waves, who would tell them?

She wondered how Darius had handled this sea voyage. The boat he sailed on had been described as a leaky tub. Maybe it hadn't made it across the channel. Was he drowned or wandering somewhere alone in the wilderness of an unknown land, lost and afraid? Mikal had told her during the night that she thought he was still alive, and Lydia clung to that hope.

She took a deep breath, trying to imagine a good future for Darius. First, he would escape from the terrible people who had him. Then he'd find himself a place to work and live a long and happy life, while she? What? Searched for him forever.

Discouraged, feeling sorry for herself, afraid to eat, Lydia shivered under another onslaught of heavy seas. Culain whimpered and tried to make himself small enough to crawl under the blanket Marius had given her. .

In the stern, Coa whinnied into the wind. The forlorn sound matched Lydia's mood. Slowly and with much difficulty she stood up and staggered toward the stalls, Culain dragging at her heels.

Poor Coa, his eyes were white, his ears flat against his head.

"Dear friend," she crooned to him. "You'll be fine, don't worry." She crawled through the railings and walked slowly toward him, giving him the soothing words that always calmed him down. He looked at her, wild-eyed and suspicious. When she touched his neck, he flinched, but slowly, very slowly, settled down. She snuggled against his warm body, rubbing his nose, his flanks, his neck, trying to keep upright against the tossing of the boat. Reassuring him, she reassured herself.

"Frightened is he?"

The voice came so unexpectedly that Lydia jumped in spite of herself.

Marius stood outside the pen, watching. She'd seen him at the tiller most of the afternoon and the night past. Right now he certainly didn't look like anyone Neptune would be proud to claim as a son of the sea. His hair dripped with water and there were long lines of salt spray etched into his face. His dark eyes, as best as she could tell in the dim light, were bleary and red.

"Shouldn't he be?" she asked a bit testily to hide her embarrassment at being found out.

"Yes, since he's a horse and has never been on a ship before. This channel can be a lot rougher than what you see now. The mare isn't afraid, is she? She's like your friend over there, Mikal. Some take to the ocean more easily than others."

"I'm not one of them," Lydia admitted.

"No, but take heart. We will be at the harbor tonight. "

"Tonight?" She needed to plan some course of action, but she had no idea what to do or where to go.

"Tonight. Depending on the tides, we will probably stay offshore until morning, but you will be in Gaul as you wished. Mikal should rest. You should try to eat. Bread usually stays down if taken with a bit of water. That's my advice, which you probably won't take."

"Thank you but I don't feel like eating yet, and I'm sure Mikal knows her own heart."

Marius laughed and sat down on a large storage crate, leaning his head back against another one. It was awkward having him stare at her so she turned her back to him, concentrating on Coa and Culain.

After awhile he asked, "Where do you go?"

"I don't know. The ship, you said, goes to Juliobone."

"This ship was heading for Tunadur until your tantrum forced me to change course. I'm only trying to figure out what to do with you now."

Lydia had nothing to say to that, but she did wonder where Juliobone was.

"All right, where exactly is Juliobone?" she asked.

There was no answer from the captain who had fallen asleep on the storage crates.

I guess I'm not very interesting, she thought, and scanned the railings looking for Mikal, someone she could talk to. Not seeing her, Lydia started to imagine that Mikal had been knocked overboard by a strong wave. Then she saw the girl's dark shape lying on a box on the far deck. Without realizing it, Mikal was taking Marius's advice. Maybe soon Lydia would do the same and try to eat.

Culain's wet nose nudged her hand. She knelt down and wrapped her good arm around his shoulder, taking comfort from him.

Suddenly the wind screeched overhead, twisting the ship until the timbers squealed in agony. A long swell lifted it high then slammed it down into a trough where it shuddered so hard that Lydia expected it to break apart. As tremors swept from fore to aft, the ship rolled far onto its side. Lydia tumbled over and slammed against the wall of the pen, her left wrist hitting with full force and causing a stab of pain so sharp she screamed. Miraculously, Coa seemed to push himself against the rails of the stall and keep his balance though his eyes and ears showed how frightened he was.

Culain came to her and licked her face. She crawled over the straw to a corner where she collapsed in tears. Her loneliness was so intense that she wondered if she had died while the boat hung in the balance. Was she now a shadow spirit doomed to wander the earth, haunting those she once loved? If so, were there no gods in the world of death to show her the way?

This mood could not last forever. She noted that Marius still slept on his boxes. Mikal slept in her spot, also. The other sailors, some throwing dice, seemed just as calm as ever. Maybe that huge crash hadn't actually happened to anyone but her. How strange the ocean was.

It would be over soon. Marius said they'd reach Gaul by evening, but probably not land in the harbor until the next morning. No matter how hard she tried, she couldn't figure out a plan of action for what came next.

The world to which she awoke the next morning was a mist of soft pink and lavender. The sun was low on the eastern horizon peeking through a light veil of clouds and dusting everything, even the surface of the sea, with pale rose. Coa stood serenely in his stall next to Kem's and the other horses, munching hay. Culain had wandered off somewhere.

The boat creaked and rolled gently now, side to side, front to back. The wide-winged sail was half furled on its boom. Gulls followed the ship, diving, swooping, calling to each other.

The smell of land had awakened Lydia from the first peaceful sleep she'd had on the boat. The perfume from warm fields of dirt, manure, and bare-branched trees was heady, mingling now with the familiar salt air of the sea. It was curious that the autumn land had such a delicious aroma. She had never noticed it until she spent two nights and a day on the ocean.

A rooster crowed in the distance. Startled, Lydia sprang to her feet and looked out over the water, half expecting to see the bird itself. She couldn't see the rooster, but only a half mile from where she stood was the coast of Gaul. The ship had already rounded the headland.

As uncertain as she felt about her search for Darius, she couldn't help but be excited by seeing this new, to her, land. "I'm in Gaul," she said to herself, amazed at the thought but proud at the same time.

Holding her still painful arm, Lydia managed to maneuver herself through the railings of the stall. The long British dress tangled awkwardly around her ankles.

"You'll have to find something else to wear in Gaul," Marius's laugh came from above where he was at the tiller, keeping the ship on course.

"I know that!" she shouted in exasperation, determined not to look at him.

He laughed. "You must be feeling better. We're almost there. Are you hungry?"

"No!" she lied and went to find Mikal, surprised that she could walk on the rocking deck without falling down. Mikal was nibbling at a luscious-looking hunk of dried salmon. The sight made Lydia yearn for some, but she wouldn't ask.

There was an expression of great peace on Mikal's face. Her mouth seemed to curve in a permanent smile. She held out the fish for Lydia who shook her head, at the same time mentally kicking herself for being so infernally stubborn.

"Take it," Mikal said. "You are hungry and I don't need it."

Unable to deny the mind reader, Lydia gave in. The salmon was heavenly. She nibbled slowly so as not to surprise her empty stomach with too much at once.

Mikal spoke quietly but her dark eyes glowed as she said, "Darius is ahead, I can feel it. We've come the right way."

Lydia felt such an immense rush of relief and joy that she impulsively flung her arms -- cast, fish and all -- around Mikal. "May the gods be praised," she said. Only then did she realize how hopeless she had been feeling.

Everything changed now. She knew her search would be successful because somewhere ahead, maybe even in Juliobone, was her brother. If not, it did not matter where in Gaul he was. Even if the whole Roman Empire blocked her way, she would find him whether he liked it or not. A tie that could not be broken bound her to him, stupid, proud Darius. She would bring him home. She smiled and said quietly, "Thanks, Mikal."

The slave girl changed the subject. "Isn't it surprising how much the white cliffs look just like Britannia? If you woke up and didn't know whether you were there or in Gaul, how would you figure it out?"

Lydia laughed.

"Now you'll be wanting bread," Mikal said, breaking a large piece in two and offering Lydia the larger part. Lydia did not refuse. The bread was crunchy and tasty. Life was good!

"The captain is a fine sailor," Mikal said, looking out to sea again.

Lydia shrugged, not knowing if he was or not. "Mikal, I hope you won't be disappointed by being in Gaul."

Mikal turned to her with a questioning look.

"I mean, there's little chance we will be going anywhere near your old home."

Holding up her hand, Mikal said, "It's all right. I'll be fine. Darius is the important one now for both of us."

Lydia nodded, feeling more warmth toward her slave companion at that moment than she'd ever felt with Diana, her former best friend.

She decided to leave Mikal to her musings and get back to the horses to keep them calm.

Marius was waiting there.

"Eat, young lady," he ordered, offering her some pieces of apple.

"I have eaten."

"Good. Try these."

Lydia accepted them. Why not?

"There is clean water in the jars, too, for you must be thirsty."

She took a bite of apple and waited for Marius to leave. Instead, he again sat down on the crate where he had fallen asleep before. He looked at her with such seriousness that Lydia got worried.

"What?" she asked curiously.

"I have to ask you a question and I know you won't want to answer. Consider my position, though. Your father is a Prefect and I am only a trader. I seem to have kidnapped his daughter. He could have me killed should I ever go to Britannia again, which I fully intend to do. It is my business to freely trade all over the Empire. You were desperate at Adairinnic and I don't know why. For you, I risked my business in Britannia. Wait! Don't interrupt, please. Just tell me what you are doing and where you are going. Are you running away from a lover? From an arranged marriage?"

"You mean you don't know?"

"How could I? You didn't say. All you did was scream about your grandmother telling you to go to Gaul. Now I must know why. Maybe you and your grandmother are both crazy. I must be crazy, too. I have never done such a foolish thing before, taking such a risk for – ." He shrugged, looking at her, shaking his head.

Lydia was beginning to realize how much Marius had done for her on this cross-channel voyage.

"I should have taken you back to your home." He laughed and added, "I wonder what the crew is thinking about you and your horses and the dog. Now back to my original question. What is going on? What do I tell your father when I go back to Britannia?."

"You have to see him?

"It's likely. How about some answers."

Lydia felt she could trust him after all he'd done, so she told him about her runaway brother and how her grandmother sent her and Mikal on this search. When the men at Adairinnic had talked about a red-headed boy, that boy was Darius.

He looked incredulous. "Are there no brave men at Tunadur to send instead of a mere girl?"

"That's an insult. Of course there are men, but they aren't Darius's sister. And I am no 'mere girl'!"

Marius sighed. "Just tell your story, lass."

"My grandmother, a brave and intelligent woman of ancient Celtic blood, sent me to Lewes to my uncle, and then my uncle sent me to Adairinnic. You know the rest. They don't know where I am but they know that I will find Darius no matter what stands in the way."

"What a better world it would be if all men had valiant sisters like you to find them when they get lost."

As much as she liked the sentiment, Lydia felt she should be honest with him. "It wasn't like that. Darius and I had a huge, ugly fight. It's probably because of me that he left Tunadur, so it's me that has to bring him back."

"Nevertheless, many men would give a lot to have a – sister – like you."

Lydia knew that Titus wasn't one of those men, and if he didn't want her, no-one else worth having would either. So Marius was wrong.

"Where will you look? Any ideas?"

"No. None."

The apple slices were sweet and juicy so Lydia chewed slowly. She finally told Marius that her only real evidence was that Mikal believed Darius had come this way.

"To the port of Juliobone? Boats from Britannia don't use it as much as others to the east. That is where the British legions will surely land if Albinus decides to bring them."

"And where will the legions go?" She was curious because of the two different discussions she'd overheard, and felt she should find out as much as possible in case it helped her find Darius.

"Albinus has set up his headquarters in Lyon in central Gaul. The legions will probably go there to join the others loyal to him. After that, it depends on what Septimius Severus does."

"And then? Will one of them be Emperor?" Lydia recalled the midnight conversation at Arundel, and Titus, and his "unborn child."

Marius replied, "Albinus hasn't the heart for what it takes to hold the Empire together. Septimius is more ruthless. But this is boring stuff."

"No," Lydia replied honestly. "My family is involved and our land. I want to know how we will fare."

"If it's Tunadur you're thinking of, you'd better hope your father doesn't give too much support to Albinus. If he does, he's likely to lose the villa and all the lands."

"But it doesn't belong to him yet. It's my grandmother's."

"That might save it. Your father seems to be a man who will not act foolishly or selfishly. Not like Brutus Marconius, who wants all the power he can get. It's men like him who risk most in a civil war."

Lydia asked,. "Civil war?"

"Certainly. The eastern Empire against the west. Do you know that both contenders were born in Africa, far from Rome?"

"That's odd."

"But this brother of yours?"

"Right. First I have to find him and bring him back."

"One boy in all of Gaul."

"I will find him."

"I expect you will."

A truce was established.

He asked then, "Why do you hold your arm?"

"It hurts again. I bumped it last night."

"Should I have a look at it?" he asked.

She wouldn't mind, but shook her head and said, "No, it will be fine." He had more to think about, as she did.

"All right then. In no more than an hour, we will be docked in Juliobone. Maybe you want to come and watch."

"Yes, I don't want to miss my first city in Gaul."

"It can be a rough place. You can hope your brother is not here. Your horses seem to have found their sea legs. When they go on land, be careful because they'll think they're still rolling on the sea. It will be hard for them to stand. You, too. It's an interesting phenomenon."

"Sounds fun," she replied, following him to the rail.

15. "The Only Thing You Can be Sure Of"

Catching the morning sun, Juliobone looked like a pearl floating on the water as the boat came near the harbor. Buildings of white plastered brick and red roofs in the Roman style lined the waterfront. Hundreds of others crowded together and rambled up the hillside behind.

There were far more ships of all kinds and sizes in the harbor than she'd ever seen in one place before. It was a daunting view, reminding her that she knew nothing about this land, its customs, its people.

"I can do this," she told herself. "I can find Darius. He's here somewhere. I can't let myself be afraid." In spite of that, she found that her teeth were chattering and she wasn't cold.

Soon Mikal came and stood by her side.

"The captain said you'd hurt your arm again. I'm sorry, I should have been taking care of you instead of –"

"Don't worry about it," Lydia interrupted. She tested her arm, moving her fingers and turning her hand slightly. "It's a lot better, I think. Only twinges when I go like that." She demonstrated and winced at the twinge.

Mikal shrugged. What else could she do?

"Where will we be going?" she asked.

"I have no idea," Lydia answered truthfully. "None at all. I'm relying on your instinct. It will all work out."

"Lydia, if you rely on instincts or mind-reading or anything like that, you rely on air. We have to have something more definite before we go into this land."

"Oh? I hoped you would say that Darius is in Juliobone."

Mikal shook her head slowly. "Do we have any money?" she asked.

"No. Only my uncle's necklace. I'd rather not sell it if we can possibly find some other way."

"The only other things we have are the horses."

"That's a no. Or there's you. I could sell you."

Mikal opened her mouth but only a cry of dismay escaped.

"I'm not serious," Lydia quickly added.

Mikal pouted. "That's not something to tease a slave about."

The boat swung in a long arc toward the harbor area. Crewmen at their oars pulled against the current. They seemed to know exactly what to do even without orders from Marius. Soon a flawless docking was made, the ropes being run around and secured to stanchions on the dock.

A small elderly man in a flapping long white tunic was scurrying toward them shouting, "Marius! We saw you from the balcony. Welcome! Horses? You bring us more horses? We don't need horses! Marius, Marius, you've lost your mind. May God preserve us, but – " Then he saw Lydia and Mikal. "What's this?"

"A moment, Julius," Marius called to the man. "And try to keep quiet, or – too late, you woke the dog."

"Dog!" The poor man leaped onto the boat, landing full force on the deck. "Marius, I don't know what's possessed you, showing up like this – what?!" Culain had ambled over to him and was settling his head under the man's hand to be scratched. "It's as much like a small horse as a dog. What is it?" The man gave a merry laugh and acquiesced to Culain, scratching him behind the ears and ruffling up the fur on his back.

"How funny his speech is," Lydia whispered to Mikal.

"I think it's lovely," The girl answered. "I feel like crying." And she did.

Lydia was uncomfortable seeing her cry. She tried to help by putting her arm around Mikal's shoulders, but she did it badly. When she saw that Mikal didn't mind, however, she kept her arm there until the quiet tears stopped.

Marius, flanked by the man he'd called Julius and the dog, spoke to his crew from the bow. "Savino, stay to guard the ships. Don't let anyone near the dog or horses. The rest of you get yourselves some refreshments. Off with you! You'll unload the cargo later."

The exodus of the sailors was swift.

Marius then spoke to Julius.

"This young woman," indicating Lydia, "is important to me. She searches for her brother who may be anywhere in Gaul or Italy or the underworld. Come, let's go to your house to talk where no-one listens. She is in need of help from you."

"Well, why didn't you say so in the first place. Let's go!"

Lydia stepped onto the deck and stumbled as the whole world suddenly lurched under her feet.

"Takes some getting used to," Marius laughed, linking his arm in hers to steady her. "As I was saying before, your horses will feel the same way for awhile, so you'll have to handle them with care."

The other man, Julius, took Mikal's arm, not knowing she was only a slave, and the four started into the town.

It was nice walking arm in arm with Marius. The streets were marvelously clamorous, crowded with people rushing about selling exotic things. A man with a monkey on his shoulder stood in a doorway watching the crowds. A monkey! Lydia wanted to stop and look but Marius shook his head and kept walking. As they went along, Lydia noticed a few people turning to stare.

"It's your clothes," Marius whispered. "They probably think you and Mikal are my British slaves. Free people don't wear long dresses like that here."

"Nor in my part of Britannia," she agreed, embarrassed. "I'd love to have my own clothes, but there was no choice."

Marius laughed. "Just think of Bearta wearing your tunic. What a picture!"

"Yes indeed," Lydia smiled at the idea. Bearta and her rough company seemed far in the past. She withdrew her arm from Marius's. The ground had long since steadied itself. When she dropped back to walk with Mikal, the two men went ahead.

"Isn't this exciting?" she asked.

"Not really," Mikal answered. "I'll be glad to leave the city. It's a bit frightening."

"True, but still, it's exciting. You're afraid of a city but on the boat you were calm as cheese. Why?"

Mikal didn't answer right away. Finally she said, "The family who owned me used to tell a story about a man who was in a boat in a storm. Everyone else was afraid, but this man wasn't. In fact, he was sleeping. When they woke him up, he made the storm go away. The father said he could even walk on water. So thinking of him, I wasn't afraid."

"You don't believe that, do you? It was just a story."

"Maybe. But it helped me not be afraid. I like to think it was true."

"That's because you were a little girl. It doesn't sound like any story I've ever heard, and I've heard a lot. Maybe they made it up."

"Maybe," Mikal agreed. "It helped me, like the old songs. Remember the one about the shepherd?"

"Yes, that was nice." Lydia added, "That owner seems a lot different from my father."

"Yes. But Quintus Antonius is a good man."

"I know."

Ahead, the men waited for them to catch up.

"This is Julius's home," Marius said, pointing to the open gate leading to the courtyard of a large elegant house facing the harbor. "His wife, Marissa, will help you with new clothes and provisions. Julius has agreed to get you on your way. Now he wants us to dine with him. Come!"

Mikal tugged on Lydia's sleeve and whispered, "I shouldn't eat with everyone. A slave shouldn't."

Remembering Adairinnic where Bearta seemed suspicious of Mikal, Lydia answered, "No. It's better if they think you're my friend and not my slave. Let's go."

Julius led the way to a wide tree-filled courtyard. Four, no five, young dark-haired children played a chasing game around a fountain, giggling and screeching delightfully. As soon as they saw the newcomers, however, they stopped and stared. One beautiful girl of about five years old broke away from the others and ran over to Marius yelling, "Papa! You're back so soon. Did you bring me a present?"

Lydia was dumbfounded. Never had it occurred to her that Marius was married. She tried hard to keep from showing how stunned she was.

Marius caught up the child easily and, with a smile that transformed his homely face into one that was quite handsome, said, "No present this time, Sera. This time I only brought these two young ladies."

Sera suddenly became shy, hiding her head on his shoulder and peeking out between her little fingers. Lydia wasn't sure how to respond, but Mikal touched the little girl's hand and said, "I'm glad to meet you." It must have been the right thing, for Sera smiled and laughed, kissed her father's cheek, wriggled down and ran off to play again.

Climbing up a short flight of stairs, they entered a light-filled dining room. Lydia found that her appetite, which had been strong when they left the ship, had vanished. Even the fruits, hot sausages and bread spread out on the large central table didn't tempt her. She kept expecting Marius's wife to appear.

Julius was explaining, "I had already started to eat when they saw your ships coming in. Marissa has replenished the stock, as you can see, so eat heartily. It may be a long day for us all."

"Julius always eats heartily in the morning," Marius explained. He figures that –"

"I'll tell it," the older man interrupted. "You always get it wrong. Well, ladies, it's simply that in an uncertain world the only thing you can be sure of is starting each day with a full stomach. Who knows? By evening I might be dead!"

"But, friend, you say the same thing in the evening when you again have a feast," Marius jested. "And look at you! You're as round as you are tall."

Julius seemed to enjoy the teasing, and answered, "So it will take me longer than you to starve to death should the time come. Sit, all, while the sausages are still sizzling. I'll have your story as we eat; that will be a fair exchange."

Lydia's heart lifted a bit under the influence of Julius's infectious joy. She'd never seen men joke with each other as he did with Marius.

Marius stabbed a sausage and wrapped bread around it. "Salt air for almost three days makes a person famished, as you well know. I tell you, Julius, your Marissa is a jewel among women for having these ready for us."

"Don't I know it! She'll be in after awhile, ladies, and you can meet her. Likes to get her work done first, and then visit. Now, the story."

In between bites, Marius explained things to Julius as he understood them. It was accurate enough so that Lydia felt no need to elaborate. When he came to the end, though, and asked Julius if he'd seen anything of a red-haired young boy on the docks or in the city, she listened intently for the answer.

"I can't be sure. Lots of merchant ships come through here."

"This would have been a small trading boat from Britannia. Three men and the boy."

"Two or three days ago?"

"Yes."

"I'll make inquiries, but he wouldn't have come to Juliobone, would he? Most people land at Bononia and then work their way down the coast, especially in winter."

"I know, but the courier was in a hurry and didn't want to be followed. There's a good chance he would have come this way and then gone through Lutetia and Lyon, and then on to Rome. We made the crossing well; there's no reason they wouldn't have, too."

"Except for their boat, which you say was smaller and old. It sounds as if it might have been some of those cut-throat mercenaries who take whatever comes their way. Not good. Not good for your brother, Lydia. But come, you're not eating!"

"Oh, sorry," she said, and took a sausage. Nibbling a bit, she soon found the taste irresistible and took a piece of fresh bread to go with it.

Marius was saying, "This one," pointing to Mikal, "is no Briton. When she speaks you'll hear that she comes from Gaul, like you, though it must have been a long while ago. Come, Mikal, won't you say something?"

Lydia, her guard up, proclaimed, "My friend speaks Latin as well as I do."

"Of course she does," Marius grinned. "But it's different, maybe not to your ear that has heard nothing else, but to mine. My speech is not the same as yours, either, because I'm from Marseille. Do you know where that is?"

"I've heard of it," Lydia hedged.

"Most people have," he said, laughing. "It's the most important port in southern Gaul, a sunny place filled with pirates and thieves."

Listening closely to his voice, Lydia thought that the only difference between his and any other man's speech was the sonorous richness of tone. When he spoke, the sound carried far without effort. When he'd given orders on the ship, it had been almost like singing. Before she could think of something to say, Mikal started talking.

"I am, yes, from Gaul as you say, but Lydia's family is my family. Lydia is my friend. Perhaps you can guess where I'm from for I do not know. I will sing a song I once learned. If you know it, you may know where it is sung."

She began, high and soft, "The Lord is my shepherd . . ."

Instantly, Julius's hand slammed down on the table commanding silence.

"Your people sang that?" he asked brusquely.

Mikal looked confused.

"You must forget it. Believe me. Trust me. If you value your life, forget that song."

"Why is that, Julius?" Marius asked, as surprised as everyone else.

"It's dangerous to even speak of it," Julius whispered. Looking intently at Mikal he asked, "Are you a slave?"

Mikal looked to Lydia who nodded. Why pretend when Julius already knew?

"Your family? By the inflections, the rhythms of your speech, I would say you lived south of here. The area around Lyon perhaps. Is that right?"

Lydia could tell Mikal was not happy with his probing questions because her head hung down and she simply shrugged her shoulders. Still, there was no stopping Julius. He seemed like one of the forceful waves that had sent the ship reeling. Time to step in.

"Mikal has been with us since she was eight," Lydia explained. "She doesn't know what happened to her family, but she says they were good people."

Marius burst out laughing, breaking the tense spell in the room. "I never would have believed it! A few days ago I'm invited to a little party at the villa of Brutus Marconius, and now look at the stew I'm in. A Christian! The girl's family might be Christian! Is that what you're driving at, Julius?"

Christian? What's that, Lydia wondered, never having heard the word before.

"It's possible," answered Julius. "Or she may be a Jew like me. Either way, her life will be worth nothing if you howl out the news like that. Down in the south, Lyon and even your Marseille, they have turned Christians into gladiators to be killed in the arenas at festival times. The weak ones don't even make it that far."

"Stop!" Mikal cried in a voice full of anger. "No more! Is it evil, this Christian thing?"

Julius shook his head, realizing how his words must have frightened the girl. Marius answered quietly, "I don't know if it's bad or not. Julius is a Jew. Sometimes that has been considered wrong, sometimes not."

Lydia knew about Jews. There were some doing business in Noviomagus.

Continuing, Marius said, "Once the Empire tolerated all religions. It welcomed all peoples' gods and fit them into the Roman lineup of gods. Jews and Christians only worship one god and no others, not even the Emperors who declare themselves gods. The authorities, whoever they may be, consider that to be rebellion against the state."

"That's stupid," Lydia stated.

Marius gave her a wry look. "I agree. You remember that in Britannia it was the Druids who were killed because they claimed Rome had no power over them?

Lydia knew that very well. Rema's aunt had been a part of it.

"All of them were wiped out except perhaps a few who went into hiding. The Empire lost a great deal of knowledge because the Druids never wrote anything down, at least nothing of importance. It was all memorized by the ones whose families sent them to the Druid schools. You see, ladies, Rome is tolerant only of those who choose to fit in."

He put his hand over Mikal's in a gesture so kind it touched Lydia's heart. She noticed how strong his hand was, with long fingers and gnarly knuckles. He kept it there just long enough, it seemed, and then withdrew it. What a complicated man, she thought. Then, out of nowhere, in her mind came the impression, "His wife is a lucky woman." It was followed immediately by an uncomfortable twinge of envy.

"Marissa!" Julius called, and his wife, a lively, tall, grey-haired woman entered the room. It was obvious she'd been hard at work already. "These young women are in a hurry. They need shawls and tunics and whatever else – leggings, boots – you have around or can conjure up from your friends. They are travelling south, first to Lutetia and then I don't know where or for how long. They need to be warm and comfortable."

"Easily done," Marissa said and smiled warmly at Marius. "It's good you're back so soon. My babies think the world of you, but you know that."

"And I of them," Marius replied with equal warmth. "Sera seems so happy here, I will be ever in your debt, you know that."

Marissa nodded and said quietly, "She is so like her mother it makes me feel young again."

This talk puzzled and worried Lydia. Mikal, bless her, boldly asked what Lydia couldn't.

"Are those children all yours, Marius?"

Marius smiled, his eyes crinkling at the corners. "Only one. The liveliest, in case you didn't notice. Marissa cares for her like a mother, just as she cares for the other children you saw."

"And her mother?"

That was the real question, thank you, thought Lydia.

"My sister. She died when Sera was a baby. On my return from a long voyage, I had a niece but no sister. I adopted Sera, as my sister had wished, and love her like she was my own."

"How good of you," Mikal said, glancing at Lydia as if to encourage her to join in the sympathy.

But Lydia's thoughts were so jumbled she couldn't think of a thing to say. She knew how often mothers died in childbirth, but somehow this was different, more immediate. Finally and, she hoped, not too late, all she could say was, "She's fortunate to have you."

Marius looked at her and smiled.

Marissa explained further, "Marius has always been like one of our own family, and it is a joy to keep Sera, believe me. I love all these young ones, but she especially shines like the sun."

Marius chuckled, breaking the solemn spell that had taken over. "Flatterer! But it's true, of course! Now we truly must plan the day. Supplies for Lydia and Mikal. After they are set, Julius and I will see to unloading my cargo. To work, Julius!"

16. She Peeked Four Times

In due time, Lydia and Mikal were outfitted with new woolen tunics, heavier cloaks and boots. Lydia felt much better being in familiar clothes again. Tunics were practical, as they could be draped short or long, depending on the circumstances. Petrus's saddlebags, with blankets tied over the tops, now held a change of clothing for each of them and enough food to tide them over should they not find hospitality on the road. Marissa urged them to take more, but both girls agreed that the less they carried, the easier it would be to pack up each morning. They could restock their supplies in Lutetia.

Marius then took them back to the ship to unload Culain and the horses.

"Remember, they might bolt when they hit the dock," he said.

"I remember," Lydia agreed. "Coa's such a baby when he's frightened."

"We'll soon find out."

As it happened, subduing Coa took all of Lydia's and Marius's combined cunning and strength. The steady dock, the noise of the port, even the smells, must have seemed like horse-eating monsters to him. Kem, however, seemed only slightly bothered by the change from water to land and gave Mikal no trouble. Culain, eager as ever to explore, needed to be tied with a rope.

"He'll be fine once we start out," Lydia said hopefully.

"Bring Kem closer, Mikal," Marius suggested. "She might be able to calm Coa down."

It was the right thing to do. When Kem nuzzled Coa's neck and brushed up close to him, the big horse stopped trembling and fighting, though his ears were still laid back on his head.

There was nothing left to do but continue the hunt for Darius. Lydia was ready, even eager. She wanted to be on the road before the sun moved any farther in the sky.

They led the horses slowly to let them get accustomed to walking again. After a mile, they came to the large arched gate at the city wall. From here, the road led southeast along the general direction of the Seine, except that the river made many curves while the road went fairly straight.

Marius handed Coa's reins to Lydia. "Now show me how you are going to mount him," he said.

"I've been thinking about it," Lydia replied. "I can use the cast as leverage but I can't grab anything with my left hand. Let me try something."

After making a few high swings with her right leg, she was almost ready to do it for real. However, for the first attempt she needed help.

"Would you hold his head just this once?" she asked Marius.

"Sure. This could be interesting."

Lydia laid her cast across Coa's withers. He made a quick sidestep, probably not happy with feeling that hard thing.

Marius stroked his head, distracting him.

Lydia tried again, this time bending her left arm so her elbow kind of hooked around the withers. Again Coa danced nervously.

"All right. Wait. I know I can do this. I just have to do it fast, like I've been picturing it. I can't let Coa have time to think about it. Walk him around a minute to help him forget."

While Marius walked Coa, Lydia stretched her legs, trying some jumps from squats.

"I'm ready."

Marius brought Coa over and stood holding his head. Lydia laid the cast slowly and gently over the withers, took a half step back, counted out "One, two, three," then stepped and leaped with her left leg while swinging her right arm and leg up and hooking it just over his back. A bit of wiggling and she was up and straight. Coa tossed his head as if saying, "That's the way to do it!"

"Worthy of a legionnaire," Marius complimented her.

"It felt good! I'll use the sling for my arm, though, because there's nowhere to put it without banging Coa."

"I remember how hard that thing hits," Marius said, rubbing his chin where a purple bruise had formed.

"Sorry, but you were going to take me home."

"I'll remember not to ever order you around again." Marius smiled. His dimple made it look as if his whole face was smiling. "Don't be surprised if people stare," Marius continued. "They aren't used to seeing two girls riding horses. They'll love Culain, though."

"You know we couldn't have taken a carriage. It would have been too slow, and Coa has never pulled one before. It wouldn't have worked at all."

"Oh, I wasn't suggesting that. I know how you are when your mind is made up. You'll be surprised at the Roman road, though. It's largely free of bumps."

"Then we can ride faster."

He nodded. "Yes, but usually the cavalry rides alongside the road where the dirt is soft. You will probably do that. The stones can hurt the horses' hooves. Anyway, Julius is a friend. If you come back this way, go to see him. He'll want to know how you fared. And so will I."

It was easy to agree to that. It was also easy to realize that she might never see Marius again. Looking down the road at the rolling countryside where most of the trees were barren but a few still held onto golden leaves, she wondered if Marius would be in Juliobone when they came back. If they found Darius. If they returned this way.

"I wonder where this search will take you," Marius remarked.

Lydia shrugged, not having an answer. She saw that Culain's tail was wagging so hard it made his rear end wobble.

"Ah, let me see how your arm is doing," Marius said in the singing voice that gave commands on board ship. Lydia complied, taking her arm out of the sling

He took hold of her elbow and left hand. Gently but firmly he maneuvered her fingers and tested the cast. "Does it hurt when I do this?" he asked.

"No," she whispered, realizing she was blushing because if felt so nice to have his hand on hers.

He smiled then and said jovially, "If it did get cracked again when you fell, Bearta's cast has kept it well set. You needn't worry. In six weeks, come back and I'll take it off for you personally."

She nodded, thinking that six weeks sounded possible. "Darius, don't be hard to find," she silently pleaded.

"*Valete et bona fortuna,*" Marius said, giving back her hand. "Good luck be with your brother that he may be found soon and be in good health."

"Thank you," Lydia said, surprised that she could speak at all, she felt so rattled.

"One last thing: Shall I tell Quintus Antonius where you have gone?"

"No! No, please. It would be best if you don't mention you saw me at all. If I'm gone very long, Mother or my grandmother will talk to him. You're safer to stay out of it completely. Trust me."

"All right. But – . Lydia, if --. There's a chance . . ."

"What? What chance? What are you saying?"

Marius took a deep breath and looked away. "If something should happen and you should die – it's always possible when one is traveling dangerous roads – then I think I should tell your father all I know."

Lydia couldn't help smiling, he was so serious. "If I die, it won't matter to me what you do, so yes, tell him."

"All right, my girl. I am at your command," Marius said less solemnly than he'd begun, and squeezed Lydia's ankle. His touch was warm and firm but gentle. "Stay safe, and hurry back. Julius will know where to find me."

He then turned abruptly and walked into the town without looking back. Lydia knew he didn't look back because she peeked four times as they rode away.

The stone-paved road was smooth, as Marius had said it would be, but better suited to carriages than horses. Lydia directed Coa down the side bank to the soft dirt path along the side.

Looking back, she saw Mikal on Kem ambling leisurely in the distance. Though she felt impatient, she knew that both horses needed to be warmed up slowly, so she waited. Still, she hoped this was not how the whole trip would be. Soon they would have to speed up. Darius could be in danger, or so far ahead they would never catch up with him.

Her main hope came from Mikal's belief that he was all right. Even though it made no sense, logically, Lydia clung to it. She had six whole weeks to return to Juliobone.

The first night, they stopped at a farm after only about ten miles. That was as far as she dared make the horses go after the long time on board ship. It wouldn't be any good if Coa or Kem became lame or weak because of having been ridden too hard.

In the morning she was up before the farm wife, ready to go. Culain and the horses seemed willing, but Mikal groaned, turned over on her straw pallet and refused to open her eyes.

Lydia shook her and warned, "I am leaving. You come! That is a command."

"Mmmmmm hmmmm," Mikal mumbled, stretching slowly and painfully.

If Lydia had not been so focused on reaching Lutetia, she would have noticed how eloquently Mikal's stiff walk and contorted face told of the pain in her body from yesterday's hours of riding.

Mikal tried to explain, "Every bone I have is bent out of shape from banging against this horse's back. I hate riding. My hips ache. My back is twisted. I'm trying, really. Really I am."

Lydia believed that if she showed sympathy, Mikal would use it as an excuse to go even more slowly, so she didn't. Besides, how could she be sympathetic when the very thing that Mikal hated was the thing that exhilarated her?

Even though she chose to ignore Mikal's soreness, she gave Coa a good hard massage before starting out to relieve any aches or pains he might feel. As usual, he loved it. Mikal started doing the same for Kem, so at least they had two contented horses even if only one of the riders was content.

The next day they went ten miles again. The farm where they stopped was near the road, and the farmer and his wife not particularly friendly. When Mikal chanced to ask if they had seen a red-headed boy with two men come through, however, they became talkative.

"Not on the road, no, but I was fishing," said the farmer, "fishing on the Seine as the sun went down, must have been four or five days ago, and there came this boat up the river, the oars pulling like mad, the sail flapping in the breeze not doing much to help. The men on the boat was makin' a heck of a noise, singing and all, so I had to look, didn't I? Paid a bit of attention, too, once I saw the boy. Standing by the tiller he was. It seemed as if it would crush him, he looked so small next to it, I can tell you that. Red hair like the sunset, made me smile. I waved to the lad and he waved back, then they were gone around the bend. Funny to think it might have been your own brother, and here you are, come looking for 'im."

Knowing now that he had traveled by boat, they didn't ask any of the other farmers about him. Lydia felt jubilant, certain she was on the right track. Darius had gone to Lutetia, where she and Mikal were heading. It almost felt as if he was so close she could reach out and touch him.

Occasionally from the road they could see the river Seine, flowing from Lutetia. "Do you remember my brother?" she took to asking it, not expecting answers.

The horses were able to go longer and farther each day until the last two when they went twenty miles. That was all Lydia dared try. Any more and she would risk hurting them. Speed wasn't as important as safety. "Be safe," Marius had ordered.

Other thoughts flitted about. First, she realized she was no longer afraid. She was heading for a place she knew nothing about, yet she felt confident. This new feeling had probably begun when Mikal told her that Marius had turned his ship to Gaul. It was the first time anyone had ever changed plans because of her.

Second, before they left, Marius had actually asked if he should tell her father about her. That had surprised her, too, because any other man would not have asked. He would have told, because under Roman law fathers had absolute power over daughters. Marius was different from other men, and she was intrigued by him.

"Remember how homely he is," she told herself, then laughed because his big ears, his unruly black hair and his dark eyes did not seem homely anymore. "At least I'm not just imagining how he is, like I did with Titus."

Late in the afternoon of the seventh day, they arrived on a hill overlooking Lutetia. The walled city was impressive, with many towering Roman buildings on both sides of the river and an island in the middle. Lydia hadn't expected that the city would include an island.

It was easy to pick out the forum among the buildings on the opposite side of the Seine. Two lofty rounded rooftops could only be the baths or temples. Lydia chose to think these were baths. How her body would love a real bath! She hoped the hours for women would be convenient because, if Darius wasn't here, they'd have to move on almost immediately.

On the island there seemed to be a large temple, and, on the side where they were, what looked like municipal buildings and homes of wealthy citizens. A few river boats moved languorously on the water, some headed for moorings along the quay, some for Juliobone and the sea.

It was disrespectful, perhaps, looking down on such beauty, to think of food, but somewhere near the forum there would have to be a market. Markets always had huge cauldrons of hot meat soups. Warm bread. Cheese..

Even the small farms in Gaul where they had stopped had proven to have much better food than in Britannia. It was full of herbs and rich flavors. The farmers themselves had been a surly lot, but the food was wonderful. She was ready to sample the fare of the city.

By the time Mikal caught up with her, Lydia had talked herself into a hunger so strong that she didn't want to waste another minute before getting to the forum. One look at Mikal, however, and Lydia realized with disgust that her slave had given up again.

Without a word, Mikal slid slowly off Kem's back and down to the ground where she stood a moment before gingerly lowering herself and stretching out on the winter-dried grass. No sound escaped her lips but the grimace on her face was eloquent.

Lydia wished she wasn't burdened with such a weakling. If Darius was here, they would leave immediately for home and Mikal's slowness wouldn't matter, but if they had to travel farther, she might have to leave Mikal and go on alone for the rest of the trip.

"Well, is he here?" she asked.

"I don't think so," Mikal answered wearily.

Lydia's hunger increased her impatience. Soon the sun would be setting, shops would close, people would head for their homes and shut themselves up behind closed doors and shuttered windows. What chance would she have of eating or asking questions if she waited any longer? If Darius had been here four or five days ago, it was likely that someone would remember him. How could you forget a boy like that?

"Go," Mikal said, eyes closed. "Go. I'll meet you at the forum in an hour, but I need to rest for this hour."

Without a word, furious, Lydia led Coa back toward the road.

"Wait." Mikal sounded pitiful as she struggled awkwardly to her feet. "I'll walk," she moaned. "You'll be looking for the stable so you might as well pay for both horses at once."

Lydia knew that Mikal guessed her plan of going on alone. And she knew that Mikal knew that she knew that Mikal knew. Mind reading could be annoying.

"What makes you think I'm going to the stable? If Darius is gone, I still want to follow him. We're not staying."

"I know. I believe that Darius was here, so all we need to do is find where he stayed and stay there ourselves. Doesn't that make sense?"

"No. How are we going to know where he stayed? Your 'talents' only go so far. Well, come on. First we'll find the stable and then go to the forum to eat and ask questions.."

It was possible Mikal was lying about Darius. Since she knew that Lydia wanted to get rid of her, she might lie to keep it from happening. If so, it worked. Rema had said that Mikal was her best chance of finding Darius. She was stuck with her.

Mikal started walking, leading Kem. Lydia called Culain and pressed her knees into Coa's flank to start down the hill. The dog ran toward her, but then turned around and walked beside Mikal.

"Go away," Mikal told him, shooing him with her hands. He wouldn't budge.

"Culain!" Lydia yelled, but still he didn't move from Mikal's side. Giving up, Lydia kicked Coa into a canter. She did not look to see how far back the others were. It didn't matter.

Once at the city gate, she dismounted and led Coa by his bridle since she wasn't allowed to ride in the city. She could tell he was nervous. A few children, whether boys or girls it was hard to say, ran up giggling and squealing. They touched Coa and then raced away. So far, the horse was on his good behavior. At least the urchins of Lutetia didn't throw things – yet.

She decided to ask the little ones for directions to the stable. They looked as if they didn't understand what she said. She repeated herself several times, each time louder than the last, but it did no good. It wasn't until Mikal caught up and asked the same question that one of the boys answered, saying the stable was on the other side of the Seine.

"They could not understand your accent," Mikal explained. She had once more proven her usefulness.

They kept going south, walking across a wide bridge to the island where a large temple to Jupiter rose on their left, and what might have been a palace or home of a nobleman was on their right. After that, they crossed over a narrower bridge onto the left bank. The buildings she had seen from a distance loomed even higher than she'd thought, towering over the street. Ahead lay the forum and food.

She turned to the west, knowing she should probably ask more directions from somebody, but not wanting to. Luckily, the stable was easier to find than she expected. High thick stone arches made a lofty barn wherein were stored massive quantities of hay and other grains, still leaving room for long rows of stalls, far more than she'd seen even in Noviomagus.

The sullen stable boy pointed out adjoining stalls for Coa and Kem, then held out a dirty hand for payment. Lydia took out the purse Marius had given her and opened it for the first time. The number of gold and silver coins inside was astonishing! She'd known the purse was heavy but had no idea of the wealth she carried under her tunic. She hoped Father wouldn't balk at repaying Marius when the time came. On the other hand, if she found Darius and brought him back to Tunadur, that should be worth most any price.

She and Mikal then left the stable and hurried off in the direction of the forum. Culain kept close to her now, tail between his legs, leery of the crowds and noises.

She had a plan. Unfortunately, her hunger would have to wait because first she needed to find the person in Lutetia who knew everything. It was logical to expect that this person would be in the forum for that was where most of the business and gossip of a town took place Either the forum or the baths, and she couldn't very well go into the men's baths. When she found this person, she could ask about Darius.

Groups of men and a few women stood around or lounged on benches talking and throwing dice. Most of the men wore ordinary togas, not gleaming white ones but well-cared-for older ones. Others, less well kempt, sprawled on steps or lurked behind columns. One of these with oily eyes and greasy hair grabbed Lydia's good right arm as she passed. She immediately whirled on him ready to strike with her cast, but he removed his hand quickly and stepped back, apologizing.

"Sorry lady. Sorry. Thought you were, you know, looking for someone like me. I've got money. I can pay well."

"Scum!"

A hard look came into his eyes and he slurred his words, saying, "You're no prize yourself, dirty woman."

Embarrassed, Lydia knew that what he said was true. Her clothes hadn't been washed in days and her body probably stank. Though she had bathed twice in the river along the way, all the long hours of riding and sleeping in barns had done their worst.

Culain had not shown a spark of bravery during the encounter.

"What a city!" Lydia sighed. "I have no idea where to begin finding anyone to talk to."

Suddenly Mikal let out a yelp and shoved her elbow into the side of a fellow who had come too close. Young, timid, tired Mikal had surprised her again.

"What was that?!" Lydia asked.

"He was reaching for your necklace," Mikal answered as the man slunk away, laughing.

"Good work," Lydia praised. The girl might be a slow traveler, but she was loyal. Culain wagged his tail.

Lydia reconsidered her plan. With their clothes so dirty, they really should find a fuller's shop. There they could purchase new clothes to wear while the old ones, two sets, were washed. Once in better clothes, they could go to the baths at the women's hours and ask questions. She was giving up on the forum and its inhabitants, even though she knew that it was men who were most likely to have answers and not women. Women stayed close to home and had little idea about the comings and goings of merchants and slaves.

"I wonder where the fuller's shops are," she said aloud.

"I'll ask," Mikal said. After stopping a couple of women, she motioned for Lydia to follow her westward.

17. Artemis Hunting for Her Brother Apollo

Lydia and Mikal hurried against the flow of people heading toward the evening baths or to their homes. Many of those passing stared and made rude comments about how they looked. Lydia ignored them. Still, it wasn't polite. If she'd had time, she would have stopped to tell them so.

In a short while, the buildings were smaller, and soon there were no more people on the streets..

The girls quickened their pace, turning down a side street that looked promising. It made a bend toward the Seine where they passed leather shops, jewelers, apothecaries, but no fullers.

The temptation to use the bridge to cross over to the picturesque island was strong. However, if night came on and the fuller's wasn't on the island, which was most probable, they'd soon be wandering in the dark. Lydia touched her heavy purse. It was reassuring but also temptation for a thief.

"I think if we take that street, the one up ahead –" Mikal spoke suddenly then speeded up until she was running. Culain gave a yip and darted ahead, veering left then turning into a narrow lane. Lydia had to rush to catch up with them. When she turned the corner, they were both waiting impatiently outside a shop with the familiar fuller's sign over the door.

"Knock! Quickly!" Mikal urged, then – perhaps Lydia reacted too slowly – pounded on the door herself.

Lydia was amazed at the sudden change in Mikal, but before she could say anything the bar inside was lifted and the door opened by a frightening looking man. His thick grey beard must have been permanently curled by the steam from the washing vats. He raised fierce eyebrows, questioning. Lydia couldn't speak.

Mikal took over. "My friend's brother was here – we must come in!"

Boldly Mikal pushed past the formidable hulk and on into the shop, with Culain and a very mystified Lydia following.

"Explain!" the man ordered brusquely, scowling at Mikal who then looked at Lydia.

Lydia took a deep breath and blurted out a quick version of the story. The fuller's stern expression didn't change. When she was finished, he growled, "Wait here," and stomped off down the hall.

"What's going on?" Lydia whispered to Mikal.

"Darius has been here," Mikal said.

Lydia was overjoyed! "What?! Happily?"

"How would I know that?"

"Because you should!"

"Well, I don't. I know he was here, though. That is enough."

The man returned followed by a young woman whose mass of blonde curls framing her small head was like a golden halo. Could this be the gruff man's brow-beaten wife?

"My daughter Gloriana," he introduced her.

"You must be hungry after your long journey," Gloriana said in a voice as beautiful as she was. "You came alone from Juliobone? How brave of you. Come to the kitchen. Mother always has a pot of stew cooking and bread for visitors. After you've eaten and washed, we will talk. Please, though, do not speak loudly. There is someone here who is hurt and needs to rest."

"Darius?" Lydia asked fearfully.

"No, no. Someone else. Come."

Lydia needed an answer. "Do you know where my brother is?"

Gloriana turned, smiled, and said quietly, "Yes."

Lydia screeched before she could stop herself.

"Shhh, please! I will tell you all I know, but you must keep quiet."

"Is he all right then?" Lydia whispered, her heart pounding.

"I don't know. At least he is in good company, of sorts. That's all I'll say until we get you washed and fed."

Gloriana had her way. Lydia and Mikal were shown to a back room which held two big tubs, one with cold water, one with hot.

"Our private baths," Gloriana's mother explained. She was a larger, coarser version of Gloriana and instantly likeable, reminding Lydia of Bearta. "This way we don't have to go at the women's hours which never suit my schedule. Off with your clothes now. I've got plenty you can use in their place. Soap is on that ledge. You'll find it does wonderful things for your hair."

When she had gone, Mikal said, "If it would make my hair like Gloriana's I'd be happy."

"Me, too," Lydia agreed. "At least I've got the curls if not the blonde hair. It's not only her hair that makes so beautiful, is it?"

"No, she is so kind, so natural and so graceful. Everything. Life isn't fair."

"What a funny thing for you to say. I'd have thought you'd be jealous of me, not of a fuller's daughter."

"I'm not jealous of anyone," Mikal protested, sounding jealous. "If I've got to be a slave forever, I'd at least like to be beautiful. That's all. That's what's not fair, don't you think?"

Lydia thought for a minute then answered, "I always thought I was prettier than Diana, but a lot of good that did me. Beauty isn't the key to anything, but if it makes you feel any better, you are quite pretty."

"Really?" Mikal looked surprised. "It's important to me." She dumped a pot of warm water over Lydia's head and explained, "I'm a slave. I have no money, no dowry, nothing. No family, either, though I'd give up everything I don't have for a family. I'll probably never get married. That's my future and it's not very bright. If I'm pretty, though, maybe someday someone will have me."

"You're wrong about that," Lydia said, enjoying the soapy massage of her head for the first time in a week. When it was obvious that Mikal didn't understand, Lydia tried to explain that people became attracted to each other by a lot more than their looks. While explaining to Mikal, she realized that physical beauty was exactly what had attracted her to Titus and not to Marius.

Back to Mikal, though, "My family will find you a good husband when you're ready."

"So I can bear tiny little slavelets? No thanks."

"All right, forget it. How about this, though? What if you still have a family of your own? What if your own parents are alive?"

"I can't think about that. I've given them up."

"Really? But why? Maybe we're getting close to them, too."

Mikal shook her head.

"What's wrong?"

130

After several tries, Mikal was able to say, "Ever since we left Juliobone, I've tried to feel some hint of my mother or father. Some trace that they are alive, but I know they've gone." Tears filled her eyes then overflowed quietly onto her cheeks. "I have felt it – my family, their spirits, their essence – all gone from here. It's empty for me, like going through a land where all is strange."

Finally Lydia understood Mikal's lethargy the last few days. She recalled how she'd thought Mikal was being lazy and hating to ride. It was hard to know what to do. She put her hand over Mikal's where it was rubbing suds into her scalp and said simply, "I'm sorry." She meant it.

Mikal nodded her head and continued to shampoo Lydia's hair.

Suddenly Lydia had an inspiration. A generous, pure inspiration! It was only the second one in her life, the first one being when she'd saved Darius by changing the amulet to what their father wanted. She asked, "If we could get a priest to sacrifice to one of the gods for your parents, which one would you choose?"

Mikal didn't answer right away.

"Come on! Which god would you want? Which one would be the best one?"

"I don't remember my father doing sacrifices, but I don't remember much of anything from that time. From what Julius said, maybe my father believed in just one god. I don't know which one it was, and Father would not like it if I sacrificed to the wrong one, would he?"

"Probably not," Lydia agreed, disheartened because her generous idea had been rejected. Then a solution came. "I've got it. We can sacrifice to your parents! Like at the Parentalia when we go to the graves and say prayers and give the dead spirits some food. Would you like that?"

Mikal actually giggled. "It always seemed foolish, if you want to know, feeding dead people."

"You shouldn't talk like that. The gods might hear. Besides, it makes me feel good to sacrifice to my ancestors. If you don't, they can turn mean."

"If you say so. But please don't feed my parents. I don't think they would like it. Maybe somewhere we'll find one of those -- what did Julius call it? – Christians and they'll tell us what to do."

"It sounded as if being Christian was about as safe as being a Druid. Better forget it."

"Yes. Hand me the soap, please." There was a pause while Mikal lathered her own hair. "Do you know what I want? I want a mirror! I want to see what I look like!"

Lydia should not have been surprised. Mikal was, after all, just fourteen. As she looked around the room, she saw no mirrors here in the fuller's home.

After the baths, it felt good to sit around the fire in the small kitchen, so different from Tunadur's in both size and feeling. She was learning that a small space can be more friendly than a large, elegant one. The stew, laced with wine and rich cream, was superb, and the family made her feel at home. What good people there were in Gaul, not including the louts hanging around the forum.

She wondered if she would have found the fuller's place if it hadn't been for Mikal. There would be no more thought of leaving her behind.

Culain lay on Lydia's feet like old times, his tail thumping on the wooden floor as he gnawed on a huge soup bone.

"You've a lot farther to go," Gloriana said in her soft Gallic Latin.

"Oh? How far? Rome?" Lydia joked, but if necessary she would go all the way to Syria, so determined was she to find Darius.

The father laughed heartily, in a better humor after a few goblets of wine. "Quite the traveler, ain't she? And broken arm not holding her back. A regular Artemis hunting for her brother Apollo. Though that funny-looking little redheaded boy could scarcely compare with such a handsome god. Well, daughter, tell her where she's going before she takes off for the Alps."

Gloriana then began Darius's story, what she knew of it, finishing with, "He didn't seem the type to run away. He was so quiet and gentlemanly. What happened back at your home, anyway?"

Lydia didn't dare tell the whole truth. If she did, they would know how awful she could be. But it had been as much his fault as hers. What explanation could she give that would sound reasonable but not cast her in too bad a light?

"Darius went against our father's will," she said. "He works in metal and refused to make something important that Father wanted."

A great guffaw came from Gloriana's father. "That little pipsqueak disobeying his father? Doesn't seem likely, does it, Mother?"

The mother smiled and said, "Not likely, but still waters run deep."

Still laughing as if it was a huge joke, the father asked, "So, what do you think of your brother being a slave? Quite a turn, isn't it, from being a Prefect's son?"

Gloriana then tried to apologize for her own brother by saying, "Hector never would have allowed it if he'd known, but Darius never said anything. The other, Acteon, he's a bad sort. Do you know the story of the real Acteon? He was a hunter who was so mean that finally his own dogs killed him. More than likely the whole kidnapping was his scheme. I wish my brother had never gotten mixed up with him."

Lydia believed her for who could not believe Gloriana. "Please tell the rest of the story."

"All right. Optimus Maximus, a Roman, fine and brave –"

Her father choked on his wine, laughing, out of breath. Gloriana continued patiently, "Optimus took the Flea, that's what they call Darius, as his own slave. He liked your brother and, Optimus being an Imperial Courier and all, he could take over property if it meant carrying out his mission. He needed the Flea – sorry, Darius – because he knew that the next courier station – that is, the next station where he could trust someone – was too far away for him to go himself. Poor Optimus, almost dead, had to send someone and he chose your brother."

Lydia couldn't believe her ears. Optimus was the biggest fool in the world to entrust an eleven-year old boy with anything so important. "Where are they going?"

"Lyon. About nine or ten days on horseback south of here where the Rhone river and the Saone come together. We don't know what the message was. Optimus only told Darius. My brother and Acteon went along to protect him. Hector is steady as a brick. Acteon is not.."

"My son will not let anything happen to the little Flea," the father stated.

"How are they traveling?" Lydia asked, knowing Darius was about as useless as Mikal on a horse.

"By cart," the father answered. "Two of the best mules in Lucius's stables. They'll be making better time than you will."

Lydia wasn't going to argue with him. Mules could go long distances even if they had to pull a cart carrying two men and a boy. She would stick to no more than twenty miles a day for Coa and Kem, and maybe not even that much.

"You'll be needing extra warm clothes and mittens because the land you pass through is higher and colder than here," the mother said. "You'll also need places to stay. Father?"

The father nodded his head. "At the morning baths I'll ask around. You'll have everything you need, including people to lodge with. Two pretty young ladies like you, carrying money, fine horses. It's a wonder you weren't murdered already."

Gloriana said, "Optimus knows a lot of places where they could stay. He didn't tell the others; I wonder why."

Her father shook his head vehemently and said, "Probably thought that rogue Acteon would rob them blind and he'd get a bad name for it. But I'd be reluctant to let anyone think these two girls were connected with that scoundrel of yours. Besides, Optimus is in the employ of Septimius Severus, and it is Clodius Albinus country where you'll be heading. Don't mention politics to anyone. You never know who is a spy and who isn't."

"Don't be mean about Optimus," Gloriana pouted. "You know we are to be married."

"Stop the quarreling now," the mother broke in. "It will all work out. You know your father is just teasing you."

"Bah!" the father snorted.

"Hector likes Optimus," Gloriana demurred.

"And what does Hector know? He'd trust anyone, he would." Turning to Lydia he explained, "My son is a fine fellow, worth ten of anyone I know. His problem is he'd trust anyone, he would. He's 24 years old and trying to get rich by hitching up with crazy fools like this Acteon. Trading, they call it! Then they come limping back up the river, nothing to show for their trip but a leaky boat, a runt of a boy and a husband for Gloriana who's more than half dead. Fine thing. My son could take over this business, but no, he wants to make it on his own."

The mother put her hand on the father's arm, a calming gesture which he received well. "My husband gets carried away. Our Hector is a fine, loyal son. Slow, yes, but a more trustworthy companion your brother could not have."

"I'm glad," Lydia said, reassured.

"Yes, but don't trust him with money. Never! Gives it away again."

"Father, you've had too much wine," the mother said.

It was true. The grapes the year before had been extra sweet and rich, making a powerfully relaxing drink. The man stretched and yawned then ordered, "To bed all. Tomorrow we prepare our guests for their journey, though if ye were my daughters, you would be staying home and helping with the work."

Gloriana disagreed. "I think it's grand, what you're doing! If I were a Briton I would be fearless, too. If, as Optimus says, Albinus means to challenge Septimius Severus, I wager that the Britons will give the Emperor a good fight!"

"Hush, child!" the father bellowed. "We're not to speak of it! Or have you forgotten that your lovesick Optimus ordered silence?"

"I didn't think it mattered here in the house."

"Don't the walls get thin in places? Who knows what the baker next door hears. Or the cobbler? If they find out Optimus is here, what will they do? So hold your wagging tongue, Gloriana."

"Yes, Father," she said, much subdued.

"Now, to bed all.

18. Betrayed by the Gods

There was a small room off the workshop for Mikal and Lydia to share. Straw stuffed inside a heavy woven covering made a comfortable mattress. Lydia found it hard to sleep because of the closeness of the room. Inside the fuller's dwelling, the air was heavy with moisture and heat, feeling like summer. Gloriana's mother had shuttered the only windows so no breeze stirred inside.

The courier in the next room snored and groaned in his sleep. She was curious to know what he looked like, imagining that he would have to be someone as handsome as Gloriana was beautiful. Otherwise why would she be so devoted to him?

What a shock it was, then, to come to breakfast and meet a thin, dark-haired little man with close-set black eyes and a hawkish nose. Nothing about him was harmonious. It was odd to watch Gloriana hovering over him like a mother with a child, bringing him fruits and broth, listening to every word.

"The Flea's sister!" he exclaimed. "I don't believe it! May both our missions be blessed, fair lady. If the Flea succeeds, he will be rich, I promise you, and you will have a brother again."

He stared impolitely at Lydia making her blush, and continued, "Your chestnut hair is nothing like his, is it? Like a rainbow he is, yet scrawny as a beanpole. Ah, let us pray he doesn't fail us for if he does, we are all paupers and probably dead besides. No worries then, right?"

Optimus laughed at his peculiar joke, obviously feeling better. His hand caught Gloriana's rear end and gave it a squeeze, an act that clearly her father did not approve of.

"Not till you are married, you blackguard!" he shouted. Optimus obeyed with a shrug and a wink of his eye.

"Your wounds must be healing," Gloriana's mother commented drily. "Our visitors will have to use their imaginations to believe you had so many cuts in you."

"I could show them if you care to see," he offered, grinning wickedly at Mikal.

Down came the father's fist on the table! "Good for nothing son of a sea snake, prove yourself a man and get into the drying room. You'll learn a trade today or you'll not have my daughter. I go to the baths. Look for me in no more than two hours."

"Can we help?" Mikal asked when he was gone.

"Maybe you will be able to do something," Gloriana agreed, "but Lydia cannot with only one arm. The work is too hard. Come, Optimus."

The three headed for the steamy workshop, and since the mother also refused Lydia's help, she was left to sit. Culain lay down again on top of her feet, quite at home in the fuller's house.

The next thing she knew, she was being wakened by the father's hand on her shoulder.

"Sorry, young one, but there's a fair distance for you and your friend to travel today." He was so much quieter, it seemed as if the baths must have washed out last night's wine and this morning's ill humor. For the first time, Lydia wasn't wary of what he would say, or how.

"I wish –" he began, then started over again. "I'd not have you go, if you were mine. A wayward brother is a bad thing, but the boy has chosen. Let him go. Why should your parents lose two of their children? It's not right, Artemis and Apollo or no." He shook his head sadly, then said, "We'll give a prayer to the gods to lead you safely, but –"

Were his eyes glistening? Lydia looked away, embarrassed.

He drew from his tunic a scroll on which was written a list of names and days.

"Your hosts," he said. "I have rich friends in Lutetia who know people all along the road. Promise you'll stop with them. Promise."

What a softy he was. Lydia promised.

"Come," he said. "We'll go to the market and buy provisions for today. Mother has your clothes ready."

He bustled about with purpose, calling Mikal away from the work and shepherding them both out the door once they had changed into clean clothes. Culain's tail was high, his ears up, as if he was ready for more adventure.

What a difference it made, walking through Lutetia with Gloriana's father and not looking like vagrants. He seemed to know everyone, as passersby called greetings or came up to speak a few bantering words with him. Lydia's opinion of Lutetia changed completely. Now it seemed like one of the pleasantest places she'd ever seen.

Suddenly she was struck by a wonderful idea. "When I find Darius and all of this is over, will you come to Tunadur for a visit? All of you? My parents would welcome you gladly. Please?"

"Me? In Britannia? That would raise some eyebrows around here. Hah! I hear they have strong ale there, is that right?"

"Yes, indeed," Lydia admitted, though she would rather not entice him on that score. He was a lot easier to get along with when he hadn't been drinking. However, ale diluted with water still tasted good, and that's what he would get.

Lucius at the stables greeted them warmly.

"Taking a trip today, are you, Fuller?"

"Not me. You know me better than that. Lots of work waiting for me."

"Bah. You've got plenty of workers to get the work done for you."

"I'm not speaking of the fullery but of the forum. Someone has to see that this town is run right."

Lucius laughed heartily and then got down to business. The charge for boarding the horses was far too low, but he wouldn't hear of taking more.

"Hector is eight days ahead of you," Lucius said. "Don't worry. He told me that Lyon was as far as they were going. Look for them there. Maybe you'll meet them on their way back. The gods make things work out for those who are favored."

"Oh, and are we favored?" Lydia asked, hoping he had the answer.

Lucius shrugged and shook his head. "Who can be sure? But they brought you to our fuller and he's always got good luck. So, *vive valenque*! Live and farewell."

"Yes, *valenque*. And thanks."

"How do you get up on this horse with only one arm?" Lucius asked.

"Watch," she said, awing the two men with her expert vault onto Coa's back.

"Excellent!" cheered Gloriana's father.

"May the gods protect you!" Lucius called as they passed through the stable gate.

It was a perfect day for a journey, cool and bright. Aside from a few short stops to graze the horses, the travelers kept going until well into the afternoon. A small stand of trees near a brook was the welcome spot to take their rest. They brought out fresh bread and cheese and clear wine (to which they added water), and relaxed.

"Poor Gloriana," Mikal sighed.

"What do you mean?" Lydia asked, surprised.

"That Optimus."

"He's not much to look at, for sure."

"It's not that. He – I suppose you didn't notice that whenever she wasn't looking, he would touch me, and not in a nice way? Gloriana's in for trouble. I wouldn't have wanted to stay another minute there. How can she be so in love with such a scoundrel?"

"It's easy," Lydia answered. "Read Ovid's love stories and you'll understand."

"I have, and I hope I never end up with someone like Optimus."

"All right. I'll make sure of it," Lydia smiled. Then she thought a bit and said, "Maybe all men are like that. Titus, for instance. Did you know he kissed me when he must have already been making love to Diana. I had thought he was so wonderful, but he was as bad as Optimus."

"Not all men," Mikal demurred. "There's your father."

"You're right.. I would stake my life on his love for my mother and his faithfulness."

It was true. Her parents seemed perfectly suited. Their ideals were the same: Make sure their children were respectable and don't be extravagant in any way. Probably there were more, but that's what came to Lydia's mind right away.

Their first stop was to be at the villa of a man called Vitruvius, but they made much faster speed than expected. Hours before dark they reached the villa, but not even Mikal had any desire to stop. After burying a piece of round bread in the soil as an offering to Ceres to forgive them for breaking their promise, they kept going.

When the sun set and twilight came, an icy breeze started up which made them pull their cloaks closer around them. The sky was cloudless, the first stars bright sparks against darkening blue. Shelter there was none. They had passed the last farm at least an hour before. Ahead loomed what looked like a small forest.

"What do you think?" Lydia asked Mikal, knowing it was time to stop somewhere.

The girl looked doubtful as she replied, "If we have to spend the night outside again, I'd rather be in the forest than here in the open."

"Not me. There might be wild animals in there like the boars at Adairinnic. Not to mention bandits, like the fuller said."

"Have you forgotten Culain? He'd warn us of any danger."

"Be serious."

"I am."

Lydia decided for once to let Mikal have her way since the open field looked rocky and uncomfortable for sleeping. Bandits could surely see them more easily, too. What would it hurt to spend just one night in the forest?

The grove of birches and bracken was growing so tightly together that it actually provided a fair shelter against the cold breeze. The beds they made of dry leaves piled high were reminiscent of the awful night in the storm near the Long Man.

"I hope the gods of this place are kinder than in Britannia," Lydia remarked.

"Of course," Mikal agreed with a giggle. "I'm sure all Gallic gods are kind."

"I'd feel better if we gave them a sacrifice."

"As you wish, but I still can't make a fire if you want to have a burnt offering."

"No need for that," Lydia informed her. "I don't suppose you would consider giving them one of your songs?"

"Never!"

Lydia sighed. "Don't get mad. I don't understand why you're so against it, though."

"I don't, either," Mikal answered. "I just know that my whole self doesn't want to have anything to do with it. I'll probably be punished for it one day."

"Probably, but not while you're with me, I hope. Anyway, the gods had better be satisfied with cold food because I'm certainly not giving them Uncle Petrus's necklace."

So saying, Lydia took a hunk of dried pork from her saddlebag and laid it at the entrance to the grove. Perhaps it would have been better if she hadn't.

Unknown creatures snuffled through the dead leaves all night long, mewling and grunting. Probably the first to arrive got the meat. Lydia hoped it was the god. The rest, gods or animals, came for the smell and left when they found nothing. Once when Lydia had dozed awhile, she awoke to find a furry tail so close that her breath ruffled its fur. She dared not move while the creature took his time investigating their bags of provisions. When at last he found a treat to his liking and shuffled off, Lydia leaped out from under her covering of blankets and hung the saddlebags from a tree limb, out of reach. Culain and Mikal, Coa and Kem slept undisturbed through the night.

How Lydia envied them! Alien, eerie noises kept her from falling into any kind of restful sleep. A pack of wolves, afar off, began calling and singing to each other. They sounded like the wolves that sometimes came out of the forest at Tunadur to raid the flocks of sheep.

Once for about a half hour she tried to wear herself out by pacing the circumference of the shelter. Through the dark limbs of winter-bare trees, the stars – the Bear, Mithras, the Bull, and Sirius the Dog Star – looked down. How strange that they would be the same in Gaul as at Tunadur. If Rema was watching tonight, would she know that Lydia was, too? Would she know how lonely it was? Lydia then remembered what Rema had said: "If I wasn't two years older than the gods, I'd join you," and she knew Rema would have been good company on a night like this.

"I wish you were here, grandmother," she whispered to the night.

At dawn, the leaves by the entryway where the meat had been were scattered everywhere and trampled almost down to the bare earth. Mikal awoke cold, stiff, and in a bad humor.

"At least you slept!" Lydia protested.

"Yes, if you can call having horrible dreams all night long sleeping. I hope you don't want to spend another night like this when we could be at one of those villas that belong to Gloriana's father's friends."

Lydia agreed, but let Mikal think it was because of her when actually it was her own choice. From now on they would use the names on the scroll for food and shelter.

Everywhere they stayed they were warmly received. They always managed to arrive before dinner and to leave just after breakfast so as not to make too much trouble for their hosts, any of whom would have been happy for them to stay longer.

Nothing in Britannia, not even Arundel or the palace near Noviomagus, could compare with the luxurious villas of the friends of the friends of the fuller. Lydia even felt a little sorry for Diana's parents who thought they had redone Arundel so elegantly. It seemed as if hundreds of years of Roman rule in Gaul had put it far ahead of Britannia in architecture.

One brisk, cold morning as they were setting out, Mikal asked, "You haven't noticed, have you?"

"Probably not," Lydia replied lightly.

"I didn't think so."

"Well, what?"

"Never mind."

Mikal began humming one of her tunes while Lydia rode in silence, refusing to ask what it was she hadn't noticed until she couldn't stand it any longer.

"All right, tell me," she finally asked, exasperated.

"I'm riding as long as you are and you don't have to slow down for me anymore."

Astonished, Lydia realized she was right.

"That's wonderful! *Mea culpa.* I should have noticed. Did Kem's back suddenly get comfortable?"

"That might be part of it, or my kidneys have adjusted, but it's also because I think I'm ready to get to Lyon and face what's there. I know it won't feel the same as when I was a little girl, and I can handle that."

"That's good," Lydia said, not really understanding Mikal's feelings. All she really cared about was finding Darius. That was what kept her going on to Lyon. "What about Darius? Is he all right?" Lydia asked this several times a day.

"I am sure he's all right because if he wasn't, I'd feel it. You probably would, too."

"I doubt that," Lydia said. "That's why Rema sent you with me. I don't have that gift. If I did, I wouldn't need you, would I?"

Mikal stared at her and finally said, "You are so proud of yourself. You think you don't need anyone, especially me. I hope you . . . Never mind. It doesn't matter."

Mikal was right. Whatever she was going to say did not matter to Lydia.

It was early in the evening of the seventh day from Lutetia. Having slept soundly and been well fed at the villa of one Cariantius, the girls had put in a solid day of riding. The plan was to make one more stop, then ride into Lyon tomorrow.

Lydia was confident that she'd managed very well so far. Who would have believed, when she left for Arundel a little over three weeks ago, that she'd find herself making her own way in such a far place as the center of Gaul? One more day and she'd find Darius and take him home. Everyone, maybe even Titus, would see that she was a girl worth a lot more than Diana or anyone else.

Mikal had been humming a peaceful tune for miles. It had become such a part of the rhythm of riding that Lydia didn't hear it anymore, nor, perhaps, did Mikal.

Culain explored ahead, occasionally darting after a winter rabbit or rummaging through wind-driven piles of dried leaves, sniffing out all the new scents by the roadway.

The air was light and warm in spite of patches of snow on the ground. Soon they would arrive at the villa of Plotius to rest their final night before arriving at Lyon.

Unexpectedly, Kem halted. Lydia turned to see what was going on. Mikal's face was white. "Something's wrong, Lydia. Look at Culain."

The wolfhound stood fifty yards ahead of them, riveted in his tracks, lips curled back over his teeth, ears flat on his head. Obviously, he had found something interesting in the thicket of small trees and bushes not much above the height of a tall man.

"It's probably just a . . ."

The dog lowered himself into a lurking hunting stance and was inching forward when suddenly he leaped, snarling and snapping.. Instantly from the brush, out stepped a small ugly man slashing a long knife at him.

"No!" Lydia shouted and kicked her heels into Coa's flanks demanding obedience. The war horse gathered all his power and charged forward into the fight. Lydia felt as if she was his legionnaire master riding into battle. So be it! No-one would hurt Culain, not while she was alive to prevent it.

The little man's knife gleamed in the dying light as he kicked at the dog while trying to keep his eye on Coa's approach. As Culain jumped, the man thrust out with the knife. There was a sharp yelp of pain, then Culain was up again, surging like a tiger toward the arm that held the knife.

"Aaaiiieeee!" the man yelled, whipping himself around, thrashing with his other arm to get Culain off him. But Culain held on and the knife fell first, then the man. He quickly rolled over, struggling to get to his feet with Culain holding tight, growling fiercely.

Before the man could stand again, Coa reached him. The huge war-trained horse reared up, his front hoofs pawing the air. The man's eyes were wide with terror.

"No," Lydia gasped as she realized what was going to happen. She closed her eyes as the hoofs crashed into the man's face. In speechless horror, she felt each jolt, heard each bone crack, as Coa pummeled the man into the ground. She didn't even realize she was screaming because the horse's cries, Culain's growling and barking, filled her head with an excruciating din.

An eternity later, as Coa began to calm down, blowing hard through his nostrils, Lydia slid off his back. A glance at the mangled corpse so unnerved her that she retched, and then vomited until nothing was left to come up. She was shivering, freezing in the air that had suddenly turned cold. Wailing in anguish, she felt betrayed by the gods who had seemed to be with her before this.

Culain nudged her with his grey young-old head and showed her his cut paw. She examined it closely and found that, though blood was oozing out, the wound was not very deep.

Hugging her dog tightly, Lydia cried, "What have we done?"

In answer, he licked her face happily.

Back home, dogs that attacked people were themselves killed. Did this count? The man had attacked first. Lydia cried for Culain.

"In the trees!" she heard Mikal shouting from far away.

Instantly Lydia was alert. Was there more danger? Through the bushes she heard noises – snuffling, shuffling, mumbling. She glanced around quickly looking for Coa, but the big horse had disappeared. A few paces off, the dead man's knife lay in the grass. Being careful not to look at the corpse, Lydia picked up the knife. Holding it in front of her, she followed Culain toward the noise. Her hand was trembling but she knew she could do what was needed, even if it meant killing. She and Culain would face this next enemy together and the outcome would be as the gods willed.

Suddenly, Culain dashed ahead. As she fought her way through the stiff branches blocking her way, she heard Culain yip and squeak (yes, squeak).

Bursting through the final layer of brush, ready to kill, she saw her dog standing in a small cart mauling a bundle of rags. From inside the rags came incoherent – but loud – noises.

"Culain!" she urged, holding the knife and scared to death. "Come here!"

Culain, his tail wagging like a windmill, ignored her.

A flash of red hair caught her eye. It took a moment before she realized what she'd seen. Instantly, she dropped the knife and raced to the cart. Tearing off the top layer of rags, she stared at her brother, all tied up and gagged like a pig. He looked even more bewildered than she did.

"The knife, I've got to find the knife," she gasped, wondering where it had got to. A minute was all it took to find it in the tall brown grass, but that seemed far too long.

Because her hands were trembling, Darius got a slight cut on his cheek before she managed to slit the gag and yank it out of his mouth.

19. The God's Vengeance?

"Darius!"

"Lydia!"

"What are you --?"

"Where did you --?"

"What is --?"

"How did you --?"

"I found you!"

"Acteon? You --?"

"That man? Coa killed him," Lydia answered in a tone that made it clear she wouldn't explain any more. "I'm going to cut that rope." The rope was wrapped so tightly around his skinny wrists that Darius's hands had turned blue. With only one good hand and no extra space to insert the blade of the knife, Lydia came precariously close to his skin again.

"Watch it! That's me, you know!"

"I can see! Stay put. I'll be right back."

"How can I go anywhere?" Darius muttered under his breath watching her hike back through the bushes. Everything was such a jumble. On one hand, he was so happy to be rescued that he could have kissed Lydia -- almost. He also knew for certain that she had come to take him back to Tunadur, for why else would she be here? He would not go.

Never could he have guessed that his quick, desperate prayer to the gods would be answered by his sister. Anyone but her! There was no understanding the ways of the gods. Maybe Mithras had planned this revenge from the beginning. If that was so, then Darius hoped that going back to Numerianus was also in the plan.

He had a feeling that his future, or any hope for a future, lay with that strange old man. At first, Numerianus had seemed so odd that Darius had wondered if Optimus knew what he was doing, putting so much trust in him. He was far too old to be a courier, for one thing. Almost bald with a long beard that flew in all directions, and faded brown eyes that never lighted on anything or anyone for more than a second, he gave the uncomfortable impression of having been interrupted in the middle of something more important. Yet, as soon as he learned of Darius's mission and heard the message, he commandeered Hector to drive the cart and rushed off, as a real courier would, not to Rome, but to the next loyal courier.

They didn't return until the next day. While they were gone, Darius kept out of Acteon's way by exploring the courtyard and outbuildings of the dilapidated farm. He discovered a blacksmith shop that looked as if it had recently been used. Great stacks of rusty iron tools covered the ground and a bellows in good condition lay in the corner by the furnace. A big lump of hammered iron looked ready to use. He discovered other implements – tongs and hammers.

When Numerianus returned, Darius told him that he would like to use the forge. The old man agreed without asking pointless questions. In fact, he seemed downright enthusiastic about it.

That was eight days ago, and Darius had made good use of his time. Unfortunately, before dawn today, Acteon changed everything. He'd crept into the room where Darius was sleeping, stuffed a gag in his mouth, tied his arms and legs, and dragged him out of the villa without anyone hearing a thing. Then, with Darius lying in the cart covered by an old blanket, Acteon drove the mules at a furious pace northward. Darius couldn't call for help, being gagged, but he hoped that Acteon would want to keep him alive so he could at least be sold as a slave. As the cart bounced along he had thought about Mithras and the amulet. Was this the god's vengeance? It wasn't fair. Darius believed he'd already been through enough.

When they stopped at this little clearing, Acteon took out a wicked-looking knife, looked at him with his piggish little eyes and said, "*Morituri.*" You will die.

"Like Ansonius," Darius thought, recalling his brother, murdered in Gaul, probably by someone like Acteon. He'd quickly sent a silent prayer heavenwards, "Gods of this strange place, whoever you are, please don't let me die yet."

Immediately afterwards, Acteon had been distracted by the growling of Culain. How, then, could Darius doubt the powers of the heavenly watchers? The only problem was that he didn't know which god had helped him. Whom could he thank? Maybe the mother goddesses had forgiven him, or maybe Mithras had been overruled in his revenge by the local god of this little spot of Gaul.

While Lydia went to find Mikal, Culain stayed with Darius, licking his face, tickling him, and smearing blood from his paw everywhere. Darius couldn't fight back so he just laughed, and that felt good.

His sister finally reappeared with Mikal right behind her. The slave looked awful. Darius wondered why she was sobbing, her face streaked with tears. When she wiped her running nose on the hem of her tunic, he remembered the perfect Gloriana. Why couldn't all girls be like her?

"Cut him loose!" Lydia ordered Mikal.

Darius closed his eyes and gritted his teeth as Mikal took the knife and began to saw at the rope. He waited for the awful moment of shooting pain when his arms would be able to move again. "Aiyhh!"

It was just as painful as it had been when Hector untied him in the boat. This time, though a film of tears welled up in his eyes, he didn't allow them to fall. Slowly and carefully he managed to pull himself out of the cart and stand up. Stretching his cramped limbs, he began to loosen up.

He waited for Lydia to say or do something, wondering what it would be. Finally she just said, "I can't believe it," and smiled so sincerely that he actually had to smile back. "I really can't believe it. What now? Shall we go home?" she asked, looking at both him and Mikal.

Everyone seemed overwhelmed. Finally, Mikal spoke up. "We might still have time to go on to the villa of Plotius. I certainly don't want to stay here tonight."

"True enough," Lydia agreed. She kept looking at Darius as if he was an apparition. "What about tomorrow? Maybe we could be home in time for the Saturnalia."

Darius hadn't yet figured out how to say it so she would understand. Even so, his traitorous tongue mumbled, "Lyon."

"I didn't hear you," she said.

Mikal helped him out. "I think he said Lyon. Oh, Lydia, could we? We're so close and I may never have another chance to see my old home. It would break my heart to leave now. Couldn't we take a little more time? We have Darius, so –"

"Quiet!" Lydia ordered. "Darius, speak up. Where did you say you wanted to go?"

"Lyon. There's a farm about seven miles north of the city. I have to go there."

"You *have* to come home!" Lydia declared heatedly. "That's why I'm here! I know all about this disgusting creature that kidnapped you. He's dead, thank the gods. I'm sure Father won't punish you, in fact everyone will be enormously happy to see you. So you don't have to go to this farmer in Gaul! Be reasonable for once."

Darius sighed. He knew he owed her his life, but he owed himself a life, too.

"I might still be someone's slave," he mumbled, hoping that would be a good enough reason to leave him with Numerianus.

"Father will have something to say about that," Lydia countered.

Unable to answer that, he merely shrugged.

Mikal started to plead again, but Lydia cut her off. "I want to hear it from Darius, not you. How hard can it be to say what he wants? I don't want to have to go hunting for him again."

Fighting her own impatience, she tried hard to look pleasant as she waited and waited for an answer.

Darius thought maybe there was hope. Opening his mouth, he took a deep breath and began to explain.

"We have to go back to the farm to show that I'm all right; otherwise Hector – you don't know him – and Numerianus – you don't know him either, will accuse me of stealing their mules and the cart; then when they find out that Acteon was murdered, they'll probably think I did that, too. Unless I go back."

"We met Hector's family in Lutetia," Lydia said, but her thoughts were on Darius's other words. Murder and robbery were punishable by death. She asked, "Where are your mules?"

"Probably ran off, like your horses. Acteon – that's the guy you killed – unhitched them for awhile and then went – you know – I guess they smelled blood and ran off. I wonder what they do to murderers around here?" The last was a brilliant addition that surprised himself.

"We're not murderers and you know it."

"Killer animals, too. Poor Culain and Coa. I know you like them a lot."

"Will you stop!"

Darius plunged ahead anyway, enjoying himself at last. "It will be big trouble for you if Hector finds out what happened to his friend. Hector hates women and animals. He's – he's big and ugly too. But if you let us go back to the farm I will say that Acteon and I were attacked by robbers and he was killed and I just happened to run into you."

Darius amazed himself with his cleverness.

"That's blackmail, you worm," Lydia said.

"Not worm. They call me Flea around here."

"You're as much trouble as a Flea, that's for sure," Lydia scoffed, trying to get her thoughts together. What was the truth? How much trouble was she in because of Coa and Culain? Would Hector be mean enough to let her be imprisoned for murder?

"Mikal, what do you think?"

Mikal shrugged her shoulders. "I know nothing of the law here. It's the same Roman law as in Britannia. What would happen there?"

Darius felt a bit sorry for Lydia. They both knew that at Tunadur, father would have both Coa and Culain killed. He'd probably behead them and offer the heads to Epona and Sylvanus, gods of horses and shepherds. It was a chilling thought.

No-one spoke for a long time as Lydia pondered the next step. There was no sound, no birds sang, no insects skittered through the leaves. The little grove felt as barren as a grave.

"All right." Lydia had made the decision. She would bide her time. It was clear that Darius wasn't going to come easily, and that she might be in big trouble if she tried to force him. She had a promise to keep to Rema and would figure out later how to manage it. "The villa of Plotius is nearby. We will go there for the night."

Mikal hesitantly asked, nodding toward Acteon's mutilated body, "What about him?"

"Ewww! I can't . . ."

All of them felt the same way, so in the end they decided to leave Acteon where he was. It wasn't a courageous or smart decision, but it was all they could do.

Lydia stood up. "We'll all have to go after the animals. Let's move the cart away from here so they won't get skittish from you know what."

Darius was elated! He got to have his way! He was going back to the farm, and without Acteon. It would be fun showing his sister and Mikal all he'd done there. He smiled, imagining what they'd think of Numerianus and Hector.

The three walked slowly through the tall grass in the direction of the horses and mules, who were bunched together.

Lydia inched her way to Coa, calling softly. His head came up and he backed off a little. "Come on, sweet boy, come on," she coaxed. The mules and Kem began backing, too, watching the people nervously.

"Good boy you are to wait so patiently for us," Lydia crooned. He must not have believed her for he stepped sideways, then backwards, then forward, then to the other side. "Easy, easy. We're going for a little ride, you and me," she murmured. His eye gradually lost its look of terror and his ears calmed down. She kept talking, patting Coa's neck and holding tightly to his reins. She could feel him relax. At last, when she could vault onto his back, she went to help round up the others.

A little way off, Darius was singing in a high boyish voice to the mule closest to him, "You stupid old nag, you had better get your four bumbling legs over here or I'll whip the tar out of you."

He had pulled up a handful of grass and was holding it out as he approached the mule. It was a pretty good strategy, though combined with the singing it made such a ridiculous picture that Lydia couldn't help giggling. She was actually starting to have a good time!

Kem was giving Mikal trouble, bolting ever closer to the woods. "I might need some help," Mikal sang in the same type of easy voice Lydia and Darian had used.

Lydia nudged Coa, guiding him toward the horse. The renegade might have felt intimidated by Coa because she stopped immediately and let herself be herded back to Mikal who took hold of her bridle and led her back toward the cart.

Culain, his tail wagging proudly, hadn't moved from the cart.

"Good boy," Lydia complimented him. He was off the seat in an instant, inspecting the mules and getting in the way as Darius hitched them up. Lydia was surprised at how competent Darius had become. Her little brother had grown up a lot in these three weeks.

There was plenty of time for talking on the way to Plotius's villa, but no-one said a word, each one being absorbed in his or her own thoughts.

As the slow undulating ride relaxed her, Lydia basked in the knowlege that her quest was over. It was almost a letdown. She speculated about how long Darius would stay home once they got back to Tunadur. Having journeyed this far, he might be hard to contain. She watched him as he stood driving the mules. Skinny, short (but not more so than others his age), white skin, freckles, red hair. He looked so vulnerable, so determined, so young, and he'd just been through a horrible experience. She felt proud of him.

The quiet, cool evening; the empty countryside, the barren trees, and the murder of Acteon all worked a spell on her. Her thoughts drifted elsewhere, to Marius. She touched her ankle where he had touched it. How is it, she wondered, that I think so often of him? Since she had promised to let Darius go back to Lyon for awhile, how long would it be before she returned to Juliobone? If she was too late, would she ever see Marius again? The chances were not good. And then, to her dismay, she realized how much she cared for him. All these emotions were too much for her. She sighed.

Darius heard the sigh and thought she was mad at him. Too bad. He was determined to make the most of the time he had with Numerianus. It might be his only chance to work as a full artisan, not an apprentice. He would do it no matter what she thought. All she cared about was getting him back to Tunadur. Her life was easy. Father would make all her decisions for her and she would agree. He would even choose who she would marry. She would never have to worry about anything. For him, a boy who did not want to follow his father's path, life was going to be a lot harder.

Setting his jaw, he stood stiff and straight, concentrating on the mules' steady, slow gait.

20. Why Not Take Big Risks?

On their way to the home of Plotius, they passed through the small town of Matisco, attracting the attention of a number of townspeople. What was so odd about two young girls on horseback and a young redheaded Celt driving a mule cart? If the people had known what these three had left behind on the road, their curiosity might have turned dangerous. Lydia was relieved that the blood on Coa's legs had been rubbed off in the tall grass. It would have looked suspicious and she did not want any more trouble.

The villa came into view long before they reached it since it was even grander than the other ones where they had stayed. However, Lydia began to have second thoughts. Her tunic was frayed and they all looked quite shabby, especially Darius. Plotius might take them for vagrants. She had just decided to turn back to Matisco where there might be an inn when a horseman overtook them, headed in their direction.

He was old, with grey hair, but muscular and he certainly rode with energy. Even though he seemed to be in a hurry, he stopped to talk.

"*Salve*, young travelers," he said. His voice was one of those hearty ones that immediately puts a person at ease.

"*Salve*," Lydia returned.

"I would guess, since it is getting late, that you are coming to my villa. You'll be welcome there. Where are you from?"

"Oh! Are you Plotius Commodius?"

"Yes, yes. Do I know you?"

"You know friends of friends who have recommended us to you. I have a scroll in my saddlebag with a note from Lutetia."

"But you are not from Lutetia by your speech."

"No, we come from Britannia."

"Britannia! You are a very long way from home! Two girls and a young lad. There must be a good story here. You, Sir Redhead, if you had a few years more on you, I'd vow you were one of Albinus's vanguard of British soldiers come to save the Empire from Septimius."

"What? Me? No!" Darius sputtered, confused and dismayed by that idea.

Plotius laughed jovially and said, "Not to worry, son. Now come, it's getting late. I will go ahead and let them know you are on your way. Hurry along." Then he galloped off.

"Well, that was interesting," Mikal murmured.

"To say the least," Lydia agreed.

The villa was the most sumptuous place Lydia had ever seen in her life. The rooms were immense with tall columns holding up carved plaster ceilings. Lydia and Mikal would sleep on the second floor in a room overlooking the formal gardens where hedges of evergreens outlined beds of roses, now leafless branches but promising blossoms of rainbow colors in summer.

After bathing and dressing in clothes generously provided by their host, the travelers joined Plotius and his wife for dinner. Aelia was just as hospitable as her husband, but seemed much younger though a narrow streak of grey highlighted her dark straight hair. Even Darius became talkative under their spell. Mikal, too, seemed quite at ease and was accepted as Lydia's friend rather than slave.

They weren't the only guests. Two young men with such muscular arms and legs they might have been gladiators, took the couch at the end of the table. Plotius introduced them as Damian and Pythias, which Lydia guessed were pseudonyms from Greek mythology. She was eager to find out more about them.

The dinner was lavish, with delicious snails in a garlic sauce, pheasant, fruits, salads, and pork roasted with apples and garlic. The wine, watered and strained as usual for dining, was velvety smooth with a rich ruby color that glowed in the light of the oil lamps. Even though she had to eat reclining, Lydia spilled nothing this time. She doubted if even Titus had ever dined in such luxury.

She noticed that Damian and Pythias were picky about what they ate, or was it that Plotius didn't allow them their choices? They ate none of the snails, pork or bread, yet took large helpings of the pheasant, fruits and salads. A strange diet, she thought, especially when they each had only one small goblet of wine and then switched to plain water.

When cakes dripping with honey sauce were brought in and the men took none, Aelia finally cleared up the mystery.

"Damian and Pythias are in training for the arena games next month," she explained. "My husband, as you probably noticed, is a very strong man in spite of his age. He was a gladiator. The best." Here, Plotius shook his head and laughed, but she continued, "Yes, you were. Absolutely the best. I was only eight when I watched him fight both a bear and a lion and win! Can you imagine anything like it? No man would fight him after the first year, so they had to match him with beasts. Finally after four years the Emperor himself, good Antonius Pius, gave him his freedom. My husband is one of the few gladiators to ever live long enough to be free."

"And earn so much money," Plotius laughed. "That was what kept me going. You wouldn't believe the prizes they gave me each time I won! Houses, slaves, gold, silver, whatever I wanted was mine. Of course everyone expected me to die the next time I fought and they'd get it all back. Temporary loans, so to speak, to be repaid on my death." More hearty laughter. "They didn't understand that I wasn't interested in anything temporary. I convinced some of my wealthy friends to persuade the Emperor to free me, and it happened. Then I invested in shipping, trading, didn't I? Made myself a fine citizen, convinced Aelia's father to let me have her and we moved from Rome to this lovely spot. Now you know a lot more about me than I know about you."

Before Lydia could reply, Aelia added, "Our life has been good, but Plotius missed the excitement of the games. After our children were grown, he started training gladiators here at the villa. He takes only men who have the potential of being the best, then teaches the arts of fighting – surviving – that he learned in the coliseums. It includes eating right, especially the last weeks before games."

Plotius continued, "Damian here will have his first combat this year, but Pythias has already won two. He'll soon be rich enough to buy whatever he wants, or whoever he wants. Of course, it all depends on winning. The loser loses everything when he loses his life."

Lydia glanced at Mikal. She was poking at her food with her fork, not looking at anyone.

Plotius smiled his charming smile and said, "You don't look too happy to hear that. Gladiators don't mind. We realize how short life can be, so why not take big risks and earn big rewards? Perhaps women cling more to life than men do. What do you think?" he asked his wife.

"Of course we do. We bring life; we like to preserve life," she answered testily as if they'd had this conversation many times. "You men, flinging your lives away in wars and games as if no-one cared about you. You know perfectly well how I feel. If you had been killed I never would have known you or borne your children, and I can't imagine what a dreadful life that would have been for me."

He looked slightly chastened and patted her hand. "It's an inborn difference, I'm afraid. But young Darius doesn't look like a fighter. What is your ambition?"

Darius blushed bright red, giving him a most florid complexion, which sent Plotius into gales of laughter.

"Your sister perhaps wants to fight. I don't imagine you got your broken arm spinning wool, did you?"

Lydia could hardly brag about being thrown from Coa in a thunderstorm, but she gave the tale anyway, sparing no details of their terror that night nor making herself appear brave when she hadn't been.

Darius realized he hadn't asked anything about her journey or her arm and saw that it had not been as easy as he had supposed. In fact she seemed awfully brave to have done it. Smart, too, figuring out where to go and how to get here. He was full of admiration, if only briefly.

The dinner ended earlier than usual because the gladiators had to rise early for training.

Soon after Lydia fell asleep, Mikal shook her awake, whispering, "I hear something. I think someone's outside our door."

One small oil lamp burned in the spacious room letting off enough light to make ghostly flickering shadows on the wall.

"What should we do?" Lydia asked softly, not having the slightest idea herself.

"You go look."

"But it would seem – what would they think of us?"

"No worse than what I think of them right now."

"You're right. Let's do it together. We can pretend we're going for a walk."

The two crept silently to the door and stood there listening. Sure enough, someone was out there. Lydia could hear rustling and breathing.

As she whipped open the door, a grey shape hurled itself at her, knocking her to the floor.

"Culain, you idiot!" Mikal whispered as she closed the door. "How did you get into the house?"

A soft, hurried knock sounded on their door. Puzzled, Mikal opened it a crack, then all the way to let in Darius.

"That scared me to death!" the boy muttered. "All that noise, then you crashing around. I thought you were being attacked."

"And you were coming to my rescue?" Lydia teased.

"Yes." To prove it, he brought out a knife he had hidden under the blankets that were wrapped around him. "Stole it from the table when I realized I'd be all alone in my room. I never trust anyone, not anymore."

Lydia couldn't help but stare at this little boy who was ready to fight for her.

"So, well . . . can I stay in here with you? I'll sleep on the floor. It's too dark in my room and everything creaks."

Lydia smiled at her brave warrior and said, "Sure. You can have the floor with Culain."

"You don't think Plotius will try to keep us here, do you?" Darius asked.

"Of course not. What makes you think it?"

"All that talk about being a gladiator. Maybe he'd want a red-haired gladiator, or even a girl one. Don't laugh. Ever since I ran away, people have been after me because of this hair. I think I'll dye it black."

That reminded Lydia of how Fulvia dyed her hair to try to match Darius's. When she told him, his happy giggles broke the eerie spell. Soon all slept deeply until well past dawn.

It was Aelia who finally came to wake them up.

"Breakfast is ready for you downstairs and a good lunch is packed to eat on the way. Plotius told me to warn you not to stop at any other houses along the way. Others will ask questions you won't want to answer. Moreover, do not mention either Albinus or Septimius. Both names can be bad luck around here."

Lydia decided to follow that advice.

When they had eaten and nothing was left to do, Aelia bid them goodbye. Plotius was training Damian and Pythias, so was not there to see them off. His hopes were high for the two gladiators. They would be fighting one of the best in Gaul, Oxenius. A murderer, he'd been so successful for three years now that some citizens were clamoring for his release. Not liking murderers, Plotius would be happy if one of his fighters killed him and won the purse.

Aelia added, "Rumors say the ladies are so fond of Oxenius that he is populating Gaul with his babies."

"Beware of gladiators, you two!" she laughed. "Not all are like my Plotius. Off you go! Come see us on your way back to Britannia. Count us as friends."

"And us," Lydia said. "Thank you for everything, including not asking a lot of questions."

"The less we know the safer we are from intrigues," Aelia noted.

21. "Numerianus is Getting Up an Army"

Culain ran ahead as they headed east to the Roman road then south. Coa and Kem stepped proudly, having been brushed and curried by the slaves in Plotius's stables until their coats shone.

As they travelled, Lydia tried to make Darius tell her more about what to expect when they got to the farm where he had been staying. All he would say was, "It's just a farm," or about Numerianus, "He's odd." Finally she gave up and rode alongside Mikal, letting the girl chatter on about how glorious it would be to marry a former gladiator and live in a fine villa like Plotius's.

Lydia knew that Mikal was dreaming too high, but she didn't say anything. Why spoil a dream even if there was no chance of it coming true? Mikal was fourteen. Lots of girls were married by that age – Aelia, for example. Plotius must be almost old enough to be her father.

Darius was enjoying himself now that Acteon was gone forever and he was heading back to the farm. The miles went past with a steady rhythm. His solo trip to Canterbury had turned into a big adventure. Someday he would see more of Gaul, maybe even Italy. He knew that Lydia had given him only a few more days of freedom, but maybe when she saw what Numerianus was doing and why it was important to stay, she would change her mind.

Lunch was eaten by the side of a brook. Aelia had selected the sweetest apples and plums for them, along with tangy cheese and crisp white bread. Water in the leather skins was clean and cold. For Culain there was a large pork bone – the dog was getting spoiled. The warm sun along with the food made them all so drowsy that they took longer than they had planned.

"Come on!" Darius suddenly leaped to his feet and began gathering up the bags. "We can't stay here. I won't be able to find the farm after dark."

Reluctantly, Lydia and Mikal started toward their horses that were grazing nearby.

"Lydia, look!" Mikal giggled, pointing to the road where a strange sight approached going south, like they were.

A massive plow horse ambled along, ridden by an enormously bulky man.

Darius looked, then took off running as fast as he could toward the road yelling, "Hector! Hector! Stop! Here! Hey!"

Lydia looked at Mikal, Mikal looked at Lydia. So this was the famous Hector, brother of the beautiful Gloriana. He was certainly not the angry, dangerous man Darius had led them to expect.

When the work horse and its overgrown rider met up with Darius, Hector hurled himself to the ground and engulfed the boy in a huge bear hug.

"My boy! I thought he had killed you!"

"Darius looks squished," Mikal whispered to Lydia with a big smile.

"He does, indeed."

The girls came forward and Lydia introduced herself and Mikal since it was unlikely Darius would do so. .

"The Flea's sister!" Hector bellowed. "You came all this way for the Flea? I vow that British women are braver than any others of the Empire!"

"I'm sure that Gloriana would do the same for you," Mikal ventured.

"You know Gloriana?" he asked, his eyes big with wonder.

"It's a long story," Lydia replied, smiling.

"Bah! My sister's a silly one, so cuckoo about that idiot Optimus Maximus she can't see straight. She wouldn't be much good at going all through the Empire looking for me – or anyone."

"I think she's grand," Darius piped up firmly.

"Oh, aye. You, Flea, are still too young to understand."

With the addition of the plow horse and Hector, their little group was quite a spectacle, if anyone had taken notice. The horse was tied to the cart since he had already gone a long distance carrying his heavy load. Hector sat in the cart beside Darius who kept driving. Because of the plow horse, they had to relax the pace of their travel.

It took Hector almost all the way to Numerianus's farm to explain how he had found them and to hear Darius's story.

Yesterday around noon he had finally realized that Acteon and Darius had disappeared, and suspected that Acteon was up to no good. The only transportation left at the villa was the old plow horse, Henric. Hector had ridden all the rest of the day, camped, then started again before dawn. By chance he'd discovered Acteon' corpse, what was left of it. It looked as if robbers had murdered him and stolen the cart and mules, leaving the body for animals to scavenge. Had the robbers also taken Darius, or had Acteon killed the boy somewhere along the way? In either case, Hector was miserable thinking he'd never see Darius again. Not having any way to dig a grave, he had simply thrown Acteon's body into the river and then headed back to the farm. It was all he could do. He had never felt worse in his life. And then, out of the blue, there was the little Flea running across the field and calling to him. Not only that, but the cart and mules were there and the two girls. How quickly everything had changed for the better.

As twilight dissolved into night, they arrived at the farm. They hadn't gone through Lyon, so Lydia guessed they were still north of the city. That was a disappointment to her since it was supposed to be such a magnificent place.

"The city is off to the southeast," Hector explained as they got the horses and mules settled into what used to be the stables but was now a crumbling barn.

Darius hurried ahead into the villa followed by the others. Inside, a pool of light shone at the end of the atrium.

"The Senator is in his study," Hector explained. "Happy he'll be to see the Flea again, I can tell you."

Lydia couldn't believe how filthy the place was. Surely a Senator could afford servants or slaves to keep the house clean. Cobwebs hung from every corner, every archway, and dust lay so thick that footprints showed on the broken tiles.

Through the doorway ahead, Lydia could see Darius talking to a long-bearded, almost bald old man who gestured so much with his head and his arms that he looked like a gander about to take off.

The room was overflowing with artifacts, scrolls, tablets, tools, gadgets of every kind, all scattered about in no particular order except for one dark corner. Stacked in that corner was a collection of rocks, midsize to large. Most of them were black, smooth and rounded, covered in dust.

"My sister, Lydia and her servant, Mikal," Darius told the old man. He turned and flapped his arms at them. His eyes darted everywhere, alighting nowhere. He made Lydia distinctly nervous.

Without any more recognition of her, the old man continued what he was saying to Darius. "Let that be a lesson to you to trust your own judgment. Shouldn't have left you alone with that Acteon. Stupid of you to allow it. Brainless of all of us," the old man scolded. "But you're back. It's a wonder your sister ever found you, isn't it? You never know what a woman will do."

What an unpleasant old man, Lydia thought. I'll show him what a woman can do. I can get my brother away from here, that's what!

"Food for everyone!" Hector announced from the kitchen where he'd been organizing some bread, leftover chicken and wine. Darius found two oil lamps stuffed in a corner, lighted them and set them on a heavy oak table in the atrium. Mikal quickly grabbed a rag and wiped off some of the dust. Hector pulled up chairs for everyone and they sat down to eat.

Lydia expected to find mold or worse on the bread, but was surprised that it was as good as any she'd had.

"This is fine fare," she complimented Numerianus, trying to start a conversation.

He looked puzzled then scowled as he answered hastily, "The widow woman from the next farm comes. Brings food. Cleans up the kitchen. I don't know where anything is in there. No, I don't bother with the house." Then he turned back to Darius, shutting her out.

Lydia saw that Numerianus had a strong hold over Darius. The old man treated her brother as if he was important, almost an equal. It would take some strong reasoning on her part to convince him to come away from here. So be it. She would bide her time for a few days. By her figuring, she still had at least three weeks to get back to Juliobone so Marius could remove her cast.

Glancing over at Mikal, she saw the girl had fallen asleep at the table, exhausted. Let her sleep now for there would be a whole lot of cleaning for her to do in the morning. If they were to stay here, the dirt and mess would have to go.

Culain lay peacefully on Lydia's foot, his nose and ears twitching from time to time to show he was listening. He might even have been imagining beating off generations of rats and spiders that inhabited the house. With her other foot, she gently massaged him behind his ears then, when he rolled over, on his tummy.

All of a sudden her thoughts were interrupted by the word "murder."

"Murder?" Numerianus asked. "But it was the horse, you say. Trained for it. Defending the dog. If the body is ever found, can't blame anyone."

Since he was a Senator, he ought to know, Lydia thought., relieved.

The old man studied the dozing Culain and pronounced, "Did you know that the Britons gave Julius Caesar a wolfhound like your Culain? It was the first one the Emperor had ever seen. Guess they wanted to bribe Julius to stay away, but he didn't, did he? You knew that? Good. Ignorant girls are abhorrent to me. Girls should have education just like boys. Both of you read? All right. Now down to business. You must stay here, of course. The road north won't be safe for quite awhile."

"What do you mean?" Lydia asked.

"Darius didn't tell you?"

'He never tells me anything."

The old man shot a glance at Darius then back to Lydia. He shook his head and said, "You will have to hear it from him."

"Darius, tell me!" Lydia demanded, exasperated. "Don't you dare keep secrets from me after all I've done for you!"

Darius looked at the floor and said nothing.

Furious with him, Lydia nudged Mikal awake and announced that the two of them were going to bed. She didn't give a fig about the dirty dishes she was leaving behind.

She found a bedroom. If the stables hadn't been in such bad condition, she would have preferred to stay out there because the room was so unpleasant. Mikal wiped off the bed for Lydia and a medium-sized table for herself. It was a lot better than sleeping on the filthy floor where the rats would come in the night.

The next morning, after almost no sleep, Lydia found out all she needed to know from Darius.

"I'm making a knife," he mumbled, leading the way to the forge.

"Why?"

"Well . . . See?"

Lydia could see that the furnace had recently been fired because there was a lot of slag around and a lump of iron in the middle of it that had been hammered to what looked like a good pitch, probably within the last week or so. A hot fire was burning in the smaller oven.

"I see it. Now tell me why the Senator needs you to make him a knife."

Darius took a long time answering,. He grabbed a pair of tongs, lifted up the five-inch long rectangle of steel that was now almost the shape of a knife and carried it to the small fire to heat.

Lydia waited.

Darius finally said, "To make weapons."

"What?!"

"Numerianus is getting up an army to fight Albinus."

Lydia couldn't believe what she was hearing. She saw how red her brother's face was growing. He must know how ridiculous it sounded.

Darius turned the tongs, heating the iron bar on both sides.

"That's it?" she asked. "He's organizing an army and you are going to make weapons."

Darius nodded and kept working.

Lydia turned and walked away, feeling as if she had stumbled into a bizarre world, a place full of crazy people where nothing made sense. She needed space and time to think.

One thing was certain. She knew enough about Albinus and Septimius to know that Darius should not be involved in anything connected with either of them.

Coa was out in the pasture. She called to him. A ride would help her to think things over. They trotted out to the dirt road and then Coa cantered easily about a mile before slowing to a walk.

After an hour or so, she knew what to do. The only way to save Darius from Numerianus was to help him with the forge. The old man's idea of organizing an army was so implausible it could never work. She would pretend to go along with it for her brother's sake. Then when the whole scheme failed, she would whisk Darius back to Tunadur safe and sound. It would be over.

She rode back to the farm, let Coa back in the pasture, and went to help Darius.

With just one hand, she couldn't do much more than put wood on the fire and give a few pulls on the bellows. They didn't speak as Darius hammered on his knife, but it was an easier silence than before.

The air was cool with a hint of snow. Somewhere to the east was the city of Lyon. Lydia wondered if Mikal would ever have a chance to go there.

Culain stayed near Lydia in the workshop just like he had in Tunadur. At lunch, Darius said to Numerianus, "I told her. You can tell her why."

As they ate the hot chicken soup and fresh rolls left by the widow, Numerianus explained, "Albinus sits in Lyon pretending to be Emperor and gathering legions around him to fight Septimius, who is actually the Emperor. When Darius arrived here as a courier, he brought the message that the British legions were coming. They should have landed one week ago today if the weather in the channel was good. That will put them in Lyon in three weeks. If Septimius got the message we sent, he will be prepared, but no matter what, he can't be here before the first of the new year. He's coming through Germania, the only route open in winter. By that time Albinus's army will be rested, maybe even bored, and ready to fight, while Septimius will be tired after weeks of winter travel. Tell me who has the better chance. Simple, no?"

Lydia wondered where this was heading.

Numerianus continued, "I left Rome to find peace. For years I taught the spoiled sons and daughters of the rich. That wore me out, but Rome itself took its toll. Everyone, including my old students, wants power. No-one is safe. I wanted to find a place where I could think and study, so I came here. Now, ironically, the war has come to me."

"You mean Albinus and Severus will fight here, in Lyon?"

"That's what Albinus seems to be planning. It's for the best."

Lydia said, "I don't call it 'best' if there's a war right here!"

Numerianus scowled, shook his head and started a reluctant explanation. "Women never see the whole picture. We must have the war in Lyon in order not to have it elsewhere. In order to save the Empire, in fact. Albinus is building a trap for himself though he doesn't seem to realize it. He wants to defeat Septimius here, where he has been in charge for many years and has friends. After that, he will have an easy trip to Rome in spring to declare himself Emperor over the entire Empire, not just Gaul, Britannia and Spain."

"And you don't want that," Lydia said.

He frowned, then his eyes lit up. "The gods may be on my side. Why else would Darius have come here, or even you. Mars himself, or Mithras, or perhaps Jupiter, or all three, may be behind it."

"I hate to ask this – no, I don't – where is your army?"

The Senator glared at her. "They will be here. The farmers in this region have no love for Albinus. He set up his headquarters in Lyon a year ago and allows his soldiers to roam the countryside taking whatever they want. With 40,000 more British legionnaires on their way, it will be even worse. They will need food that the farmers have saved for their own families. The farmers hate this, but now they will see that they can fight back. With my steel they can make javelins, arrows, and swords that can beat any legionnaire's."

Lydia looked at Darius to see how he was taking this.

He looked at his soup and explained, "Numerianus thinks he has invented a better steel. When I'm done with the knife, he'll know if it worked or not."

"Why do you have to be the one to do it," she asked. "Surely there are other blacksmiths around with more experience."

Numerianus cleared his throat.

Darius scowled.

"What?" Lydia asked.

Darius began, "The iron out there, the lump –"

"Yes," she said. "Where did that come from?"

Darius looked at Numerianus, who reluctantly said, "Three of the blacksmiths near here came to see what my idea was. They set up the forge, which took a lot of doing since it was old and in bad shape, and then they gathered up scrap iron from the farms. They brought charcoal and even some coal for the furnace . . . "

"Very generous of them," Lydia commented.

He nodded but his eyebrows came together in a scowl. "The furnace heated up over three days, and then they put in the iron. In the night, after they left, I added my secret ingredient – some of the meteorites from my study. You saw them in the corner. Pure iron. The next day when they found out, they argued that I'd ruined their work. I said a few things back."

"So they quit?" she asked.

"Not then," he answered. "Not till after it was melted and they'd hammered the daylights out of it clearing out the impurities. That's when they decided it felt different and that they'd wasted their time. Now no-one will come near here. They call me the crazy Senator."

At this point, Mikal gathered up the plates and left the table. Then Hector came and sat down to eat his stew and rolls, unaware of the conversation taking place.

Before Lydia could say anything, Numerianus explained, "All Darius has to do is make a good enough blade to show the blacksmiths that if my iron is shaped and tempered correctly, it will turn into the best steel in the Empire."

"You're a dreamer," Lydia scoffed.

"Yes," he answered firmly.

After a short silence, Darius asked her quietly, "Will you help me?"

Hector looked up, interested.

She nodded. She really had no choice.

22. "It's Politics"

Inside the villa, though no-one but Lydia and the widow woman noticed, Mikal had cleared out most of the visible cobwebs and the worst of the dirt. For the first time in who knows how long, sunlight was able to penetrate the glass on the windows to make graceful shadow patterns on the clean tile floor.

Out in the foundry, Lydia watched Darius working on his knife. She wasn't sure what she could do to help, since her left arm was useless. It was even awkward working the bellows, but at least it was something.

The knife had taken on a beautiful shape and texture, more steel now than the molten iron it had started out as. She was as curious as Darius, but more doubtful, about whether the secret ingredient Numerianus had added would actually work.

At lunch, the Senator had a suggestion that neither of them liked at first.

"Why not let your sister work on the edging and polishing of the blade while you start another knife? The sooner we can have two finished, the better."

By the time lunch was over, and each had been able to think about that idea, they grudgingly agreed that it was a good plan. Because Lydia wouldn't need to be shaping the steel with the hammer, she should be able to manage the filing, polishing and sharpening with her good hand while the other held the knife steady.

Darius had his own ideas of how to do it, of course, but reluctantly turned that part of the job over to Lydia. Searching the tool shed, they came up with enough files of varying sizes and in fairly good shape to get the job done.

Using her left arm in the heavy cast as a brace, Lydia was able to get a good angle on the steel and, over the next two days, file it until it had a sharp edge. Polishing, sanding and waxing were tedious jobs, but as the blade began to take on a beautiful finish she didn't want to stop until it was finished.

Numerianus had said not to put a handle on it, so they would just let the tang act as handle for now. It was, after all, only a demonstration model.

"Time for the test," Darius murmured.

"Now we see," Lydia agreed, her hands shaking as she handed Darius the knife.

They were alone in the forge, having decided that they didn't want Numerianus or anyone else to know before they did whether or not the new steel worked.

"Watch your fingers," she warned as he held the tang awkwardly, ready to slice into the thick-skinned pumpkin he had picked in the garden.

"Here goes," he said, hardly breathing.

In went the blade and out again like magic. The squash didn't move. Darius touched it and it fell into two perfect halves.

They looked at each other and nodded. Numerianus's steel worked!

The old Senator was delighted, even smiling as they showed him what the blade could do. He was even happier when they told him that Darius almost had the second blade ready for Lydia's finishing touches.

"Now we can show the blacksmiths how wrong they were," exulted Numerianus. "They can see for themselves that I was right. Hector can take the blade around and show them how well it works. I'm sure they will want to make the weapons for my army when they realize that now they will have a good chance against the soldiers. I'm sure they will!"

"But it don't have a handle on it," Hector protested. "It's just a blade and a whatever-you-call-it."

"Looks aren't important," Numerianus scoffed. "If they decide to help, they can make swords out of this steel of mine and put handles on any way they want to. Mostly, though, they should make javelins and arrowheads. Those will be safer weapons for them to use even though they aren't as fancy."

Hector, who had been brought up in a fullery and not a blacksmith shop, was not sure that a blade with no handle would be good enough to convince anyone, but he chose not to argue.

"All right," he agreed with a shrug. "I'll take it around and show them all. See what happens."

Mikal was curious about the blade, never having had a chance to see it, so when Hector got back from showing it to the blacksmiths Lydia took it to the kitchen to demonstrate its powers to Mikal and the widow woman.

When they saw how easily it cut through even the hardest bones, and even pierced one of the iron pots, they were amazed.

"Can we keep it here to use for awhile?" asked Mikal.

Lydia couldn't think why not, so she left it with them. In the morning, the knife had disappeared. Mikal was frantic, having looked everywhere for it.

When Numerianus found out, he was furious. "How could you let it out of your sight?" he shouted at Lydia. "It was not a kitchen knife. It is priceless, don't you understand?"

"I guess I don't understand," Lydia snapped. "Why does putting a meteorite into the mix make a difference? Is it from a sky god?"

"Hmpf. I thought you had a brain, girl. Don't you know that all the iron we melt has other metal in it? When it first comes out of the fire, it gets hammered to get rid of the impurities, but they never go away entirely. Some can even be useful, but we never know ahead of time how that will work out. A meteorite, however, is pure iron. Nothing but iron. It is a gift from the sky god, if it pleases you to think so."

Subdued, Lydia said, "I didn't know all that."

"Now you do so make use of it. Hector can spread the word to the farmers and find out where your knife went. It was a foolish thing to do, don't you forget that."

He stomped back to his study and slammed the door.

Lydia was angry, too, at him. She hurried back to the forge and began working on a bit of scrap iron to make a votive figure for Apollo, the god of artisans and metalworkers. When you give statues to the gods, they sometimes help you get what you need, and she needed to get the knife back.

Working quickly, without paying attention to what she was doing, she laughed when she saw the result. Her little man was bald with a long beard, looking like a small version of wrinkled and worn Numerianus. Gods don't care what the figures look like, she reasoned, so she would put this one on the secret altar she had made in her bedroom. It was the first statue she'd made since the little Minerva got lost.

Hector was surprised when, just the day after he'd demonstrated Darius's knife at the farms, several blacksmiths showed up asking about the "new steel." Each had been impressed enough that they took some of the "lump" to work with in their own shops. Each day following, more smiths came until the first lump was gone and the second lump was taken from the forge ready for hammering. This time, all ten blacksmiths showed up and hammered in shifts until the lump was ready to cool and be separated into useable pieces.

Around this same time, early in November, an impressive stranger drove out from Lyon in a richly ornamented chariot. A neighboring farmer, seeing his approach, warned his own blacksmith and then hastened across the fields to warn Numerianus. No-one from Lyon could be trusted, it being Albinus territory. Darius quickly began hammering on a scrap iron scythe and hid the knife away. Lydia ran to the kitchen to work with Mikal since the widow woman had not shown up for several days.

The man's errand was to Numerianus, who invited him into his study, the only room still in its original disordered state because Mikal hadn't dared clean it.

After an hour, the stranger left and Numerianus reappeared in the workshop.

"Where's your sister?" he asked.

"In the house, I guess."

"Get her."

When Darius came back with Lydia, Numerianus told both of them, "You have a commission."

They stared at him, not understanding.

"That man brought an order for a gladiator sword, one with an eighteen inch blade," the Senator explained. "It has to be stronger and truer than has ever been used before in the arena. Have you heard of Oxenius?"

Darius felt faint. Oxenius, the rival of Damian and Pythias. Of course he'd heard of him.

"That was his servant. Oxenius has been testing out swords made by the legion's armorers, the ones from Britannia who are supposed to be so good, but he hasn't been satisfied. He wants better. Somehow the blade you two made, the one that disappeared, ended up in one of the soldier's hands, who took it to an armorer --"

"The widow woman! She must have taken it!" Lydia cried.

"Possibly. This servant of Oxenius happened to be at the armorer's at the time and heard what the soldier said. The armorer scoffed – laughed at him, can you imagine? Didn't even try it out, but the servant, whose job it was to find a good swordmaker, asked to have it. When he showed Oxenius, the gladiator told him to find us. He even returned the blade."

And there it was on the table.

"The bad thing is that now, because of the widow woman, the army knows – and the gladiator knows – that we have good steel and that there is a Briton working here. A man, of course. I guess they wouldn't have believed that a boy and girl could produce such a knife. Anyway, since Britannia belongs to Albinus, they assume I am loyal. We're somewhat safe because of that as long as we're careful. Oxenius is a Briton like you and wants Celtic interwoven designs on the handle and guard and scabbard. The fancy work is to be done in bronze and silver with set-in precious stones. He has provided all that. The blade will be unique, the only one in the known world. This time it will have two parts. You can use the iron we already have for an inner core, but the outer shell with the sharp edge will be of pure meteorite. Have you ever seen that done?"

"Not with meteorites," Lydia said, "but we've seen them use different types of iron in the core and the shell."

"Darius, you are looking doubtful."

The boy couldn't think how to answer. He wasn't sure if he or Lydia had the skill to do it, having only made two knife blades in their lives and never one like that. If, by some miracle, it turned out well, then Oxenius would use it to fight Damian or Pythias. To do that to Plotius wouldn't be honorable. And the decorations. Did the Senator have any idea how much work that entailed?

"There's no pure meteorite melted," Lydia interjected. "It's impossible. How long do we have?"

"You don't need a large amount of meteorite for the shell. Put it in the fire now and it will be ready by tomorrow night or the next day, I'm sure. You have about three weeks."

Darius looked at Lydia for help.

"What if we fail?" she said. "What if he doesn't like it?"

"Then he finds someone else to do the job. In fact, he probably has two or three armorers working on swords right now. He'll decide which one he likes best. If he chooses yours the money we get will make it possible to buy more supplies."

"To make more weapons," Lydia stated.

"Yes. It's politics, girl, and sometimes you have to play the game. If Septimius is the winner, so will we be."

Darius had been thinking.

"No," was his answer.

The Senator scowled, "For what infernal reason?"

Darius then explained the problem of Damian and Pythias, trying to make the Senator understand about being honorable. He was dumfounded when Numerianus laughed.

"It's not funny!" he yelled.

"No, no, I know that. This is why I laughed. Oxenius will never fight your gladiators. He is so good that no human being is allowed to go against him. They bring in bears and tigers and other animals. Don't worry, boy. Your 'honor' will be intact. What do you say now?"

"Plotius said Damian and Pythias would fight Oxenius."

"Not a chance, believe me."

Darius looked at Lydia who shrugged and nodded, so he did, too. It would be a huge challenge, but maybe, just maybe, it would turn out well.

Because the sword required so much work, Hector had to work the bellows and hold the tongs and other unskilled but necessary chores. Darius needed both arms to wield the heavy hammer over and over. When Hector was needed elsewhere, Mikal took over and proved to be fairly good at it.

One of the neighboring blacksmiths came to work on the inner blade which didn't need to be as perfect as the outer one.

As strong as Lydia was, with one arm she could only hammer for a short time if someone else held the iron with the tongs Sometimes she held the iron while Darius or the other blacksmith worked on it. . Even so, her right arm ached so badly it brought tears to her eyes and she had to rest far more often than she wanted. After a few days of trying to work that way, she decided her arm was healed enough. She'd lost track of the days, but thought it must be close to six weeks since they'd been in Adairinnic.

She asked Mikal to find a way to get the cast off.

"Too bad we're not back in Juliobone," Mikal remarked innocently.

Lydia blushed, thinking the same thing.

"I will try to be as gentle as Marius would have been," Mikal promised as she cut through the cast. It was hard going, requiring a sharp saw, steady hand and strong arms. "I'm glad I don't have your knife," she said. "That is so sharp it would have cut through the cast and your arm, too."

"We didn't tell you? I guess not. It's back. Numerianus keeps it in his study."

Mikal scowled. "I've been worrying all this time. I wish one of you had said something. I can be trusted, you know."

"I know that," Lydia agreed, "but I don't think the Senator trusts anyone. Maybe it's because you worked with the widow woman."

"Bah!" scoffed Mikal.

At last the cast fell away, exposing skin that looked as if it came from a tomb.

Lydia stared. "Ewwww. Ugly," was all she could say. Her arm had been so long hidden from light that it was shriveled and white. Worse, when she lifted it up off the table, it flopped back, weak, not at all fit for hard work in the forge.

"I should have kept the cast on," she whined. "At least it was solid and strong, not like this lump of jelly that used to be an arm."

"Stop feeling sorry for yourself," Mikal scolded. "You know as well as I do that it will be fine in a little while. Just take it easy. Don't overdo it."

At first, she could hardly hold onto the tongs, but her arm gradually grew stronger just as Mikal had said it would.

Both she and Darius separately planned designs for the scabbard and hilt to would be added at the end, and both knew that the other would probably not like what they designed.

Once Darius asked to see the chain Uncle Petrus had made for Lydia.

"Copying?" she snipped, laying it on the table for him. She suspected he was going to use the ideas for the sword decoration.

"Never!" he denied. "Petrus himself would not have minded my learning from his example. See the way the leaves have that special twist before they go under the bar? That's what I'm trying to do. It gives strength and also allows extra space where a stone can be set in."

Lydia was unimpressed. "I knew that, Flea."

"Don't call me that."

"Yes, Master."

In the evenings Lydia was stiff and sore all over from lifting the heavy hammer and pounding the stiff iron. Mikal gave her long, deep massages to ease her muscles and joints..

"I do not want to look like a blacksmith!" Lydia wailed as the slave rubbed oil into her skin each night. "Please say that my arms aren't getting as big as trees."

Mikal dug in the harder. "Don't be so vain," she scolded. "Your arms are strong and smooth. Lye soap and sheep oil are working miracles."

"Maybe, but the soap isn't as gentle or nicely scented as the soap Gloriana's mother made."

"We need stronger stuff to get rid of the grime from the forge, even on your hair. Stop complaining."

Lydia and Darius were surprised at how easily the two steels of the blade welded together compared to how hard it had been to get them to the right shape and thinness for that step. The meteorite steel took an extraordinarily sharp edge after much filing and sanding. The eighteen-inch blade with its black edge was, in fact, a beautiful weapon, but now it needed decorating..

Just before the three weeks were up, brother and sister worked before dawn and on into the late evenings to finish up the elaborate scabbard, done in bronze and silver on a wooden shell covered in leather.

To avoid arguing, they had to divide the work between them, each taking different parts for their own designs. Numerianus made them promise that neither would criticize the other's work. No-one was surprised when they broke that promise several times a day.

Even the requirement to make the decorations Celtic in style, with intertwining motifs, led to quarrels over which motifs to use, and which leaves of which vines, and whether or not to include animals, and if the designs should be freeform or geometric. Each had definite opinions and hated compromise. Numerianus, never the best diplomat, found himself meddling often in order to keep them focused on finishing the job in time.

That was another problem. They couldn't agree on when or whether the decorations were finished. When one would say yes, the other would find a tiny spot for another garnet or emerald, which would lead to another leaf of bronze somewhere else to balance it out.

It finally came to an end when one afternoon, followed by Hector and Mikal who had faithfully worked the bellows and kept the fire, they walked into the Senator's study and announced that it was finished.

"What a relief," Numerianus exclaimed. "The farmers tell me that soldiers have been nosing around asking about the steel, but so far no-one has given us away. I feel that won't last forever, so you finished just in time. We should go to Lyon tomorrow and show the sword to Oxenius for his approval. Hector, you must stay here and keep things going, but Mikal deserves a chance to see where she lived, isn't that right?"

Lydia was amazed that he'd remembered. The surprised look that came on Mikal's face showed that she, too, had given up hope.

Numerianus continued, "Don't look so shocked. Of course, I remembered. I have another reason for going. As a Senator I will be able to see the Governor of the province. It's time I include him in our plans before I get arrested for starting a revolution."

"Which side is he on?" Lydia asked, fearful of the consequences of choosing the wrong one.

He laughed and said, "Whichever side wins. Right now he has Albinus with 500 Roman soldiers living in the town, and 40,000 from the British legions camped outside of town, so he pretends to support him. I can make him see that being on our side will be his best bet if Septimius triumphs. When we attack, it should be with official approval, even if it's only secret approval. Otherwise he will have to label us rebels and put us to death in the arena. Simple, no?"

"No!" declared Lydia, recoiling at the idea and wishing she'd never agreed to let Darius stay with this madman.

He smiled, and with a shake of his white swirling beard said, "Don't worry. Tomorrow we'll take the cart and pick up a few of the weapons our farmers have made to show the Governor. They'll be well hidden from other eyes, of course. It's time we all got away from here for awhile."

Darius did not want to go. He didn't want to be around if Oxenius hated the sword and scabbard. He had put every skill he had into them and he knew that Lydia had, too. If it wasn't good enough, he didn't want to know – yet. A gladiator who had won every fight for three years was not someone he wanted to face.

Numerianus would not let him stay behind. "In an uncertain world, you have to take advantage of every opportunity."

"This is torture, not opportunity."

"Seeing Lyon and its most famous citizen is opportunity. You'll get through it."

Darius didn't believe him but realized there was no use arguing. He rode in the back of the wagon with Mikal and sulked.

Lydia, on the contrary, was excited about going. Even if the worst happened and the sword was rejected, it would mean no more money for weapons, and that was a good thing. Why not enjoy the day? The chance of seeing one of the most important cities of the Empire after weeks of working on the farm, was too good to miss. She wore her one tunic that had no burn holes from the forge, and a blue shawl given to her by Plotius's wife. With Mikal's help, her hair seemed to be behaving itself. Most of it was pinned up on top of her head, kept in place by the few hairpins that had survived her travels.

By fast horseback, the trip would have taken only two or three hours at most, but by cart and mules the time stretched to over four. It promised to be a lovely day, not too cold, overcast but dry. Lydia wondered if deep winter with its gales and high drifting snow ever touched this part of the world.

As the sun rose, the city on the distant hill caught the rays and shone like a small marble sculpture. It grew in size the closer they came until Lydia realized it was the largest city she'd ever seen, much larger even than Lutetia. On the outskirts they passed two extensive graveyards that looked like miniature cities themselves, cities for the dead.

Inside the gates, Lyon was a busy hub of noise and activity. It rose from the bottomlands of the Saone and Rhone rivers and grew up the hillside to a high plateau.. Ordinarily, they would have had to leave the wagon and mules outside the city during the day, but Numerianus, as a Senator, was allowed to bring them in, along with a driver. Lydia got down to walk with Mikal and let Darius take over the driving. Walking felt good after the bumpy wagon ride.

They had approached from the north, which put them on the plateau overlooking the amphitheater and temple of Augustus. Government buildings and impressive houses lined the streets, the largest ones closer to the edge to take advantage of the view. Here were also the governor's mansion and, as it turned out, the home of Oxenius the gladiator.

"I remember this," Mikal said unexpectedly.

23. "I Was Invincible"

"I remember," Mikal affirmed. "I remember looking down at the amphitheater and all the rest, just like we are now. Our house faced out to the view. There was a balcony where you could watch everything. On the street side was a huge gate with carved lions." She was getting more and more animated as the memories became clearer. "Lydia, it was on this very street, I am sure of it."

This shook Lydia's curiosity wide awake. "Darius, slow down," she called to him. "Mikal says her house is on this street."

"I hope not," Numerianus mumbled from his seat next to Darius.

Mikal was overflowing with excitement. The farther north they walked along the ridge, the more grand the homes became. Lydia was afraid for her friend, afraid she was imagining things. Mikal stared at each house they passed, but only those on the outer edge, the largest ones with the best views.

Where the street curved at the end of the hill, Mikal began to run, Lydia following.

"Around the bend!" she cried. "There you'll see a big house with a tower. Next to it – oh, Lydia, it's here – it's my house! It is! Look!" She stopped, staring at the house where a number of people were lined up as if to go inside.

Lydia was baffled, not understanding a thing that was happening.

Darius stopped the cart.

After a moment, Numerianus stepped down onto the ground, sighed, and said quietly to Mikal, "So that is your house. Now you know for certain that your parents are really gone. Hope – what a traitor it can be to us." His voice trembled as he put his arm on the girl's quivering shoulders and continued, "I had heard that Oxenius bought this house from a priest of Augustus, the one who had the former owners – Christians – killed. Your parents."

Mikal nodded.

"How wrong the killing was. Not all of Lyon approved. But the priest was powerful and the old governor had no reason to stop him. It was just after I came. Fifty massacred at the festival of Augustus. *Tantum religio potuit sundere malorum.* So much wrong could religion induce. Believe me when I say that the Christians taught Lyon a hard lesson. Your parents, their names?"

"Jacobus and . . . and . . ." Mikal could not speak her mother's name.

"It's all right. Never mind. Darius, drive slowly past the gladiator's house and stop just beyond it. See? It is just as Mikal said it would be. The tower, then the lion gate and then the house with the balcony. What a long line of people are waiting to see Oxenius. Probably more than are awaiting the Governor. Ironic, no?"

"Tell me," Mikal asked Numerianus, "Did Oxenius kill Christians in the arena?"

"No," he answered firmly. "He has never, so far as I know, killed Christians, though he has killed many criminals like himself."

Mikal nodded.

"When we go to present the sword, you may stay by the cart, or will you come in?" he asked.

"I will come," she answered without hesitation. There was a resoluteness in her eyes that Lydia admired. If what had happened to her, happened at Tunadur, would she be able to be so brave?

"Darius, tether the mules to the post there. We won't stay long, just long enough to see if Oxenius approves of the sword."

"I'll stay out here," Darius declared.

"No," the other three said at once.

"Wait. One last thing," said Numerianus. "In case Oxenius is superstitious, no-one must mention that Lydia had any part in making the sword. No telling what he might do if he found out."

For once, Lydia was glad to be an unknown contributor. She held Mikal's arm as the four of them walked to the mansion. Numerianus pushed through the crowd to the front door and talked to the slave there. A moment later he motioned to the others to come forward. Darius carried the carefully-wrapped sword.

The girls covered their heads with their shawls, which made them feel less noticeable as they walked into the impressive entry hall. It was filled with statues of gladiators, warriors and fierce animals, the walls painted in sea blue without any pictures. Lydia saw Mikal staring at the floor mosaic, a Medusa head surrounded by fruit and fishes.

"For good luck," she whispered to Lydia. "The Medusa attracts all the bad luck away from you. It used to scare me, though."

"I can see why," Lydia smiled and took Mikal's hand, finding it cold as ice.

From the entry hall they were led to a huge atrium. On a sunny day it would have been filled with light, but today it was softly shadowed. Mikal nodded in recognition. At the far end the light was brighter.

"The balcony," she whispered.

But they weren't going there. They followed the servant down a corridor to the right lined with marble columns, then a turn to the left and into a lovely perfectly square room. Here the walls were painted in a lighthearted scene of deer and rabbits in a meadow with birds flying overhead. In a tree was a bird nest with blue eggs in it. The columns were tiled in shades of peach and gold.

Mikal's hand clutched Lydia's more tightly.

"My mother's . . ." she whispered.

A huge stone table set on four massive legs carved like lions, was the only furniture except for the large semi-circular stool upon which sat the great gladiator himself.

Lydia pulled her shawl more closely around her face, feeling sorry for the beasts he would face. Against this commanding man they wouldn't have a chance.

More impressive than his appearance was the sense of authority radiating from him. It was so powerful that she managed only a brief glance before looking away. The skin on his face was tight, hard, as if chiseled from humorless stone. His light blue eyes seemed to glow with life and energy. He was almost clean-shaven with a wild mass of shoulder-length black curly hair.

Irreverently, Lydia thought of the rumored little Oxeniuses all over Gaul and could hardly blame their mothers for desiring children by him.

She realized she hadn't been listening to anything being said.

Darius was slowly unwrapping the sword. The boy's hands trembled, his fingers got mixed up trying to undo the knots, his cheeks were as bright red as his hair.

"I had no idea I was giving this commission to one so young," Oxenius said ominously. His deep voice had the tones of Britannia in it.

Lydia looked up and smiled.

Suddenly Oxenius roared at Darius, startling them all, "Your name! The old man calls you the Flea but I know better. Your name!"

Darius was struck dumb, staring in fright. No-one else dared answer for him.

"Never mind," Oxenius murmured, scowling. "I will see the sword."

Staring at the floor, Darius opened the final fold. There lay the finest work he or Lydia had ever done. He was thinking it might be the last work they would ever do. He was ashamed, knowing it couldn't possibly be good enough for this demanding giant. He felt sick. A failure. His vision blurred as he turned to Numerianus and fainted.

The old Senator knelt to help the boy. "He'll soon come around," he whispered.

Oxenius ignored the comment, stood and grasped the sword. Balancing it in the palm of his hand, he showed no emotion as he studied the intricate scrollwork and interlocking vines, the inlaid gems and enameling that had taken so much extra work. He then drew the sword from its scabbard, running his finger along the blade – but not the black edge - right to the point. Suddenly, he turned, held the sword high at his side and thrust it directly into the center of a statue of Mercury, naked except for his winged sandals. The blow was so clean and swift that the blade went all the way through without budging Mercury a bit. Oxenius withdrew it, turned it on its side, lifted it over his head and with tremendous force whacked it against the edge of the stone table.

Lydia gasped.

The sword was intact.

Looking intently at Darius, who was now sitting up, Oxenius said, "You are Darius. Your sister is my sister Lydia. The sword is perfect."

Awestruck, wondering if she'd heard right, Lydia stared at him. "Ansonius?"

He nodded.

She screamed "Ansonius!" and ran to him. He enfolded her in his arms so tightly she could hardly breathe. Gladiator, criminal, murderer, or not, this was her brother who sang bawdy songs as she rode with him coming home from Lewes. Huge sobs broke forth from her and for once she didn't care.

A slave appeared outside the door. Ansonius ordered, "I am seeing no-one else today. Clear the house and close the gates. We will be on the balcony."

So saying, he led them all back through the corridor, through the atrium and out onto the balcony. Lydia walked in a daze and then collapsed into one of the chairs at a small table. Darius looked as shaken as she felt, and Numerianus's eyes darted about faster than ever. Mikal, who had other things on her mind, stood by the railing overlooking the amphitheater. Lydia couldn't stop staring at Ansonius, taking each part of him deep into her memory.

"Where do we start?" he asked bluntly.

Lydia shook her head; Darius shrugged; Numerianus looked uncomfortable.

"All right, let me put it differently," he continued in a low roar, his face stern, "What in the name of the gods are you doing here? What has happened at Tunadur to bring you so far? Who is this old man? Who is the girl? How did you get so good at metalwork, Darius?"

Knowing Darius wouldn't speak, Lydia found her voice. "I came to Gaul to find Darius who ran away because of a quarrel we had over an amulet. Tunadur is fine. Father is a Prefect now. This old man is a Senator from Rome who is having Darius and me make – uh, farm implements. And the girl is Mikal, who came just before you left. That's our story, now how about yours? We thought you were killed. That's what we were told."

"Tell me about Mother."

Lydia told what she thought would interest him. Then she asked again for his story, but Numerianus interrupted.

"This is highly unexpected, and I must leave you all to get reacquainted. The Governor is expecting me, so if you don't mind, I'll go."

"Go," Oxenius ordered, and the old man scuttled off to the cart and the weapons.

Oxenius stood and walked over to the railing near Mikal, looking out to the countryside but saying nothing. When she could stand it no longer,

Lydia asked, "Why didn't you let us know? You could have sent a message. Why didn't you return home?"

Ansonius whirled around and faced them, a savage glow in his eyes. The story he told seemed wrenched from deep within his soul and gave him much pain in the telling.

Attacked by outlaws on the road between Lutetia and Molodunum not a week after leaving Tunadur, his companions were slain but he was captured and taken prisoner. What they hoped to gain, he didn't know. Ransom, perhaps. Before anything was done, however, a small group from Chatti, a land north and east of Germania, heading home, came upon them. A fierce battle was fought, his captors were killed and he was badly wounded. His rescuers took him with them to Chatti, not part of the Empire. Unable and unwilling to speak, not understanding their language, not sure what sort of people they were, he allowed himself to be cared for while planning an escape. After a time, he picked up some of their words and they learned some of his so they could talk in a rough blend of both.

There was a girl, pleasant, generous. Not pretty, she had thick blonde braids to her waist. Gertrun. The way he pronounced it gave a softness probably very much like the girl herself.

"I loved her," he said, his expression hard as carved stone.

Many months went by. His wounds healed but he stayed with the Chatti. There was no way to get a message to Tunadur. One day a detachment of renegade Roman soldiers found them.

Without provocation the soldiers attacked. Grabbing an axe, he fought back as best he could, but had to see his foster father beheaded with one stroke of a sword, his foster mother stabbed and dismembered. Worst, his Gertrun was raped. Ansonius slashed through the skull of the man who was on top of her and then he saw that she was already dead. Before being taken prisoner, he avenged her death by brutally killing seven Roman soldiers.

The Romans took him to Marseille where he was trained to be a gladiator.

Marseille, recalled Lydia. Where Marius is from.

The training took a year and fueled his hate. Once in the arena, he found great satisfaction in killing, each time remembering Gertrun. By killing others, by winning the battles, he prolonged his own death. That kind of suffering was good. It seemed as if he could never kill enough to blot out the picture of Gertrun. His hate for the Romans ran deeper than anything else in his life.

He looked at Lydia. "Could I write this to our father at Tunadur?"

She shook her head.

"No. I will never be a free man again. My mind is broken, filled with evil thoughts. Why is it that the gods play such tricks on us? Here I am, far richer than Father ever dreamed of being. The ladies visit me, throw flowers to me in the arena; the people cheer me when I walk through the street. Little children try to touch me just to say that they have done it. That's today. After the next games there will be a new hero. I know it. It was foretold to me, and now I see its fulfillment in you."

"What do you mean?" Lydia asked, alarmed.

Ansonius stared at her. She returned his look, hoping to send him a softer message with her eyes.

Finally he spoke, low and solemn. "I knew it was you, Lydia, when you smiled. No other girl in the world has that smile. Then I realized the red-headed boy was Darius. He was so young when I left, just about six. You see how you have tricked me? I am the champion of gladiators because of my hate, because I lose nothing by dying except my chance to kill more people, or animals or whatever they throw at me. Up to now, that has been my source of power. But now you touch me, you look at me like that, and I feel something inside me that had been lost. My heart beats differently, not hammering with revenge but throbbing with the desire to regain my life. Not having anything to live for, I was invincible and didn't care. Now I yearn to live. That will cost me my life."

No-one could speak in the awkward silence that followed.

The high clouds covering the sky brought an early twilight, promising snow before morning.

Ansonius walked again to the railing where Mikal stood. The picture of the two of them together reminded Lydia of how Marius had stood with Mikal, pointing the way to Gaul. How long ago that was, not in time, but in spirit.

"Why are you here?" she heard her brother ask.

To spare her embarrassment, Lydia answered, "She's my friend. Rema sent her with me to find Darius when he ran away."

"Sent her? Then Mikal is a slave, not a friend. Don't lie to me, sister."

Once, it would have been a lie, but now Lydia realized it was the truth. She said, "Mikal is my friend and that's as true as that you're my brother," then added, unable to stop herself, "This was her house before she came to us."

Ansonius touched Mikal's shoulders and turned her to him. He looked like a giant next to an elf.

"It's true, I can see it in your face. I swear that if I were a weaker man I would fling myself off this balcony and not have to listen to any more. Look at the three of you! You have no idea what I'm saying, do you? Bring disaster and think it's a family reunion!"

He laughed, not happily but enough to break the uncomfortable mood he'd created in them all.

"All right then," he continued. "We shall have a party to celebrate!"

Taking Mikal by one hand, he returned to the table and declared, "We will live these few weeks I have left! A party tonight with musicians and the best food in Lyon. No dancing girls. Pity. You will all stay with me until the Saturnalia, then, poof! All will be finished. You will return to Tunadur and forget you ever saw me. I will be dead, with no memories to trouble me. Hah!"

Lydia thought of Numerianus and the little army he was organizing, the widow woman who had disappeared, Coa and Culain, even Hector, and knew that they still needed to help the old Senator until his army was ready. She hated to spoil things for Ansonius, but she couldn't stay and play while their help was needed elsewhere.

"We can't stay that long, Ansonius."

The gladiator exploded in fury, unaccustomed to being refused. "What is more important than I am?" he demanded.

With a heavy heart, Lydia explained about the army of farmers and how Numerianus still needed their help. When she finished, he no longer looked angry. "I understand and I envy you, having a purpose. Me, all day long people come to ask me for money or – other things. Ordinarily I would start training for the games, but since I am meant to die anyway, I don't have to train anymore."

He stood and walked to the railing, stood there a moment, and then came back to the table. "I will come to see this farm of yours. To see where the clever Darius does such fine work. A good plan? Yes?"

"Yes!" Lydia, Darius, and Mikal agreed together. Ansonius seemed more like Lydia's lost brother now, in spite of how much he'd changed, inside and out. There was so much life in him, how could it be possible for anyone or anything to end it? She needed to find a way to save him and bring him to Tunadur the same as she was going to bring Darius. No superstitious prophecy could be allowed to take him away from her.

Just before dinner, Numerianus returned with the cart, the weapons, and good news from the governor.

"He is in favor of our plan," he announced. "He agrees with me that Albinus appears to be staying here, waiting, but he also says the British legions are eager for war. Imagine! It's been years since such an army has marched through this land and even more years since a battle has been fought here. If my mother were only alive to see this! She wouldn't believe it was me, the cranky old schoolteacher!" He was as excited as a young boy, his pale cheeks spotted with dots of bright red.

"How much time do we have?" Darius asked, more concerned with the practical than the poetic at that moment.

"Four weeks to finish getting the weapons ready, then three days' march to meet Albinus's special unit that's bringing a fortune to him. If we stop them and get the treasure, Albinus won't be able to pay his troops. Angry soldiers don't fight well, or so the theory goes."

Ansonius scowled and said, "So, Senator, you would sacrifice my brother and sister for your own vain glory?"

Numerianus looked him straight in the eye and answered, "Nay, gladiator. They help of their own free will. But they will not fight. We have two hundred farmers, and we are making good weapons. These men are willing to risk their lives to defend their farms and the Empire from Albinus. If you are a friend of Albinus, I plead with you to guard this news for the sake of your family."

"Once I was on my way to join the army of Septimius Severus," Ansonius answered. "By an ill stroke of luck, my fate turned out to be quite different, isn't that right, Lydia?"

She nodded.

He continued, "Emperors' games are not mine, but if I had to choose it would still be Severus. Now, enough of serious matters!" he declared. "Tonight, at least, we will celebrate. I see the table is ready for us, and the musicians. Mikal, you lead the way. Do you remember?"

Mikal walked with a sure step toward the dining hall where a sumptuous feast was laid out with couches surrounding the table. Slaves, both men and women, lined the wall to be of service when needed. It would have been hard not to notice that the slave girls paid particular attention to Ansonius, and who could blame them?

"So," he laughed, looking at Lydia. "What will you tell Father when you see him, assuming you will see him before I do in Hades. Will you tell him all?"

"Maybe you can tell him yourself – in Tunadur, not Hades."

"No chance, little sister. No chance."

Lydia mused over this while she ate the delicious food. He was so fatalistic about dying. There would be a way, somehow, to not let it happen. She would say an extra prayer tonight and ask how it might be.

The musicians played softly but none of the slave women danced. Lydia guessed this was unusual. When a harpist began a new, tranquil melody, Mikal asked shyly, "Could I sing? I used to sing that tune with my other owners. Would it be all right?"

Lydia was alarmed. Didn't Mikal remember what Julius had told her about singing her songs, how dangerous they might be? It didn't matter because Ansonius had already agreed.

The musicians began again and Mikal joined them, singing in her light, clear voice,

"Turn to me and show me thy favor,
For I am lonely and oppressed.
Believe the sorrows of my heart
And bring me out of my distress."

"Not long ago that would have gotten you in trouble around here," Ansonius said seriously. "I know the song. The Hebrew King David wrote it in ancient times, long before the Roman Empire began. I believe your family was Christian when they were killed. Perhaps they were Hebrew converts. At any rate, in this house were many paintings and mosaics of Hebrew stories. Do you remember them?"

"Some, yes."

"Good. I'm sorry the priest had most of them removed except for my audience room and the Medusa at the entrance, but that is Greek, isn't it?"

"I think so."

"You know more than you are saying, don't you?" he asked pointedly.

"Perhaps. I'm not sure. My father and mother taught me many stories, but I was very young."

Ansonius said. "Even today I've heard there are people who want the death of Christians and even Hebrews. Keep quiet about Mikal's history."

"Yes, we've been told that before," Mikal said.

"Believe it."

Hours later, when the milk and wine and delicacies were gone, and the musicians had left, all agreed it was time for bed. Darius had fallen asleep on his couch. Picking him up like a puppy, Ansonius carried the boy to his own room, explaining that he didn't want him to be frightened by waking up alone in a strange place. Several of the slave women started to go with him, but he motioned them to stay away.

Numerianus had a room to himself, while Lydia and Mikal shared Mikal's childhood room.

It was hard to leave Ansonius. Lydia watched his every move, memorizing him so she could tell her parents how remarkable he was. She was certain they would be proud of him in spite of whatever crimes he may have committed.

Mikal drove the cart back to the farm, with Numerianus sitting next to her. Occasionally there was a short conversation between them, but Lydia paid no attention. She and Darius sat in back, each deep in their own thoughts.

A light snow began to fall as they drew nearer the farm. The mules became almost frisky, tossing their heads when the big flakes tickled their noses. Mikal hummed a solemn tune.

The big house was cold and lonely compared to Ansonius's mansion, but a fire in the fireplace soon warmed the kitchen. There, they ate some of the food that Ansonius had given them, and soon after, went to bed.

24. "There is No Time!"

Lydia awoke screaming from a nightmare of blood and death, dismembered bodies and crowds of people shouting for more.

When Mikal shook her awake, Lydia grabbed her tightly.

"We must save Ansonius! Where is Numerianus! I need him right now!"

"He's in his study."

"So early?"

"So late. The sun is up."

"I overslept! Don't let me oversleep! Not till Ansonius is safe."

"You were so tired."

"Next time, if there is one, make me get up anyway."

She pulled her blanket around her and ran barefoot through the corridor to Numerianus's study. Not bothering to knock, she burst in and found him poring over an old map.

He looked up, eyes glaring. "Heavens, girl, what ails you?"

"He can't be allowed to fight in the Saturnalia! We have to get him out. Get a pardon like Plotius has. There is no time to lose. You must see the Governor today. You know him, you talked to him. Come on! We have to go!"

"Calm down. You must have patience, girl."

Lydia knew he would say something ridiculous like that.

"There is no time!" she shouted. "He will be killed!"

"Not today he won't. There are almost four weeks to the Saturnalia. We've got an army to prepare before then."

"To Hades with your army! It means nothing, not compared to my brother. If you won't go to the Governor, I'll go alone."

"No, no." The perplexed look in his beetle-browed eyes kept Lydia from dashing out the door. "I must not have told you yesterday. It's obvious that I did not or you would not be here fussing at me. Well, I have a lot on my mind lately."

She had no time for this. "Tell me what?" she demanded.

"Patience. You always rush me so." He shuffled some scrolls.

"I'm leaving!"

"Stop! Your manner is most annoying, young lady. You don't know that I explained everything to the Governor and now there is a strategy, a plan."

"This has nothing to do with my brother! Hurry up!" she pleaded, unable to bear it.

"It has everything to do with him. It's a good story, girl. Too good to rush through the details. Come back here! The governor and I decided it was not in the best interests of Gaul to delay Albinus with only my little army of farmers against his best. Now remember my aging brain and don't be angry with me when I tell you that we decided to give your brother his chance to earn a pardon."

Lydia stared at him. "You have my full attention."

"I thought I might. The governor will speak with Ansonius today, but the choice will be his. He may not choose the way you would."

"Then I have to talk to him. I must go!"

Numerianus shook his head. "I think not. Realize the life he's led. He's a gladiator. He's been in love with death for a long time. In his eyes this reprieve may be no good thing."

Lydia hated to think he might be right, but it made sense. She needed somehow to force Ansonius to choose her way and life!

"When will I know?" she asked.

"I don't know. I do know, however, that the Governor likes him and will use his considerable powers of persuasion on him. The conditions are that he must join our army and lead the fighting. Let us hope he appreciates that dying in battle would be more worthwhile than throwing his life to the lions. Cheer up, girl. You look as if you're already mourning for him."

"I had a dream –"

"Pshaw! Dreams aren't worth the telling, believe me. Ever since the rumor got started two hundred years ago about one of those fortune tellers predicting the murder of Julius Caesar on the Ides of March, everyone wants to know the future. Charlatans, every one of those so-called seers. Now, what do you know about reading maps? Take a look at this."

As suddenly as that, his mind switched from Ansonius to his army. The map was of Lyon and the area north of it showing hills and valleys, rivers and streams. The villa of Plotius, near Matisco was marked with an "A".

"What about Damian and Pythias?" Lydia asked. "They would be good additions to our army."

"Perhaps. I don't think Plotius will let them go. They're worth a lot to him alive."

He seemed to be lost in the map until suddenly he looked up, surprised that she was still there.

"Out to the forge with you!" he ordered. "Stop wasting my time. Darius is as important to this war as Ansonius. You let that big brother of yours decide his own fate."

Lydia stomped out, furious at the way he treated her. If she needed to interfere with Ansonius's life, she would. Maybe he didn't understand how much she wanted him to live. Perhaps her brother was choosing at that very moment. She remembered how on the balcony he said he felt like leaping off it to his death.

Other sisters might be passive if their brother wanted to die, but not Lydia. She raced back through the corridor to the kitchen.

"Mikal, I'm riding to Lyon to talk to Ansonius. Are there any clean clothes?"

Mikal shoved the plank with loaves of bread into the oven, saying "Let me come! I'll ride Kem. I'll even gallop. I'll race you. Let's go!" She already had her apron off and was wiping flour from her hands and arms.

"Stop!" Numerianus stood in the doorway fairly burning with anger. Glaring right through Lydia, he said, "Today your duty is here with Darius. He's been working alone for two hours already. If someone must take a message, send Mikal. She's got nothing better to do, but you will remain here. That is an order and it is a righteous one. You must learn you cannot always have your own way!"

"You big toad!" She shouted after him as he returned to his study. "Let my brother die! What do I care? I'll work in your stupid forge till my arms drop off and then you'll be sorry!"

Mikal put her hand on Lydia's shoulder and vowed, "I'll ride so fast you will never know I've gone."

"What makes you so brave all of a sudden?"

Mikal smiled and lowered her eyes. "I like your brother. It would be terrible to have him die like my parents did. I think I can make him see that."

"Please say the right words to him. If you succeed, I will love you as a sister," Lydia declared and even kissed her cheek. "Hurry back. I'll be frantic until I know his decision."

Numerianus called from his study, "Settled? Then to the forge with you, Lydia."

The old man was closing his door when Mikal called, "Wait! Since I am going to Lyon and Lydia will be in the forge and Hector is gone to the other farms today, you will have to watch the bread. Thirty minutes – half of the hourglass. Make sure it doesn't burn and keep adding vegetables and water to the stew so it doesn't get low. And stir it often."

"Where is the widow woman?" he demanded.

"She hasn't been here for two weeks, and you know it. It's up to you."

Lydia stifled a laugh at the way Numerianus tried to find a way out of his new job. He sputtered, then coughed, then shuffled around and finally growled at Mikal, "Show me what to do – but I won't be peeling carrots!"

As day wore on to evening, Lydia checked the road countless times without ever seeing Mikal returning. If the girl had ridden fast, she could have been back by now. Kem's tracks from the morning had disappeared under new snow. Lydia worried that Mikal might have been caught in a storm but reminded herself that the snow couldn't be much worse at Lyon than here. What could be keeping her?

From the villa, Numerianus called, "Dinner! Time to quit!"

Darius looked so surprised, Lydia realized she hadn't told him about their substitute cook. He was so focused on making helmets that even the news about the possible pardon for Ansonius hadn't gotten through to him.

It was true that Darius was working so hard he had no thoughts for anything or anyone else. At first, Lydia's fidgeting bothered him but he knew that if he said anything she'd get mad and he couldn't waste time dealing with that. The rhythmic heating, hammering, heating, bending, heating, testing of the metal worked hypnotically. The longer he worked, the more his body seemed to be absorbed in the process until he was no longer a thinking person but rather an armor-making machine.

It is no wonder that when he heard Numerianus yell "Dinner", it didn't make sense to him. It wasn't Mikal's voice. It took a few seconds for him to come back to the world, and then he realized how very hungry he was.

A veil of clouds covered the moon and stars. On the post by the entrance to the villa Lydia had hung a lantern, its faint light magnified by the reflection of the snow. That was odd, too. Darius had no idea that it was a beacon for Mikal should she be anywhere nearby.

When he entered the kitchen and saw the burned loaves of bread, he asked in his innocence, "Where's Mikal?"

For no reason that Darius could understand, Numerianus barked, "What does it matter? Eat your food and be grateful you've got it. Don't complain about the carrots, either. Unskinned carrots are healthy for you."

Darius nodded and sat.

The meal lacked flavor and conversation was nonexistent. With Lydia acting like a nervous cat, Numerianus sulking and fuming, and Mikal gone off by herself somewhere, he wished Hector was there to lighten the mood.

25. There Was No Victory That Day

After Numerianus and Darius went to bed, Lydia stayed in the warm kitchen, waiting. All night she watched, dozing and waking, keeping the fire going. Before dawn, she stood and stretched, her muscles stiff from being curled up, sometimes on the hard floor, sometimes on the bench and sometimes on the table.

Looking out the doorway into the yard, she saw that no new tracks ruffled the snow which was now about six inches deep. Her spirits fell. She should have gone to Ansonius herself. Later she would take Coa and search for Mikal and Kem who probably got lost somewhere. While she was doing it, she would ride on to Lyon and see her brother. Meanwhile, she might as well start the fire in the forge to be ready for the day's work.

She was leaning over the firepit in the workshop stoking the coals when Mikal rode into the yard. Lydia didn't see or hear her until Mikal grabbed her from behind, almost scaring her to death. That was forgiven instantly as she saw the radiance that glowed in Mikal's face. It was the only answer Lydia needed.

Smothered by Lydia's hug, Mikal tried to explain, "I got up when it was still night and rode fast because I couldn't wait to let you know. He'll be coming here as soon as he gets his affairs in order. The Governor has made him captain of our army! Secretly, of course."

"Mikal, I love you forever!" Lydia exulted.

Not that day but the next Ansonius arrived with a long train of wagons and attendants. The saddle and bridle on his magnificent black stallion were so heavily inlaid with bronze and jewels that they must have weighed well over a hundred pounds. Oxenius's bronze helmet, for he was dressed as a gladiator, gleamed like a mirror, with three ostrich plumes waving audaciously in the breeze. His breastplate was polished bronze, shining like gold. Every inch of leather on his boots and his tunic was heavily decorated. Around his waist was buckled the new bejeweled sword.

His wagons formed a circle in the yard, drawing close together to have enough room to unload.

When he gave the sign, the drivers whisked off tarpaulins covering a cargo of grain, armor, weapons, tents and pots in unbelievable numbers.

Lydia and Darius gaped at the happenings from the area of the forge, giving Ansonius, or rather Oxenius, the full stage for his arrival.

Numerianus came bustling into the courtyard. "Welcome, Oxenius! I am humbled to have you here."

Everyone who knew Numerianus was surprised at his courtesy, a trait that rarely showed itself. Oxenius dismounted, giving the reins to one of his servants, and followed the Senator into the villa.

Lydia breathed a sigh of relief. It was extraordinary that he was here and that all these people had come, too. They were quickly organizing all the paraphernalia he had brought, setting up a camp in the open fields around the villa.

Darius wondered if any of them was a metalworker. It would be nice to have more help.

Lydia knew Ansonius and Numerianus were meeting in his study and wished it looked less like a shipwreck. Not her problem.

To Darius she said, "I think we're in for a busy time of it. Ansonius does not appear to be a repentant criminal, does he?"

"Hardly," Darius agreed. "Do you think all these people are staying here?"

"Yes indeed. Our brother does not do things in a small way. I wonder what his neighbors in Lyon thought, seeing such a parade leaving his house. I wonder about Albinus's soldiers seeing it."

"He took a chance, didn't he?"

"He did. I wish I knew more about what was going on, don't you? Wouldn't it be nice if some of his people are armorers?"

Darius grinned. "He brought a lot more weapons, which will make our work lighter."

"I'm relieved. We couldn't possibly make enough for all these men."

"Did you see how he was wearing the sword?" Darius asked with a cute, shy smile.

"I sure did. He's awfully proud of it, I think."

"I'm sure glad it didn't break when he banged it on the table."

"I was scared to death."

Darius then returned to working on a helmet.

Lydia watched her little brother working so hard. He was still so scrawny and awkward and young that she felt quite tender toward him, at least for that moment. All the work in the forge had strengthened his muscles, but his arms were still thin as sticks.

She smiled at him and said sincerely, "Your part of the scabbard looked magnificent."

Darius looked at her, surprised. "Thanks," he mumbled. "So did yours."

While they continued their work, Numerianus coped as best he could with Ansonius. The gladiator was on probation, it turned out. If he proved himself in this little skirmish, he would be freed. If not, the Saturnalia right afterwards would claim him. Under those conditions, he was determined to make good. Obviously his desire for instant death in the arena was not so strong as before.

Ansonius brought news of Septimius Severus. Some of it confirmed what Numerianus had already heard from Darius as courier. Septimius, it seemed, had sent most of his army ahead through Pannonia and Germania while he detoured to Rome. There, he once more had himself proclaimed Emperor, but no-one took those things seriously as long as rivals were alive to contest them. The Governor expected Septimius to catch up with his army and enter Gaul from Upper Germania, having avoided the mountain passes by taking lower routes along the rivers. That would be around the first of January.

"That's good news," Numerianus commented but was cut short by Ansonius.

"If the Governor knows, don't you think Albinus knows also?"

Numerianus had no answer.

"Hitch up a cart and go tell your farmers that we meet here tonight to begin training. Tell them to say goodbye to their families. It may be the last they see of them. In three weeks time we must be ready to do some damage to the legions."

Numerianus didn't argue. Off he went to the barns to find Hector and tell him to spread the word. However, since Hector was needed in the forge, the old man himself, acting in his role as a Roman Senator, drove the cart into the countryside to muster his peasant army.

That evening a massive bonfire was lighted in the yard around which 196 of the region's farmers and laborers gathered to hear their charge.

Until then, only 87 had committed themselves, but when Numerianus told them that Oxenius the Gladiator was the general, more were eager to volunteer. Old and young, they all were enthusiastic about putting on armor and being soldiers for Oxenius.

Lydia, Mikal and Darius watched from the house as Ansonius spoke to the crowd, building them to a fever pitch of willingness to follow him wherever he led. He was a gifted orator. Lydia guessed it was a learned thing since none of the rest of her family had it. Her father had agonized over the decision to be Prefect of Noviomagus knowing how much in the public eye he would have to be, including making presentations and sacrifices every festival day.

Voices were raised with shouts of *"Ave! Ave! Ave!"*

Lydia realized that, like it or not, she was involved in a civil war, the outcome of which would determine the future of all her family.

The army's spirit was high under Oxenius, so high that after nine days they talked him into letting them have a little skirmish against a band of soldiers that had been plundering some of the farms to the south. It would let them test their weapons and their skill. Reluctantly, Oxenius agreed, meeting them in the afternoon and riding south to the area where the soldiers were known to be doing their mischief.

There was no victory that day for Oxenius, but he hoped the defeat would humble his troops enough that they would be more serious about training. The lack of discipline shown by them was a severe disappointment. They didn't pay attention to commands and forgot the plan of attack, losing too many arrowheads and javelins when they had to retreat. Several were wounded after getting into close combat with the soldiers, who were well trained to fight with short swords.

Slinking back through the woods, the militia knew they had been routed.

The next afternoon when training began again, Oxenius once more gave a rousing speech. It was the best way to bring their confidence back, for a defeated army must not feel as if that will always be their fate.

At the climax of his speech when everyone was pumped with enthusiasm under the spell of his voice, a thin man riding a swift horse galloped into their midst and skidded to a stop at the general's feet. Before Oxenius could say a word, the man leapt from the horse and cried loudly,

"Sir! Optimus Maximus, Imperial Courier for his Excellency the Emperor Caesar Septimius Severus, with news for your ears only!"

Lydia and Mikal burst out laughing. The crowd turned and stared at them. It was not good to laugh at Imperial Couriers even if they looked like this one.

The girls tried without success to look solemn. Ansonius turned to the crowd and excused himself to go into the villa and speak with the courier. Instantly, Lydia rushed ahead to the study, meeting Numerianus coming out.

"My old teacher!" Optimus exclaimed, clapping him on the shoulder.

"Why are you here?" the Senator asked gruffly.

"I bring a message, of course, for you and the gladiator."

Lydia found a darkened corner of the study where she could be not exactly hiding but not exactly visible either.

"What a mess," Optimus exclaimed seeing the mess.

"Hold your tongue, Courier," Oxenius ordered, glancing at but ignoring Lydia. "Comments on the décor are unnecessary. Give your message quickly – and it better be important – or you'll be a piece of shredded meat."

The cocky man cowered ever so slightly and said, "Sorry, sir. You'll thank me –"

"I will be the judge of that. Out with it.."

"The British army comes."

"I know that already. Is that your pitiful message? The whole countryside knows that the Britons are coming. Most of them are already here, did you know that? Why do you think those men are out there training in the snow? We are not shooting dice here!"

"Yes. No. I would not bother you with old news. There is more."

Lydia wondered if the insolent Optimus had any idea how many men Oxenius had killed. One more wouldn't change his standing with the gods.

"Now!"

"Ah. You'll thank me for this, yes you will. Aiiiieee!"

Optimus screamed because Ansonius had grabbed his sore shoulder and squeezed. The pain made words flow from his mouth. "Albinus is bringing a detachment of British cavalry 200 strong, his best. They have crossed the channel and should be at Lyon in eight days. They would be faster but they carry a large amount of gold with them. A great treasure of gold in mule-driven wagons. They don't expect any trouble in Gaul, so they and the horses ride mostly unarmed except for their leather tunics and swords. Their armor and weapons come by oxcart." He then had the gall to add, "Do you thank me now?"

Ansonius loosened his grip and let him go. "Sparing your life is my thanks."

"*Gratias.*"

"Sit."

Optimus obeyed.

The two then conversed, Ansonius asking questions and Optimus answering in a more serious manner than Lydia had seen before from him. When the talk ended, Ansonius's opinion of the courier had obviously changed because he added him to the army as a captain. Hector was the other captain because of the respect he commanded with the farmers. In a legion they would have been called centurions, but this was only a rebel army so Ansonius called them "captains." He, of course, was the Gladiator, at least until the end of the battle.

"Hector of Lutetia?" Optimus cried in amazement. "He's my brother-in-law."

"I wouldn't be surprised. What a family reunion. Come with me. There isn't much time if we have to fight in eight days."

To Lydia it seemed that Optimus underwent a complete transformation after that. He had a talent for organizing people without antagonizing them, which she wouldn't have thought possible. Before retiring for the night, the 196 men had been grouped in ranks of ten, which were then separated into two equal units, one headed by Hector the other by Optimus. Twenty extra men brought by Ansonius were deployed to repair armor, make quivers for arrows, cook food, and keep the camp clean while the others were training. Some of them were skilled enough to help in the forge.

Numerianus at that point was not included in the military organization, a fact that seemed to hurt his pride. Lydia noticed; Darius even noticed, but Ansonius didn't seem to notice. In fact, he seemed to go out of his way to ignore the old man who had conceived the whole outrageous idea. Lydia was working up the courage to have a talk with her brother when Ansonius himself went to speak with Numerianus.

What went on is between the old man and the gladiator, but when they came out, Numerianus had a job. Because of his knowledge of history and the local area, Numerianus was in charge of strategic movements.

There would be lookouts every five miles along the approach who would pass the signal when the cavalry was spotted. At a certain place about ten miles north of Lyon, almost due east of the farm, Numerianus knew a place where the highway was bounded on each side by heavy forest. Having read extensively in the writings of Julius Caesar, he suggested an ambush. Farm wagons driven by oxen and loaded with farmers hiding under straw would start across the road making a roadblock, while other wagons did the same from the rear, and then the rest of the farmers, who would have been hiding in the forest, would attack with bows and arrows and javelins all along the column of horsemen. Those in the wagons would join in. The idea was to have a quick and deadly surprise attack without getting too close to the cavalry swords.

"The driver of the wagon will be committing suicide," Optimus noted.

"Not at all, for he will not be seen. Instead, there will be a man-sized puppet in the seat manipulated by sticks attached to his neck and arms. Stuffed with straw, he will appear real to the cavalry."

"Ingenious," Oxenius complimented the Senator. "I think it could work. Let's ask our captains what they think."

Hector and Optimus agreed, so that part of the plan was set. On another point, Optimus screwed up his face to look both doubtful and arrogant as he made a suggestion that went against Ansonius's grain. He said the farmers might not want to wear the armor being made for them since they had heard that the cavalry would un-armored. After all, the farmers were only local people defending their lands from a British overlord. Why not let them wear their regular clothes, maybe putting some armor underneath if they wanted? It would give them a small advantage since the cavalry wouldn't know as quickly that they were fighters.

Hector joined in on Optimus's side.

"Look at it this way," he reasoned. "Wouldn't it be better for us to meet the cavalry without armor? It makes it fair. Besides, these soldiers won't have a chance against us, armor or no. We're too good and our swords are the best."

Oxenius argued, "The soldiers will be wearing heavy leather tunics, which are almost as good as armor. You have no idea how skilled they are with their swords. They will overpower you. Our army looked terrible in the one battle we fought, and they might fall apart again. It's foolish not to use every advantage you have."

Numerianus disagreed. "Strategically it's a level field. When the battle comes, our farmers will be in the wagons or hiding in the forest. They will be throwing their javelins and shooting their arrows, both from a distance. In the surprise attack, it will be hard for the cavalry to regroup fast enough, so hopefully the farmers won't have to engage in hand-to-hand combat. The ones who have swords know how to use them and are confident that our swords are the best. They will fight well if they have to."

In the end, Oxenius made the decision to allow each man to choose for himself what he would wear. For his part, he would wear his gladiator costume, for he was still a gladiator until the battle was won.

26. A Ghastly Trick

Only nine of the men had been so badly injured in the skirmish with the Romans that they couldn't come for training the next morning. The 187 were determined to erase the disgrace the fight had brought upon them.

Out in the fields, hay bales were set up as targets and the men were made to run, fall, leap and turn before throwing their javelins or shooting their arrows into the bales. This taught them to ignore distractions and focus on their targets, which were demolished more quickly each day of practice.

Twenty of the men were given swords made from the part-meteorite steel and ordered not to use them until the battle. Oxenius hoped they would not have to fight with the swords at all. They were meant for close combat, man to man, the type of fighting that legionnaires excel in. Oxenius wanted the farmers to concentrate on using their bows and arrows and javelins, weapons for fighting at a distance. Those would give them a chance of success. When it was all over, they could use the sharp blades of the swords on their farms for castrating calves and horses.

Those who wanted to use horses were allowed to with the warning that the horses of the Romans were trained for combat. Ansonius rode Coa in a demonstration that was sufficiently awe-inspiring that all of the horsemen decided to try their luck on foot instead.

The farmers had already been running five miles each day to build stamina. Their food was grain with thick stew and nut cakes washed down with watered wine. It was the same training regimen Oxenius used, which was enough evidence for them all to see that it worked. Their few weeks of training would be up against a group that included professionals with years of experience.

Under any other leader, the people might have seen how foolish the dream was, but Oxenius the Gladiator made them believe. They loved him for his reputation in the arena, for his goal of freedom, and for his charismatic personality. He could be mean as a wolverine to them and they only performed harder. Many of them didn't care which Emperor won the crown, but they did care about Oxenius and their own families, proving it by their hard work.

Lydia, in the forge and blacksmith shop morning till late at night with Darius, was so busy she couldn't think. Some of the local blacksmiths came by to help whenever there was a break from training. After every practice there were knicks and breaks in the weapons to repair. Most of the farmers had chosen to have at least some steel armor underneath their clothes, and these were always needing adjustments to allow free movement of their arms. Four of Oxenius's men who had been detailed to help in the forge had a hard time getting it right, so that meant having patience, which was never Lydia's strong point.

Many of the local women came to be close to their men even though Ansonius forbade any co-habiting until the battle was over. Mothers brought their children and busied themselves helping Mikal in the house and in the yard, or sitting around gossiping while peeling potatoes and carrots for the ever-simmering stew. Mikal never refused the women's help, but truly her job would have been easier without them.

A few times she asked about the widow woman, but none of the women seemed to want to give her an answer. Did they not want her to know?

The younger girls were more trouble and no help at all. They watched the men drilling, and the men watched back. It drove Oxenius wild enough to threaten all of them with beheading and various other dismemberments, but his threats only caused the girls to giggle and scatter momentarily. Soon they would return, standing in groups to admire the younger men who enjoyed showing off their new-found prowess in killing. Of course they had the best teacher in Oxenius, who hadn't survived that long without inventing some unique ways of taking lives.

Four days before the battle, a message came from the Governor that all of Ansonius's property, except the mansion, had been quickly and quietly sold to trusted people who would keep it secret until after Albinus fought Septimius, probably in February of the next year. The money from the sale was safe at the Governor's mansion. The Governor wished him luck, saying he would offer a sacrifice at the temple of Mars in the morning.

In further news, the Governor wrote that the legions of Albinus were continuing to dig concealed pits and other fortifications just north of Lyon. That indicated that the legions would stay near Lyon instead of marching into Germania to meet Severus's forces before they entered Gaul. Albinus was counting on the gold the British cavalry was bringing to help pay the expenses of the army that had grown to 65,000 men. Hopefully, Numerianus's little band of farmers would be able to stop that from happening.

With Septimius drawing nearer each day, and Albinus staying put, it looked more and more as if the stalking lion was hunting the scared rabbit.

Two nights later, news was received from the scouts that the cavalry was only eighteen miles away, stopping for the night. Hector had already arranged with farmers closer to the battle site to let the army use some of their ox-driven wagons, so runners were sent to alert them.

Since equine units always rode on the soft dirt alongside the roads and not on the hard stone, the wagons would be used to block these. They would look just like normal farm wagons carrying grain to Lyon to feed the legions. The soldiers should not be suspicious of them even when they didn't move out of the way. A dozen armed farmers in each wagon would be hidden under the grain. Each wagonload of men had given their puppet driver a name – Puck, Homer, Laieus, and Mops.

More wagons set out from Numerianus's farm to be ready to carry back the wounded and any bounty they might gather, including the gold. It would be dangerous for them to loot the bodies or take the cavalry's wagons, since the soldiers must remain unknown to the enemy for the safety of their families.

The site chosen by Numerianus was ten miles north of Lyon. His farm was about ten miles west of the place. The farmers started on foot before dawn, marching by the light of a half moon.

Oxenius was in front, riding his black stallion and resplendent in his helmet and tooled leather armor, the sword hanging at his side. Hector led the first company on foot, a thick leather vest over his normal clothes. Optimus, of course, insisted on fancier dress, so Oxenius gave him some chain mail from his own supply of armor. He rode his little horse since his leg wound was still giving him trouble, while the second company followed him on foot. The stars seemed close and bright in spite of the light from the moon. One could have lifted a spear toward the sky and touched Mithras's sword.

It was a silent march. Old snow on the ground helped the men see where they were walking. No clang of metal on metal, no words, were heard, only the crunch of feet on snow. The breathing of the men and horses made fog in the cold air.

The women had risen early and watched quietly as the soldiers departed. Even the young ones were awed by the scene. What had been a game was now reality. At the end of the day some would be widows, some fatherless or brotherless, some without their lovers. If the battle was lost, they would all lose their lands, their homes, and possibly their own lives.

The forge, usually the hub of noisy activity, was silent, its fires banked.

The kitchen was empty. None of those left behind had any desire to eat or cook, but they didn't want to go home, either. Each felt some comfort in the company of others. They milled around the yard in spite of the freezing cold and the patches of ice that had formed over puddles of water. Even the small children played quietly, sensing that this day was not like other days.

Darius decided he couldn't stay at the farm doing nothing but waiting to hear the outcome. Having worked so hard to help the army, it didn't seem right to stay behind, so about two hours after the army left, he set out on foot. It was easy to follow their trail through the fields.

The sky to the west glowed pink as the sun began to usher in the day.

By midmorning, Lydia needed to get away from the women at the farm and Numerianus.

"It's possible that Titus could be coming," she whispered to Mikal before starting out. Since the soldiers were bringing so much gold, it seemed reasonable that Titus would be in charge.

She took Culain with her and followed the army's trail for a few miles, then branched off, staying well away from the battle site, not having any desire to be closer.

What a mess she had gotten herself into. Trying to stop thinking about it, she walked in huge circles until she was exhausted. How would today's events affect the south coast of Britannia, her father, her family, Tunadur? Which side had they supported? Marius hadn't thought much of Albinus's chances, but that was weeks and weeks ago. Things changed.

Maybe the future of the Empire depended on this tiny band of farmers armed with weapons developed by a madman, some of them made by a young boy and a girl. Lydia felt almost hysterical, it was all so stupid. What had they been thinking?

Darius had stolen closer to the chosen battle than he had wanted to because he couldn't see through the thick trees. Now, from his vantage point on a small rise, he had a view of the part of the road where the first ox-wagons were waiting. The soldiers in the forest were well hidden. He saw no hint of them. His hands and feet grew cold. He wrapped his cloak around himself and waited.

After a time, the earth beneath him began to throb with the pounding cadence of 200 horses trotting along the roadside. Pressing himself into the dirt of the knoll, he peered over the top. Out of the north they came, their bright colored standard waving in the breeze. Even without armor they were a magnificent sight!

To his horror, Darius saw, in the lead, the finest horseman in Britannia, Titus, riding Zephyr, the finest horse to come from Tunadur.

Darius dug his nails into the frozen earth to stop himself from leaping up and shouting a warning. Seeing the man so proud and handsome ripped Darius apart. What a ghastly trick for the gods to play. This was their final revenge for the horrible amulet.

As the soldiers drew nearer, he kept reminding himself about Ansonius. Over and over he repeated, "Ansonius will be free. Ansonius will be free." He hated Caesar Albinus and Septimius. What made men want power so much that they caused horrible things like this to happen? They never cared about people, just power.

The farm wagons blocked the horses. Titus and the standard bearer yelled at them to move out of the way. The hidden soldiers moved the driver puppets, making it look as if they were trying to obey. Titus and the others came closer to the wagon and the whole column of horses stopped, trapped without knowing it.

"Charge!" yelled Oxenius, racing out of the trees with his sword drawn straight toward Titus.

Simultaneously the farmers leaped from the wagons throwing their javelins as the men in the trees attacked the sides of the column with bows and arrows. Any retreat was cut off in the rear by the other ox-drawn wagons.

Darius watched as Titus fell from Zephyr and then saw the horse fall on top of him. The boy was mesmerized by the ghastly sight and couldn't move. Oxenius was attacking others, thrusting his sword into one after another, the sword Darius and Lydia had made.

The battle continued, with arrows flying, javelins finding their marks, and some of the soldiers fighting back, running on foot into the woods to attack the farmers. The cries of dying horses pierced the air. Darius watched, sickened by the sight but unable to move.

A soldier ran toward him from the trees, sword drawn, blood flowing from his arm. Suddenly Oxenius appeared, grabbed the man from behind and ran his sword through him.

"Get out of here! Get out now!" Oxenius shouted at Darius, turning to rejoin the fight.

Scared into action, Darius stood up and ran in what he hoped was the direction of the villa, avoiding the trail made by the farmers that morning. The dim sun was more than three-quarters through the sky, meaning that in a few hours the day would be over. When he couldn't run anymore, he walked. Head, shoulders, arms drooping, he was in such a stupor that he didn't notice anything as his footsteps plodded steadily over the snow-covered plowed field.

Perhaps an hour later, maybe two, he came upon his sister. All the emotion of the past hours welled up in him as he looked at her and remembered everything.

"Get away from me!" he screamed, starting to run again. She was a monster. Never would he be able to erase Titus's horrible death from his mind. He wanted to blame her or the amulet. He couldn't admit that his own pride had made him help make the sword that had sliced through Titus's heart.

Oh gods! Darius hated everyone! Many times Titus had spoken kindly to him at Tunadur. Never never could Darius have guessed that this would be how it ended.

Breathing hard, he knew he couldn't run much farther. He turned around to see where Lydia was, lost his balance and slammed so hard into the dirt his breath was knocked out of him. Paralyzed, he tried to gasp with lungs that couldn't move for a long time.

He dug his fists into the crusty snow, grabbed a handful of snow and rubbed it on his face. The shock of the cold against his flushed skin rekindled his breath, but his soul hurt so much that he lay back down. The silence was peaceful. He found that he didn't care if he never got up again. He hoped Lydia and Ansonius would die, too. The world would be better off without them all.

Perhaps he could find peace in the ground, deep deep in the dark warm earth mother. He would gladly serve the mother goddesses in death if they would offer him forgetfulness.

The screams of battle that had haunted him were gone. A few icicles hanging from a juniper reflected sharp rays of light, but the swords and armor that had flashed in the battle now faded from his sight.

27. How the Gods Must Laugh

"Darius."

His sister was only a few steps away. He kept perfectly still as he lay on the cold ground. His arms, his legs, were numb and at odd angles to his body. The dead and dying soldiers had lain so. If only he could stop breathing.

"What's wrong? Darius!"

The snow that had melted around him had re-frozen into black ice. Lydia took the final steps toward him and knelt down, touching his hand. It was very cold. His face was cold, too, as were his arms and legs. Her brother was freezing!

She started rubbing his ankles first.

"Stop!" he ordered in a weak voice, unable to stand the touch of her hand.

"No," she replied simply and continued to rub gently. At last she asked, "Can you walk?"

He clamped his lips shut, refusing to answer.

"Oh? Well, here you go!" With strength that came from weeks at the forge, Lydia hoisted Darius to his feet where he jerked himself free and stood on his own, wobbling and dizzy, yet grudging her any more victories over him.

She could sense the hate emanating from his frozen little body. Lydia wisely held her tongue, but also stayed close enough to catch him should he fall. She desperately wanted to know what he had seen of the battle, but did not dare ask, not yet.

"It's probably two miles home from here," she said quietly.

Darius gave a miniscule shrug of his narrow shoulders and tried to lie down again.

"No," she said, taking his arm, which he immediately and firmly withdrew from her hand. He took one small step forward and stopped.

"We're going to walk, Darius. We have to get back to the farm. Now!"

He stood rooted to the spot. A branch from the tree lay on the ground. Lydia picked it up. Never had she hit her little brother with anything other than her own fist, but she lifted the branch and brought it down across his shoulders.

Darius yelled, stumbling away from her which proved that he was capable of movement.

"Walk!"

Thus began a slow ponderous trudge with Lydia imagining the horrors that Darius must have seen. How many of the local farmers had been killed? Where did her loyalty lie? Why did a person have to choose? Oh, how the gods must laugh at the ambitions of human beings, she thought.

Lydia finally asked the question. "What happened?"

Her brother's mouth was set, his ears were red, his eyes glistened, and he didn't speak.

With sinking heart the truth, the certainty, hit her. "Oh gods," she moaned, almost fainting herself.

She willed herself to stand up straight and keep walking, leaning on the tree branch. She would have to be stronger than ever now. Her charge from Rema was still in force, so she would protect Darius as well as she could. She knew, as everyone did, that enemies of the victor had very little chance of surviving, whether they were old, young, male or female. Nonetheless, she would get Darius back to Tunadur even if armies or emperors stood in her way.

She did not know what she would find at the villa. There was a glow from that direction. It could be the surviving cavalry putting a torch to the whole countryside. If so, she and Darius would stay hidden until it was safe. What would they find? Lydia hoped that Mikal and Numerianus had escaped before the soldiers came.

She walked behind Darius with the branch ready as he kept up a slow but deliberate pace. It was like leading a balky mule. Whenever he stopped altogether, she enforced her control.

"Walk!"

"No."

Whack!

Step taken.

"Walk!"

"All right!"

Progress made.

As it grew darker, she silently thanked the gods of the forest for the sight of his small figure ahead of her. It was an odd prayer, given what lay ahead for them, but it was about all that remained for her..

The night settled in, a waxing moon on the eastern horizon, a few early stars. The steady crunching sound of Darius's footsteps was echoed by her own.

To the north, she thought she saw movement. The realization slowly came that a procession was winding its way through the countryside. Dim sounds of cheering and songs began to reach her ears, mere whispers by the time they traveled over the fields. She stared harder. The procession seemed to be heading toward the villa of Numerianus.

Roman soldiers would not behave that way.

So, the farmers had won.

Numerianus's impossible army had won.

Ansonius had won. If he was alive, he was a free man. She was so exhausted and cold that she could only move her mouth into a very tiny smile of relief at that thought.

Suddenly her heart almost stopped. If Ansonius won, and if Titus had led the cavalry, he was probably dead. Her knees gave way and she fell to the ground. She gasped for air and gulped it in, grateful that it froze her throat before reaching her lungs. Now she understood what was wrong with Darius.

He had stopped walking, waiting for her.

When she regained the strength to stand and catch up to him, he spoke coldly, "You killed Titus."

"No!" she cried in anguish.

"The amulet was false. It brought bad luck."

He must be right. How else could the rough, scarcely-trained farmers have won over expert cavalry? Lydia could not fathom the depth of trouble and anguish she had caused to everyone by simply changing a silver amulet.

Her despair turned to rage and she spat out the words, "Mithras is a weak god of war if he let himself be overpowered by our Celtic mother goddesses."

Darius shrugged and started to walk faster. Not until he was a long way ahead did Lydia move to follow.

Sounds of the celebration grew louder. Against the light of the fires and the shadows of the night, Lydia thought she saw someone either standing right in their path, or walking directly toward them. Her inclination was to duck behind a tree to hide, but then whoever it was would think Darius was alone and might attack him.

Mikal's voice called softly, "Darius?"

"Yes," Darius answered and stopped.

"I knew you were coming," Mikal said when Lydia caught up. "The others were worried when Culain came back alone, but somehow I knew you were all right. I mean, not hurt. What's wrong?"

Lydia could only shake her head, unable to speak, and Darius was silent.

Getting no response, Mikal chattered on, "Ansonius is being wonderful. You should have seen him and heard his speech. See the bonfire? Everyone's dancing now, everyone who can. He wants to see you both as soon as you get back. He didn't even get scratched! I wish I had been there to watch him!"

Darius spat out the words: "Yes, my brother slaughters at will. I wish to the gods he wasn't my brother!"

He had to get away from them, so he started walking quickly toward the villa, fuming all the while. He hated himself. He'd been playing a game in making all the armor, testing the new steel. How had he let himself be so blind as to forget what the purpose of it all was? Stupid! He had been so stupid!

Lydia and Mikal exchanged a glance, stunned but not truly surprised by Darius's reaction. Together they followed him.

In the courtyard ghostly shapes danced in front of a huge bonfire accompanied by laughter, pipes, songs and merrymaking. Avoiding the revelers and pushing through the crowd at the doorway, the three elbowed their way into the kitchen. Many women bustled around in the small room tending large pots of water and medicinal herbs boiling on the fire. Innumerable strips of bloody cloths made a gory pile in a corner.

A cacophony of sound came from the atrium which had been set up as a hospital for the wounded men. Lydia wished she didn't have to go through there to reach the study where Ansonius was waiting. She was squeamish and hated seeing anyone badly hurt.

Keeping her eyes averted, trying to ignore the pain-filled cries, Lydia led the way to the study door. The three of them entered, shutting out the commotion and smells of the outer room. Ansonius stood while Numerianus and Optimus were seated at the table. Hector was not there.

"Ah! I was worried about you." Ansonius looked so happy that Lydia wished she could forget about her own torment. "Sit down, please," he said. When they had done so, he congratulated Lydia and Darius. "You have worked hard and successfully. Without you, the battle and my life would have been lost. I thank you more than you will ever be able to imagine. Now I want you all to get back to Tunadur. Forget what you have seen and done here. Leave tomorrow."

Darius said no. He wanted to find a cave somewhere and disappear.

Ansonius countered with, "Lydia, you and Mikal must get the boy out of here and out of Gaul. Take him to Uncle Petrus if he won't stay at Tunadur. But get him to Britannia!"

"Yes," Lydia agreed. "But I'm taking you, too."

Ansonius, standing victorious and massive at the end of the book-strewn table, shook his head.

"I can't go home yet. We will have to keep this area safe from those loyal to Albinus until Septimius comes. There will be more skirmishes, but none of this importance. Before I can see our father in an honorable way, there are five years of my life to atone for. The Senator and I will stay here until the war is over. If Septimius is successful, I will give him my house and the money recovered today from the cavalry, which is considerable. It will be enough to gain us some good favor. Numerianus, meanwhile, will be my teacher and healer, showing me how to live in this so-called civilized world."

"Will the money buy your freedom?" Lydia asked.

"I have my freedom now by the promise of the Governor. I also have plenty of fortune for my needs. I am hoping the cavalry's treasure will buy me a clear conscience so I can live the rest of my life in some sort of peace. The old Senator will show me if that is possible, won't you, my friend?"

Numerianus nodded but fidgeted uncomfortably.

"What is it?" asked Ansonius.

"I – sometimes a person – it was necessary in order to raise the army – it wasn't – yes, it was."

"What? You are not making sense," Ansonius said impatiently.

"All right then. You call me friend, and that title is true. You call me schoolmaster and that title is also true. But when you call me Senator, that title is false. I pretended in order to raise the army, so people like the governor and these farmers would think it was an official army. What will Septimius do to me when he finds out?"

Ansonius answered, "We'll deal with that when we hand over our treasure to him. Riches have power to soften the hardest heart."

He continued, "Optimus will accompany you three as far as Lutetia and see that you get safe transport from there. He's vowed on the legendary beauty of his Gloriana to be trustworthy of this charge. The countryside may not be safe now, so you will keep clear of the main roads. You will need his wiles to get by."

"What about Hector? Couldn't he come instead?" Darius asked, wondering where he was. He would much rather go with his former kidnapper, if he had to go, than with Optimus the Imperial Courier.

"Didn't you see him in the other room?" Ansonius asked. "He got several bad cuts, lost a lot of blood, but the prettiest girls in the countryside are hovering over him like amorous butterflies. He has agreed to stay and manage the farm for Numerianus. The whole region is ready to show him their thanks by taking turns working for him to get this rat-trap nice again."

Ansonius then poured a goblet of wine, took a sip and went on, "When you get to Britannia, it will be necessary to be silent about what you have done here. Two hundred British soldiers, not the highly trained professionals we expected, were killed in the battle. Their families will want vengeance if they find out your role in it. However, Septimius will save our family because of me even without knowing about you. Others who were close to that cavalry unit or helped them will not be so fortunate."

He added that tomorrow he would send Numerianus to Lyon to claim the signet ring of freedom from the governor, and to collect the money from the sale of his belongings. He was too well known to go there himself.

As Lydia took the cup from her brother, her hand shook because she needed to ask, "Was it you who killed Titus, the leader of the cavalry?"

A puzzled look came over his face. "Yes. You knew him?"

Lydia nodded and plunged on before her emotions could get in the way. "Did you notice if he was wearing a silver amulet with Mithras on it?"

Ansonius frowned as if trying to remember. Finally he answered, "No, I am almost certain he was not. I didn't see anything like that. Of course, one doesn't look for amulets when one is attacking. Is it important?"

"It is. If he was not wearing it, that's important."

Darius then spoke up. "It could have been hidden by his tunic or anything. Just because you didn't see it doesn't mean it wasn't there."

"Of course," Ansonius agreed. "It could have been hidden, but I don't think it was. A soldier would not hide his connection to Mithras from his enemy. At any rate, his body and the others have been thrown into the river. Anything valuable left on him would likely have been looted by the farmers so you'll never know. If this is a point of contention between you two, forget it. Don't let it trouble you further."

Lydia handed the goblet back to him and he then passed it to Darius. The boy held it a long time, staring at the blood-red wine, wishing he had the courage to throw it onto the tiles. After a long time he took a sip.

Ansonius spoke quietly. "Think of Tunadur. Remember the long stretches of downland covered with fine horses and sheep, the fields of barley and grain. Tell our parents I will return when I have earned the right to do so."

Darius nodded. He could deliver that message. He knew how thrilled his parents would be to hear this kind of news. And then he would leave Tunadur to live and work with Uncle Petrus.

Ansonius then put his large hand on Mikal's shoulder and said, "Mikal, take care of my brother and sister. Help them learn the peace I have seen in you. Will you promise me this?"

Mikal blushed and nodded.

The former gladiator then turned to Lydia. "You have given me my life, sister. When you and Darius walked into my home in Lyon that day, you'll never know the shock I felt. I confess my knees shook together like saplings in a windstorm. I was so afraid of what you would see in me. Artemis should be your name, sister – huntress of lost souls. And Darius is Apollo the artisan."

Lydia wished people would stop using that analogy. She wasn't feeling at all heroic. Then she remembered, "I have something for you," she said, reaching under her tunic for Petrus's chain of interlacing vines she took it from from around her neck. "Our uncle made it," she told Ansonius. "Please wear it as a promise that you will return to us."

He held the beautifully crafted chain in his hands and examined it. His face was full of yearning and pain.

"I want so much to be worthy to return, Lydia. But until I can truly call myself healed of the life I've led – forgiven, even – I will have to be an exile. Pray to the gods for me. Mikal, pray to the Christian god if you ever know him. I need all their help. Tell Father about the sword. He needs to know that Darius is ready to apprentice to the best shop."

Darius then confessed, "It wasn't all me. You need to know that Lydia did half the work on it."

"What?"

"Yes. We didn't want you to know in case you were superstitious about women making such things, but it was the only way the sword could be finished in time."

"I see. The two different styles of decoration on it, yes?"

They nodded.

He then looked at Numerianus and said, "My family is full of surprises."

28. "I Don't Want to Marry a Man from Bath"

Their return journey was treacherous. All of Gaul that cold winter was in a state of alarm. Roaming bands of ruffians invaded villages and farms, robbing and terrorizing the peasants. There was little hospitality along the roads. Four people with three horses and a two-mule cart looked suspicious to many. Optimus was forced to take them on the lesser traveled road by the Loire river to avoid meeting soldiers or even civilians who might steal their horses, mules, carriage, food and money.

The indirect route added several days to their journey. As Ansonius had predicted, Optimus proved himself useful, managing to charm their way to a warm meal and a hay loft to sleep in each night. However, he was not so different in other ways. He still called Darius "Flea" and teased him about being a slave, and flirted with Mikal though she never gave him reason to hope. As ever, his mouth spewed out an unbearable stream of egotistical chatter from dawn to night.

When they reached Lutetia, Gloriana was thrilled to see them again and to hear Optimus's stories that grew more embellished with each telling. Lydia, Darius and Mikal strolled around the city, each day discovering an area more beautiful than the one they'd seen the day before. They stayed several days with the fuller's family whose friendly home was a good place for each of them to think things over. None of them was ready to cross the channel just yet.

The three had heavy secrets. Some families on the south coast would be ruined and some would prosper because of what they had done. How Lydia wished that everything could go back to being the same as it was before two power-hungry Emperors interfered in her life. But then what about Ansonius, and Hector, and crazy old Numerianus?

Finally they had to move forward to face whatever was coming..

Optimus offered to go on to Juliobone with them, but Mikal objected strongly.

"I can't stand him," she complained to Lydia after his wandering hands had provoked her wrath yet again. "I never want to see him again. He's married. Make him stay with Gloriana, the poor girl."

Gloriana's father selected two honorable men to accompany them to Juliobone. They were good company and didn't ask questions.

Arriving at Juliobone, they immediately sought out Julius and Marissa who had given up hope of seeing them again.

"We thought you must have returned on another route, missing us altogether! It was so long ago now, we were sure you had already gone," Julius said. "So this is your red-headed brother. Ah! I remember something now! Not but a few hours after you left, Marius was at the dock unloading cargo when a fishing boat from Adairinnic showed up. The men, a scurvy lot, were asking about the red-haired boy and the others. Marius remembered that Mikal guessed that Darius had been here, so to throw them off, he had one of his sailors tell them that the boy had been taken to a different port altogether. Hah! You might have had even more adventures if Marius hadn't stopped them."

"Has Marius been back here?" Mikal asked, quickly glancing at Lydia.

"Let's see, yes, he came back here. It must have been around six weeks after that. Yes, I think that was it. He asked about you, but of course I had nothing to tell him."

"Julius, remember what he said about her father?" Marissa said.

"Oh, yes! Your father! Marius decided not to go to back to Britannia again because of the chance of seeing your father in Noviomagus. What could he tell him? Marius is an honest man and would have a hard time lying to anyone. Since none of us knew what had happened to you, he thought it best to stay away from there. You could have been alive, or dead, we had no idea."

"Do you know where he went?" Lydia asked hesitantly, realizing that would have happened close to two months ago.

"I think he was going to Africa, to warmer waters. Most ships stay off the ocean until March or so because of winter storms. We're used to him being gone for a long time."

Lydia hadn't realized how much she had looked forward to hearing about him, maybe even seeing him. Still, her spirits were lifted by the fact that he'd asked about her even though she'd been nothing but trouble to him. She knew she was imagining too much, but it was more pleasant to think about that than the other things that crowded unpleasantly into her mind.

Mikal piped up, "Did Marius leave a message for us in case we did show up?"

Lydia blushed a little, not much, waiting for the answer.

Julius looked at Marissa. "Do you remember?" he asked.

Marissa smiled at the girls. "I believe he said that if we saw you, to tell you he was happy you had a safe journey and would see you again."

That was almost enough for Lydia. She tried to picture how he would look saying it, his dark eyes smiling. She tucked the thought away to draw it out again when she needed it.

"Would you like to leave a message for Marius?" Marissa asked.

Lydia didn't hesitate. "Please tell him that it is safe for him to return to Britannia."

"I certainly will do that."

Julius and Marissa seemed to understand that the young people needed time to work out whatever was troubling them and to benefit from the peace of their home.

Marissa's cooking healed hearts as well as bodies. Darius, especially, began to eat more than he had in weeks and to even carry on a simple conversation.

Sometimes in the evenings Julius brought out his lyre so he Mikal could sing the songs he played.

Lydia found herself spending time with the children, surprising herself by enjoying their company. They never asked questions she couldn't answer. Stories remembered from her own childhood were exciting to them. Sometimes she even made up stories. It was amusing watching Sera laugh at the funny parts. She had a dimple like Marius's.

Two weeks in Juliobone under such hospitable conditions did much toward, if not erasing then at least finding room to hide, unpleasant memories and remember good ones.

It was time to find a boat to take them home. They could even face crossing the channel in winter, though the crossing was worse than the first time for all of them, even Mikal, because of strong winds from a brewing storm. Experiencing it together made it almost bearable.

They arrived at the port in Noviomagus early on January 25, 197 AD.

Once ashore, they were relieved to find out that Quintus was not in town. Using their connection with him to get the loan of a horse for Darius at the stable, they set out for Tunadur, hoping that Coa and Kem were strong enough after the channel crossing to make the nine-hour trip in one day.

The horses seemed to understand they were home. Maybe the earth felt different here and the grass tasted sweeter. Whatever the cause, both horses went briskly after the first hour, ears alert, tails high. Culain raced ahead most of the time, occasionally scaring up a rabbit from the brush. Darius, an inexperienced rider, handled his bay mare well enough, or perhaps it was that the horse enjoyed getting out on the Downs with such good company as Coa and Kem.

The weather was cool and breezy, making the riders pull their cloaks tightly around them. At noon they stopped to eat the fruit and bread they had bought in Noviomagus, letting the horses graze for about an hour. They kept going, taking a more northern route in order to avoid going near Arundel . Seeing Diana was not in Lydia's plans.

There were regular breaks for the horses, which added some time to their journey so that it was night when they reached the ford over the Adur. An almost full moon lighted their way home where Lydia was not at all surprised to see both of her parents and her grandmother waiting outside the villa for them.

"We've been gone three and a half months. You'd have thought they would have had a burial ceremony and forgotten us," she marveled as they drew near.

"They didn't do it for Ansonius, and he was gone for five years," Darius reminded her.

Lydia laughed. It felt good to be home again!

The news about Ansonius being alive was like a miracle. The cloud that had hung over the home for years, lifted. Quintus, after hearing about the sword, finally admitted that Darius's future was as an artisan, and his talent was too large to be kept at home. Soon Darius was hard at work in Lewes as an advanced apprentice to Uncle Petrus.

As for Lydia, she was content to see Darius recognized for his exceptional talent. Making beautiful objects with metal was all he had ever wanted to do, whereas she had lost her interest in metalworking.

Very soon after their arrival, Lydia insisted that her parents address the question of Mikal's freedom. After they heard of the extraordinary things Mikal had done for her, it was an easy decision to make. When Mikal was asked how she felt, however, Lydia was surprised to hear her say that the thought of being free scared her. She had no family and nowhere to go. She didn't want to have to leave.

"That's easy to solve," Lydia declared. "You can stay as my companion. Can't she, Father?"

"Yes, of course. I will start the necessary legal work immediately," declared Quintus.

"Wait a minute!" Mikal insisted. "I should have something to say, and this is it. As much as I like Lydia, I can't spend my days simply following her around as a companion. I want to work like I have always done. I want to be useful and to learn."

Quintus was obviously perplexed by this turn of things, so he turned to Angwyn for help.

"That's no problem, Mikal. Just say yes. We will let you learn and do all that you wish, since that will benefit us, too. All right? And you can continue to be Lydia's friend."

Mikal smiled brightly and said, "Yes!"

Lydia was surprised that the change in status didn't make Mikal completely happy. She'd thought the girl's sighs might be for Chaton the stable boy, but that wasn't it. She was no longer interested in him nor he in her.

Mikal made up a love song and sang it day and night. It was so maudlin that Lydia finally had to plead with her not to sing it in her company:

I wander along the hidden paths;
The forest glades silence my cries.
How can I live and my love not here
To pity my lonely sighs."

The two girls often rode along the beaches, talking together of what they couldn't talk to anyone else about. It was on one of their rides that Lydia learned of Mikal's feelings for Ansonius and that the song was about him.

Remembering how the whole female population of Lyon and surrounding areas had felt about Oxenius the Gladiator, it was no surprise that Mikal had fallen under his spell. Had he returned her feelings, though? He'd seemed especially tender toward Mikal, so Lydia thought it might be so. The girl was so young, as young as Aelia was when she married the much older Plotius. It was something to think about and it took her own mind off thoughts of Marius.

In late February news came of the final victory of Septimius over Albinus. The legions fought about 60 miles north of Lyon. Albinus's troops were pursued back into the city, which was sacked and burned by the victorious Septimian army. Albinus himself was trapped in his house by the Rhone River and committed suicide.

The punishment doled out to those on the south coast who had supported Albinus was severe. Septimius sent envoys to carry out widespread executions, including that of Brutus Marconius, father of Diana. Arundel was given as a prize to some strangers from Gaul. Diana and her mother were spared but had to move to a small house in Noviomagus.

Lydia's family was safe and her father didn't understand why, since he had supplied many of the cavalry's horses. Those who suffered losses resented the fact that Quintus didn't, but the consensus became that the Romans needed him to remain as Prefect and so left him alone.

One day in April, Lydia's mother pleaded with her to visit Diana. "Now that she's lost both Titus and her father, she has no-one but Fulvia, so you can imagine how lonely she is. Their house in Noviomagus is not as fine as Arundel, of course, but they will think you are looking down on them if you don't go. Your father visits them whenever he's in town and he says they continue to ask about you."

Of course her mother could never understand the depth of the problem with seeing Diana. She requested a compromise. "Let me go after the mares have foaled and the rest of the lambs have birthed. Tar and the others cannot handle it alone."

That was a fact. Since so many of the south coast men had died, women were doing twice the amount of work now, filling in for them. Anyone who could help with the spring births was invaluable, and Lydia was one of the most skilled, along with her mother. Quintus, also, worked like everyone else, doing whatever was needed to keep the farm going.

Rema defended Lydia's plan. "Diana will survive this," Rema said. "In May she will have her own baby to keep her busy. Lydia is needed here."

Angwyn was forced to agree. "All right!" she said testily to Lydia. "Stay. But I can't understand why you're so afraid to see Diana."

"I'm not afraid."

"Yes you are. Surely you're not still angry over that Titus. You're lucky to have escaped him."

"I have no anger about Titus," thought Lydia. "It's the secrets I can't tell that are the problem, the ones that will hurt everyone if they are discovered."

On a warm spring day, she rode out to visit Petrus and Darius at Lewes. Her brother was flourishing under his tutelage. When Lydia told Petrus she'd given the chain to Ansonius, he was pleased.

"So it served a good purpose?" he asked.

"Yes. Or at least I hope so." Lydia replied.

"That's all we can ever do, isn't it? Hope."

It had been seven months now since she'd seen Marius. He had slowly drifted into a far corner of her mind. Almost the only time his memory surfaced was when she saw a ship out in the channel,. She would stare hard to see if it might be his. It never was.

The new colts and fillies rambled over the hills beside their dams, kicking up their heels, racing each other on stiff new legs and growing strong on their mothers' milk. But as much as Lydia loved horses, her favorite babies were the lambs. Watching them, she laughed and felt almost at peace.

Culain took to wandering farther and farther until sometimes he was gone for days at a time. A few times Lydia despaired of ever seeing him again, but he always came back looking pleased with himself and wagging his burr-encrusted shaggy tail. The two-year-old puppy had grown into a long-legged grey-haired giant. Lydia hoped that the long journeying in Gaul hadn't filled him permanently with wanderlust. Tar decided it was time to train him to fight wolves like the other hounds. That would keep him home and out of trouble.

On the 14th of May, Diana gave birth to a healthy blonde baby boy. Quintus Antonius brought the news himself to Tunadur and asked, not ordered, Lydia to come back to Noviomagus with him when he returned.

Whenever Father was back home for awhile he became more cheerful. He rode out with Lydia to check the horses and sheep. Though he didn't talk much, he seemed less tense and hard. Maybe being a Prefect and seeing the suffering of his people since Albinus's folly had made him more satisfied with his own lot. Whatever the reason, Lydia enjoyed their outings and hoped he would stay longer – so she could stay, too.

It wasn't to be, of course. Only two weeks after Diana's baby was born, Quintus announced that he and Lydia would leave for Noviomagus in the morning and he would give a blessing to the boy. Normally the baby's father would do this, so Quintus had volunteered as a family friend and Diana had accepted. It was a simple ceremony. The baby was laid at the father's feet, and if the father picked it up, the baby was given a name and the chance to live. If the father refused, the baby was left somewhere to die, or to be rescued and raised by whoever found him, never to know his real heritage.

Lydia actually felt relieved to be going. It was time to lay old feelings to rest.

"May I bring Mikal with me?" she asked, wanting her nearby since she was the only one who knew how hard the meeting would be.

Quintus hesitated, then agreed on the condition that the girl would be able to ride the nine hours straight, for there could be no stopping at Arundel.

"Mikal is a fine horsewoman now," Lydia assured her father.

"All right then, bring her along. She can be of help to you."

"Oh? How?"

"With your hair, for instance. It seems to be out of control whenever I see you."

"I don't mind."

"I'm aware of that. But perhaps in Noviomagus where you are the Prefect's daughter, you could – no, it doesn't matter. It isn't important."

The next morning dawned with rain everywhere. It was a slow slog until mid-day when the sun finally broke through the clouds and they were able to make up some of the lost time. Once in the town, they first took the horses to the stables, then went to Father's town house to clean up before visiting Diana and Fulvia.

It was the first time Lydia had seen the Prefect's impressive town house. Most of the landowners on the south shore had homes in the town for doing business or attending festivals, but because the Prefect spent more time there than the others, his house was better kept than most. Three permanent slaves kept it constantly ready for Quintus and his visitors.

After cleaning up in the small bath suite, Lydia and Mikal joined Quintus for supper in the dining room, complete with couches.

As they ate, her father surprised Lydia with a subject he must have been pondering for some time.

"There is a man of good standing who lives in Bath. He has heard about you and wants to marry you."

Lydia almost choked on a piece of ham.

As she was coughing, Quintus continued, "You're more than old enough. If you wait much longer, your opportunities will disappear. We don't have many men left around here, especially of your rank, so this may be your only chance."

Lydia glanced at Mikal who wasn't looking back. No help there. What if Marius never returned? Worse, what if he didn't care about her! She had no assurance he felt anything at all for her. It was her imagination that had convinced her that his kindness, his concern, even the touch on her ankle meant something. Still, if there was any hope at all . . .

"I'd rather wait a little longer, if you don't mind," she pleaded. A brilliant idea struck her just in time, "You and mother have such a perfect marriage, I want someone who I can love the way you love her."

Quintus's mouth curled up into the best smile she'd seen lately.

"All right, I'll give you a few weeks, no more," he agreed. "Lucius Barinius is his name. He is of honorable character. His wife died. He has several older children."

The name was familiar. Where had she heard it before? She couldn't remember.

"Are his children as old as I am?" she questioned.

He shrugged. "What does it matter? You will be taken care of, that's what's important to me."

With a sinking heart, knowing that Marius could now hide forever in her memory, she murmured, "Yes, Father."

The rest of the lunch was grim. Mikal kept bursting out in little fits of giggling until Quintus ordered her to control herself.

When they had all finished eating, mostly in silence, Quintus held audience with a few people who couldn't be kept waiting. During that free time, Mikal insisted on re-fixing Lydia's hair.

"Why? This is how I've worn it for ages."

"I know. Ever since we left Britannia for Gaul, but I think it's time to change it into something more stylish, especially now that you're almost betrothed to a man from Bath. After all, it's important to me if not to you, that Diana does not outshine you."

"I don't want to marry a man from Bath, and you know it," Lydia declared. "Did that name sound familiar to you? It did to me."

Mikal thought a moment then shook her head.

"It's probably my imagination. Anyway, I don't have any bad feelings about Diana and Titus. That's all behind me. The problem is – you know – the secrets." What's ahead of me, she could have added, is a miserable horrible life as a stepmother to children who will hate me.

Since Lydia put up no more struggle, Mikal had her way with her hair, finishing up by sticking another jeweled pin in it. "I think you'll find that Diana hopes you will forgive her."

"Why should she?"

"Sometimes you amaze me, how ignorant you can be about people," Mikal said, handing Lydia the mirror.

She checked her reflection and had to agree that she looked better than she had in a long time. It might not be important, but it felt good.

The slave knocked on the door and said that Quintus was ready to leave. The girls joined him and walked in the warm evening air the short distance to the house where Diana and Fulvia had been living for the last three months.

Fulvia herself answered the door. The woman would have been hard to recognize except for the tuft of crimson that still topped her head in spite of the grey trying to overtake it. The main difference was the weight she'd put on. Lydia guessed that she was one of those unlucky ones who eat during crises. Her stola, an overdress worn by married women, hung like a tent on her large figure, but at least it was a tasteful subdued pink. Though her face lacked the vibrancy it once had, her smile of greeting seemed genuine.

"Welcome Quintus and Lydia and – and --?"

"Mikal," Lydia filled in for her. "This is my friend Mikal."

226

"I think I've seen her before somewhere. Do come in, come in! It's so good to have visitors, especially old friends. How we've missed you, Lydia. Visiting in Gaul were you? Quintus said something like that, I think. Isn't that right, Quintus?"

Father nodded politely.

As Fulvia led them to the reception room, they passed by the family shrine where an oil lamp burned in front of a bust of Brutus Marconius. Next to the bust, reflecting the flickering flame, was the silver amulet. Lydia felt she had to ask about it though her heart was afraid to hear.

Fulvia sighed loudly. "Yes, dear Titus gave it to Diana before he left for Gaul. He told her to give it to his child if anything should happen to him Of course, you know –"

"Yes," Lydia said quickly, trying to hide the joy that surged through her when she realized that Titus had not been wearing the amulet when Ansonius killed him.

"Tragic, it was," Fulvia declared. "But losing my poor Brutus was worse."

Lydia didn't know what to say and was grateful when Quintus uttered a few of the right words.

In a moment, Fulvia was chattering on, "Someone's already here, a lovely man who seems to be quite taken with poor, sad Diana. I believe, Quintus, you know him."

The man, his back to the door, was sitting on the couch holding Diana's tiny baby. Diana, the picture of motherly pride, smiled, watching him croon to her new son.

Lydia's heart died as she recognized the black hair, the large ears, and the low, melodic voice. Mikal quickly grasped her arm.

Then Marius turned. As his eyes met Lydia's he stared in astonishment.

Fulvia's chatter continued, " – the trader, Marius. Brutus was quite fond of him and he's been kind enough to –"

Marius erupted with "Lydia!" and leaped over the back of the low couch. Realizing what he still held, he shoved Diana's baby at the nearest person who happened to be Quintus.

Grasping both of Lydia's hands in his, a wide smile brightened his face – how could she have ever thought he was plain? Lydia saw that his eyes, deep rich brown with golden flecks, were starting to glisten.

All she could do was smile in wonder and hold on.

Mikal let go of her arm and stepped away.

"Mikal, too! This is wonderful!" He did not let go of Lydia's hands.

Lydia knew he would be happy at the news, "Mikal is free now."

"Is it true?" He turned to Mikal and saw her face. "Yes. That is good news."

Fulvia twittered, "Oh, she was a slave? This girl is a freed woman?"

No-one paid her any attention except, perhaps, Diana.

Marius held up Lydia's left hand and asked, "Your arm is healed?"

"A long time ago."

"Yes. It's been too long." How tender his touch. "I wanted so much to know . . . I was so far away . . . How have you fared?"

"Well enough," she whispered, her voice having been lost somewhere.

"Wonderful," he smiled. "I saw Julius three days ago, which is how I knew I could come once more to Britannia. I cannot tell you how happy I was to hear you were alive. Now I will confess to your father. Quintus Antonius, I kidnapped your daughter and took her to Gaul to find her brother. Can you forgive me?"

"I had no idea," Quintus said, confused. "Lydia?"

"Another time, Father," she said hastily, not daring to have any more revealed in front of Fulvia and Diana. "It's a long story. I had to get there somehow and Marius was the victim."

"Well, Marius, I accept your apology, and await the rest of the story . . . later."

"Sir, believe me when I tell you that it was one of the great adventures of my life."

"You have my full and grateful thanks," Quintus said, handing Diana's infant to Fulvia who, for once, was speechless. "Perhaps, Marius, you would like to visit us at the Prefect's house in the morning and discuss my children's trip with us? It seems that when Lydia searches for something, she finds it."

Marius's eyes found Lydia's again. "I would love to come."

The warmth and joy in his face took Lydia's breath away.

"I must take care of business now," he said, "but I will see you tomorrow."

He then turned to the others. "Fulvia and Diana, thank you for your hospitality and congratulations to you. May little Titus bring you joy forever."

Fulvia saw him to the door, leaving Lydia, Mikal and Diana to get re-acquainted. It went fairly well, all things considered.

29. "What Were You Not Telling Me?"

Marius arrived at the Prefect's home early in the morning while the sun was making long purple shadows across the patio where they were all seated. The servants had laid out bread, cheese and fruit on the table along with cool water. With Mikal's help, Lydia had taken an extraordinarily long time to get ready. From the way Marius looked at her, she knew it was a good job. She looked at him with an equal amount of pleasure. In fact, the other two, Quintus and Mikal, were hardly noticed.

The talk went like this:

"Tell me about your search for Darius," said Marius with a smile that showed his dimple.

"Julius told us you lied to the men from Adairinnic who were after Darius."

"Julius? Who is Julius?" asked Quintus.

"An old friend in Juliobone."

"Yes, Father, a friend, and his wife, who take care of Marius's daughter, Sera."

"Oh? You are married?"

"No. I adopted my sister's daughter."

"Ah."

"On with your story, Lydia," said with that wonderful smile again.

She really didn't want to tell it in front of her father.

"Mikal, why don't you tell it? It's your story, too."

Mikal obliged, telling much but leaving some parts out, too, especially about Ansonius. Even without many key points, the story hung together well enough. During the narration, Marius's hand found Lydia's, which made for pleasant listening.

At the end, Marius said to Lydia, "Darius is fortunate to have a sister like you. I called you Artemis before, and I do so again."

She smiled at him and said, "Please don't." How to change the subject? A brilliant idea came to her. "Tell us about your voyages. Where did you go for so long?"

Marius laughed a bit and said, "A trader goes wherever the wind blows and the cargo sells. After I left Juliobone last October, my ships went to Spain and Portugal, then sailed through the Pillars of Hercules into the Mediterranean sea. There were stops at Carthage, Marseille, and then a lot of time on the Rhone river. All in all, a successful voyage."

Lydia could hardly imagine such faraway lands, let alone that the man holding her hand had actually been there. Indeed, had been there often. She began to feel quite provincial in spite of her adventures in Gaul.

"How long will you be in the city?" he asked Lydia.

"I'm not sure. Father?"

"I had planned to do some work today and return to Tunadur tomorrow."

"Then would it be all right, Quintus, if your daughter and I took a ride into the countryside today? I take it she rode here on Coa? I can get a horse from the stable."

"We're giving Coa a rest, but she has a good horse. You can take mine if you can ride well."

"He's an excellent horseman, Father," Lydia blushed.

"Fine. It's settled. You may go as soon as you like."

"Thank you, sir."

Lydia quickly changed into her older tunic which was easier to ride in. It was thrilling to have a whole day of being alone with Marius far out in the surrounding countryside. There was so much she didn't know about him. For that matter, he did not know what she was really like. If he knew, would he still like her? Was there any chance at all that he would offer to save her from a marriage to Lucius in Bath?

They went slowly until they were free of the city then galloped out past the neighboring farms, finally slowing down to a walk, chatting amiably about nothing until Marius said, "What were you not telling me last night?"

She looked at him, wondering what he was guessing. It could be anything.

Explaining his question, he said, "Mikal's story was similar to the one you told Julius, but your father seemed surprised at some of the elements, as if he hadn't heard them before. That made me think that there was even more you have been holding back. If you can't tell me, I understand.

However, I am a safe person to share it with if it's the sort of thing that is bothering you. I am not connected here. As a matter of fact, I have very few connections and no power anywhere, to affect anything."

Lydia thought back to the two meetings where she'd overheard him speak. Both times he had been respected as a voice of reason, urging the men not to join in the war. He had more power than he thought.

"You can trust me," he said.

She took a deep breath and said, "The secrets concern families on the south coast. They concern Ansonius, my older brother who was the gladiator."

"Did I hear you right? Your older brother was a gladiator? Ansonius?"

"Yes, you've probably heard of him. He's famous."

Though it looked as if Marius had more to say, Lydia hurried on, "The secrets concern Darius and how our family will be treated by our friends if they ever find out. We've lived here for generations, even before the Romans came. If the neighbors knew what the three of us did – my older brother, me, and Darius, even Mikal -- they would find ways to ruin us."

"That's a heavy load for you to carry. Let's stop under those trees and sit and talk."

So they did. The horses stayed close by, nibbling on the fresh grasses.

Lydia told him everything in complete honesty, from the amulet to the sword and even Titus. When she was done with the telling, she was exhausted but relieved of the burden. Marius was quiet for a long time. When he finally spoke, Lydia was taken by surprise.

"I had considered asking you to be my wife, Lydia, but . . .."

What had she expected? Her confession had turned him away. She had trusted him, but he hadn't known how completely evil she'd been. Now that he knew, he didn't want her. She put her thoughts into words though speaking them tore her apart.

"If I am not worthy of you, I understand. I have done terrible things and I don't blame you."

He took her hand, brought it to his lips and kissed it tenderly. Her own lips trembled and then her eyes betrayed her by crying uncontrollably.

"Lydia, Lydia, please don't cry," as he wiped tears from her cheeks. "I fear I am no match for a woman like you. You are more like Juno, queen of the gods, than Artemis. What you did in Lyon and before then to the amulet, was heroic, even if it seems now, to you, to have brought great trouble to your family. I have been thinking about you all these months, imagining what you were doing, even who you are, and I never came close to the truth."

Lydia tried to speak, but her throat caught and more sobs broke forth. She had held in her secrets so long, and now that they were out, they had robbed her of the one thing she had desired. Marius!

"Now you know the truth and you don't like it," she choked out.

"Wrong, Lydia. I love you for it. But how did I know when I fell in love with a young hysterical girl eight or nine months ago, that she would turn out to be so much more, such an ideal woman?"

"You are an idiot!" Lydia yelled at him, breaking away and trying to stand up. "Ask anyone! Ask Mikal! Ask my family! Ask Diana! You don't know me at all if you think I am any sort of an ideal anything."

She stumbled, tripped over her tunic, and fell in a heap on the grass, crying and wishing she was someone else. Anyone else. Anywhere else.

Marius took her in his arms and held her tight, though she fought hard to get away.

"Easy, calm down. Lydia? Sweet Lydia?"

"How can I be sweet Lydia to you? You think I'm a wretched goddess. I am not a goddess! I am me! I need you, Marius." And in a quieter voice, though she hated to admit it now, she added, "I'm pretty sure I love you."

She felt his lips on her forehead and couldn't breathe. Then he pulled her close and asked, "Did you really say you love me?"

"I think so."

"Can I help you decide?" he asked, kissing her hand.

She took a deep breath and whispered, "I love you even if you can't love me."

Marius shook his head and laughed. "Amazing. I don't understand it, but so be it. So be it. We can work this out, get to know who we both are. Together." He gave a long sigh before adding, "It's going to be rough sailing for awhile. Are you willing? Should I talk to your father?"

She nodded and needed to blow her nose. Lifting up a corner of her tunic, hoping he wouldn't mind, she blew.

He laughed. She laughed.

"What will our life be like, Marius?"

"I haven't dared to think about that until now. I was so surprised to see you yesterday, and so sure you would refuse me today, that I didn't think ahead. Just keep smiling that amazing smile of yours and we'll be all right."

"That's ridiculous!" she grinned.

He took her face in his hands, brought her near and kissed her fully and completely for the first time. She was amazed at how extraordinary it felt to be kissed by someone who loves you and you love him.

"Marius?"

"Yes, love."

"I still get seasick."

"We can work that out."

Acknowledgements

I thought The Amulet was perfect twenty-five years ago when I packed it away in a box. Ack! Re-reading it last year, I realized how wrong I was. After a lot of rewrites, each one of which I thought was the last and final version, Elaine Verdill agreed to take a whack at it. She taught me a whole lot about how what the writer thinks she's written and what the reader actually reads can be two different things.

Rowen Bahmer of the younger generation and an excellent writer, earned my undying admiration and applause for his critique.

And there's Gerald, my Latin instructor at the University of Colorado. Short, plump, with a quirky sense of humor, the class all loved him. Most of us even loved Latin.

Thanks to the early readers, some of whom enjoyed The Amulet enough to urge me on with great enthusiasm.

My traveling partner, Mary Peterson, endured many hours in Roman ruins when we returned to France last spring after fifty years. I appreciate her patience and understanding, and her willingness to go wherever I needed to go.

I am forever indebted to readers who like The Amulet and recommend it to their friends

Finally, thanks to the computer industry which has made writing and editing infinitely easier than it used to be.

www.ingramcontent.com/pod-product-compliance
Lightning Source LLC
Chambersburg PA
CBHW070606130626
46556CB00001B/291